A

World

I Never

Made

James

LePore

THE
STORY PLANT

The Story Plant
The Aronica-Miller Publishing Project, LLC
P.O. Box 4331
Stamford, CT 06907

ISBN: 978-1-61188-031-1
Visit our website at www.thestoryplant.com

For information, address The Story Plant.

First Story Plant Hardcover Printing: April 2009
First Story Plant Trade Paperback Printing: February 2012

For her unfailing intercession on behalf of all those who seek it, this book is dedicated to Thérèse Martin, a child of France who died in 1897 at the age of 24 and who, in 1925, became St. Thérèse of Lisieux.

Acknowledgments

I am grateful to my wife Karen, to my daughters Erica, Adrienne, and Jamie, and to my friends Greg and Joy Ziemak for their unwavering support and their thoughtful and insightful comments.

I am also profoundly grateful to my friend and editor, Lou Aronica. This would not have happened without him.

Last, a special thank you to my brother Pat for his deep and steadfast loyalty to me and to family.

And how am I to face the odds

Of man's bedevilment and God's?

I, a stranger and afraid

In a world I never made.

A.E. Housman, *Last Poems*

~ 1 ~

Paris, January 2, 2004

Dad,

I don't owe you or anybody an explanation, but I think you'll appreciate the irony of a suicide note coming from a person who has abhorred tradition all of her life. I met a young girl on the street the other day who looked into my eyes and told me that Jesus was waiting for me in heaven. She was fourteen or so, selling flowers on the Street of Flowers, and had the look of a young Madonna. The red roses I bought from her were the last thing I saw before pulling the trigger.

If, as you read this, I am actually with Jesus in heaven, I will be one shocked woman. I doubt it, though. Megan Nolan is no more. Go and have yourself another daughter. It's not too late, and the odds are very good that she will turn out better than I did. If I were famous, I would be joining the long line of suicides known to history. But as it is, in a matter of days, if not hours, my life and death will be as anonymous and as forgotten as a stray breeze.

Megan

P.S. You know how I feel about being buried.
Please, no service and a quick cremation. Don't
let me down.

Pat Nolan read the note for the first time sitting in the cramped office of Assistant Chief Inspector Geneviève LeGrand at the Seventh Arrondissement Police Prefecture on Rue Fabert. When he was finished, he looked over at Madame LeGrand, sitting across from him at her cluttered desk.

"One less hegemonic, imperialist American pig to worry about," he said.

"Pardon?"

Pat shook his head, and then watched as the bored look on the middle-aged inspector's face—she was perhaps fifty or fifty-five—was replaced, in quick succession, by a widening of the eyes in surprise, their narrowing in concentration, and finally a slight smile.

"You are perhaps weary from your traveling, Monsieur Nolan," she said, looking at him with what seemed to be a bit more interest than when he first entered her office and accepted her invitation to sit.

Pat was, in fact, jet-lagged. He had arrived in Paris from New York the morning before, slept as if drugged all day, and then, when he went out looking for a late dinner, got caught up in a walkabout involving thousands of beautifully dressed Parisians celebrating the New Year. His inner clock reversed, he had managed to fall asleep at seven AM for an hour before having to get up for his nine olock meeting with Inspector LeGrand.

"I must be."

"Would you like some coffee?"

"No, thank you."

"I am sorry for your loss."

Pat nodded his head, keeping his acknowledgment of this declaration as perfunctory as its delivery.

"I will not keep you long."

"You have a job to do."

"Yes, I do. The note is in your daughter's hand?"

"Yes."

"Did you know she was ill, Monsieur Nolan?"

"No."

"She had last stage ovarian cancer. She would have been dead in another few weeks. You did not know this?"

The police building, which looked to Nolan like a church, was a three-story affair located about a block from the Seine. Assistant Chief Inspector LeGrand's corner office was on the third floor. Through the window behind her, Pat could see one of the bridges that crossed the river. It also looked like a church, or rather the type of bridge that a church would have if it needed one. Next to the bridge on the near bank stood a large tree. Settled on its numerous leafless branches were, he estimated, two hundred crows or black birds of some sort. Some watched a barge pass slowly under the bridge, others seemed to be staring directly at him. Megan had decided as a teenager that the crow—arrogant, malicious, intelligent, cunning—was her totem. He wondered, collecting his thoughts, remembering his only child, if she was sitting in that tree. If she was, was she looking at the barge or at him?

"No, I didn't."

"Autopsies are required in France for all cases that are possible homicides. You understand it had to be done quickly in case the entry wound was inconsistent with suicide. We would want to start searching for the killer as soon as possible."

"I understand."

"There appears to be no doubt that she was a suicide. Our investigation is almost complete. I have only to ask you one or two questions."

"Go ahead."

"Do you know why she came to France?"

"She was a writer. She could work anywhere. She loved Paris."

"Did you know she was living in Morocco?"

"No." Though he had spoken to Megan on Christmas day, prior to that he had not seen or spoken to her since the Christmas before. They were in Rome at the time, and she had told him then that she was thinking of heading to Sicily and possibly North Africa. "I take it she was."

"She had a Moroccan diplomatic visa."

"What is that, exactly?"

"It is issued by their minister of Foreign Affairs. It allows a person to stay indefinitely in Morocco. It appears that she was there for some four months. Did she know people there?"

"Not that I know of."

"She must have known someone very important to have secured such a visa. They are rarely issued to anyone outside the highest diplomatic circles."

"Have you made inquiries in Rabat?"

Pat watched Inspector LeGrand's eyes narrow again. He could almost hear her thoughts: *A semi-intelligent question coming from this American cowboy? Did he actually know that Rabat was Morocco's capital?* Under different circumstances, it might have bothered him that he was perceived as a caricature by the haughty and bored Frenchwoman sitting across from him. As it was, he just wanted to get to the end of the interview as quickly as possible, to get the identification of Megan's body over with, and to figure out privately how it was he was supposed to grieve.

"Yes," she replied. "The Moroccan official who vouched for her diplomatic status is out of the country. Did she ever mention any Moroccan friends or acquaintances?"

"No, never."

"When did you speak to her last?"

"On Christmas Day."

"Where was she?"

"She said she was in Paris."

"Where in Paris?"

"She didn't say."

"And she didn't tell you she was ill?"

"No."

"Do you find that unusual?"

Through the window behind LeGrand, Pat could see the crows beginning to stir. One of them had taken flight and then circled back and attacked another one on one of the top branches. They left the tree and continued their fight, if that"s what it was, in the air, while the rest raised their wings and lifted their beaks, no doubt to express their contempt—or glee—at the spectacle above them.

"No," Pat answered."I don't."

"Were you estranged from your daughter, Monsieur Nolan?"

"Yes and no." Pat had been avoiding asking himself this question for twelve years. His answer surprised him in that it wasn't a definite yes.

"I see. Well … She arrived in Spain from Morocco on May 16. She checked into her hotel in Paris on December 24. She must have traveled by rail or bus because her name does not appear on any airline manifests from Spain or anywhere else. We do not know where she was from May 17 to December 24."

"What about her credit cards?"

"The last charge was at a hotel in Casablanca on May 15. There is no record after that."

"So she might have been in Spain?"

"The EU's borders are open now, Monsieur Nolan. She might have gone anywhere in those seven months."

"Have you checked the hospitals, clinics?"

"Yes. There is no record we can find of her receiving treatment for her cancer. She killed herself on December 30. Her concierge says she had one visitor, a woman who arrived on the thirtieth and stayed for a half hour. Do you know who that might be?"

"No," he answered.

"She came to Paris often. Who were her friends here? Her associates?"

"I don't know. I thought you were certain it was suicide."

LeGrand looked down at her paperwork before answering and Pat took the opportunity to study her. *Were you estranged from your daugbter, Monsieur Nolan? The EU's borders are open now, Monsieur Nolan.* Her voice not quite neutral, not quite professional. To the pain of Megan's death was now added the pain—the dishonor—of having to expose their failed relationship to the contemptuous eye of Inspector Geneviève LeGrand. *French* Inspector Geneviève LeGrand. He would not, at least, give her the pleasure of showing in the slightest how he felt.

"I am," the inspector said finally. "But it is a curious suicide. Your daughter did not live an ordinary life, Monsieur Nolan. Her passport has dozens of entries in Europe and

North Africa over the past ten years. She never returned to America. Was she ever married?"

"No."

"Are there other next of kin? Her mother? Siblings?"

"No. Her mother died giving birth to her. I've had no other children. Are we done? I'd like to bury my daughter."

"Bury? Her note talks of cremation."

Megan, who held strong opinions on many subjects, had never mentioned any squeamishness about being buried. But there it was, in her neat cursive hand, and he would abide by it.

"That's what I meant."

"The body is at the morgue at the Hospital of All Souls, not far from here on the river. I have arranged for one of my officers to take you there to officially identify it."

"Can I have the note?" Pat asked.

"I will give you a photocopy. The original must stay in the official file."

"I would like to visit her room."

"Mademoiselle Laurence will take you there."

"Mademoiselle ... ?"

"She is the officer who will accompany you to the morgue. She must be present at the identification."

"I see. Are there any male police officers in Paris?"

"They are busy hunting hegemonic imperialists."

Pat Nolan was careless about his looks. Some would say he could afford to be. A lifetime spent outdoors had kept his six-foot-three, two-hundred-twenty-pound body trim and supple, and burnished his naturally high color to a reddish gold, a perfect setting for his clear, forthright, and often piercing eyes. The lines around these eyes and on his brow when it knitted in thought added a depth and interest lacking in the faces of men who are young or who haven't lived much. His thick black hair, swept away from his forehead and carelessly long, framed a face that was handsome in a wry, laconic way. His feelings, more often than not, went unexpressed. Much more often than not. But Inspector Le-Grand had turned human for a second and so, despite his predilection to dislike her—to caricaturize her—he smiled. He could see her features soften for a brief moment when he did.

"Yours is not an easy job," he said, rising and extending his hand to Inspector LeGrand, who also rose. For a second, they made eye contact. *You have been touched—physically and sentimentally—by the prototypical American bête noire, Pat thought. Have no fear, you will survive.*

"Where are you staying, Monsieur Nolan?"

"Le Tourville. Do you know it?"

"Yes. Officer Laurence will collect you there. Say at noon? She will have your daughter's effects and a copy of the note."

"Thank you."

"*De rien* ... Monsieur Nolan."

"Yes?"

"I am quite sorry for your loss."

~ ~ ~

Inspector LeGrand's words echoed in Pat Nolan's head as he stepped outside of the police building and turned right toward the river. *Your loss.* For almost thirty years, Lorrie, his twenty-year-old bride, had been his loss. In the summer of 1974, he had married Lorraine Ryan—impossibly young and beautiful—impregnated her, and dragged her to Paraguay where he had been offered a job operating an earth mover at the site of what was to become one of the official Seven Wonders of the Modern World, the Itaipu Dam. Six months later, Lorrie was dead of eclampsia and Megan—the name Lorrie had chosen for a girl baby—was lying in an incubator across the border in Montevideo, Uruguay. Two months premature, sticklike, she clung tenaciously to life, oblivious to Pat's weekend visits and haggard look. *If she lives and if it is your wish, we will help you place her for adoption,* one of the sisters at the hospital had told him, her face grim, as if she had read his angry, tortured thoughts. In the end, he had not given Megan away. But he had come close. He and a crew of five hundred had merely been in the midst of shifting the course of the Paraná River—the seventh largest in the world—around the eventual construction site. A one-point-three-mile long, three-hundred-foot-deep, five-hundred-foot-wide diversion. He would never get work like that again, not with a child to care for. That was his second loss. Or was it his first? The intervening years had blended the loss of Lorrie and of his big dreams into one, and then blurred them and worn them down until they were no longer separate and no longer hurt. They were long years, in which his sticklike girl baby had grown up and run away. Loss on top of loss.

Megan, who had left Bennington at the beginning of her freshman year and gone directly to Europe, claiming that America was so bourgeois she could not take another minute of it, had since then made her living writing and, not to put too fine a point on it, seducing men. The writing, mostly for women's magazines like *Cosmopolitan* and *Glamour,* she could do from anywhere, which facilitated her lifelong urge to move from place to place, which in turn afforded ample venues for meeting men willing—gladly willing—to pay for having her on their arms and in their beds. Pat had met one or two of these victims early on and quickly got the picture. There would be no son-in-law or grandchildren in his future. No Sunday dinners with the family in rural Connecticut or Westchester when he got old, with a fire burning in the fireplace and football on the television. This wound also healed over in time.

Instead of getting a civil engineering degree and designing megaprojects around the world, he went into business with his older brother, Frank, building homes, strip malls, and car dealerships in the tristate area. When Frank had retired last year, Pat sold Nolan Brothers. He wanted no part of the office work that Frank had handled for thirty years. Since then he had been entertaining offers to manage projects, large and small, near and far, from companies and architects he had met in the course of a long career of completing jobs on time and at or under budget. He had brought a folder of these offers with him, and started looking for a not too pretentious café where he could sip coffee and read through it to kill time until twelve o'clock.

He found a place on a corner across from the Pont de la Concorde. It was nearly empty and its outdoor tables were set up to take advantage of the surprisingly balmy weather: fifty degrees Fahrenheit or so under a cloudless pale blue sky diffused even in the dead of winter with Paris's famous silky light. Pat expected the waiter to sniff at him, and he did, his large Gallic nose rising higher with each step as he made his way from the front door to the table Pat had chosen in the full sun near the sidewalk. In his jeans, worn-out workboots, and thick black sweater, his Americanness was obvious.

Parisian condescension was not new to Pat. He had spent Christmas with Megan in Europe, usually Paris, for the past twelve years. In between they talked on the phone a few times and occasionally she sent him a short letter or a cryptic postcard. The Christmas just past had been the first one since she left home that they had not spent together. And neither had he heard from her since he left her in Rome the year before. She had finally called on Christmas day.

A few days later she killed herself.

Pat sat now, and instead of looking at his folder, which he carried in a canvas knapsack slung over his shoulder, he sipped his coffee and reviewed that last conversation.

"Dad, hi."

"Hello."

"How are you?"

"I'm fine. Where are you?"

"Paris."

Pause.

"Where have you been?"

"Traveling. No place special."

Pause.

"How are you?" (Megan).

"I'm okay."

Pause.

"I'm sorry, Dad."

"For what?"

"That Lorrie died and not me."

"Is that why you haven"t called?"

"I'm calling now."

"How long will you be there?"

"I'll probably leave tomorrow or the next day."

"Where to?"

"I'm not sure exactly."

"Megan ..."

"You're angry, I know. I've had a hard year."

"A hard year?"

"It's almost over. My birthday's coming up. You can bring me a present."

"Megan ..."
"I'm sorry, Dad. I have to go. I love you."
Click.

One of Megan's former lovers, a famous novelist, had described a beautiful, twenty-five-year-old female character as having the ability "to slip in and out of your psyche in a matter of a few hot and thrilling seconds, exposing the thing you loathe most about yourself while whispering a promise of joy to your secret heart. Afterward you wanted more, oblivious to the bruise on your soul." When the book came out, Megan sent Pat a copy of the page on which this passage appeared with a note on the margin that read, "Dad, I would sue this guy, but the writing's so bad I'd be too embarrassed." Pat knew the Megan the spurned writer was describing. The heartless Megan. Megan the cynic. This knowledge was one of the few ties that he felt bound her to him. Other fathers felt more positive things of course, but this was *something.* Something to cling to. He did not know the Megan he talked to on Christmas day, the one planning to kill herself. Such a bitter thing not to know, invalidating as it were their tenuous bond, exposing it for the sham it was.

Pat walked along the river after finishing his coffee, then turned away from the water in the neighborhood of the Eiffel Tower, which was teeming with tourists, who, trance-like, were streaming to the giant structure like insects to the sacred seat of their queen. His hotel was in this neighborhood, as was the Rue des Fleurs, which he decided to visit before being "collected" by Officer Laurence. He knew from looking at his city map the night before that it ran only two blocks, from Rue de l'Universitè roughly southerly to Rue de Montessuy. When he made the turn from Rue de l'Universitè onto Rue des Fleurs, he saw a city worker in hip boots using a hose connected to a truck that followed him slowly as he methodically sprayed the sidewalk on Pat's side. Rather than backing up, Pat stepped into a doorway that turned out to be the foyer of a small apartment house. There, squatting before him, was a woman arranging bouquets of flowers in two large wicker baskets.

"Would you like to buy a bouquet of flowers, Monsieur," she said without looking up, apparently deducing from his shoes and jeans that he was a man. "For your daughter? Your wife?"

The woman's hair was pitch-black, and at first Pat thought she was one of the gypsies who pestered the tourists in virtually all of Europe's capitals. Then she stood and Pat saw that she was not a gypsy and not a woman, but rather a girl of thirteen or fourteen with large luminous eyes set in a pale face of immaculate complexion and indecipherable national origin. The foyer was small, only ten feet by ten feet, but its richly paneled walls reached up some twenty feet to meet in a darkly latticed cathedral ceiling. The floor beneath them was a pink-and-gray striated marble. The transom above the front door was made of stained glass of pale blues and greens, and the light spilling from it cast the girl's face in an angelic glow. Outside, the street washer was passing. The girl, holding a bouquet of roses in one hand and wiping the other on her poorly cut cloth coat, smiled and said, "The street cleaner has sent you to me."

Pat could not find his tongue for a second and then, without thinking, he reached into the back pocket of his jeans and withdrew his wallet, a slender beat-up leather affair with little in it except some cash, his driver's license, two credit cards, and a picture of Megan. This he slid from its clear plastic cover and showed to the flower girl.

"This is my daughter," he said. "Do you know her?"

"*Oui, Monsieur,*" the girl answered. And then, switching back to her lilting schoolgirl's English, "She told me you would come."

"She told you I'd come?"

"*Oui, Monsieur.*"

"When was that?"

"When she purchased flowers from me last week."

"What kind of flowers?"

"Roses. *Comme ça.*" She looked down at the bouquet in her hand and then back up at Pat.

"What else did she tell you?"

"*Rien, Monsieur,* just that you would be coming."

She's dead, Pat wanted to say. *I'm too late.* But he could not form the words. He heard them echoing in his head, but though he tried he could not get them to his lips. Then suddenly he was crying, holding his hands to his eyes to hide his tears. Embarrassed, he opened his wallet again and began fumbling in it for euro notes to pay for the bouquet. The girl, however, gently clasped her hands over his, forcing them to close the wallet and at the same time deftly placing the flowers into his right hand. There was more comfort in her touch than Pat had felt in years. He stood there mute, wondering at the sweetness of this child who was a head shorter than him but whose presence seemed to fill every corner of the small room.

"She was troubled, Monsieur."

"Troubled?"

"Yes, Monsieur. It is good that you have come. You must go to her."

There was no point in telling the girl that Megan was dead, that in a few minutes he would indeed be going to her, but only to her corpse.

"I am going to her now," he said.

"Have faith, Monsieur. You will be led to her."

~ 2 ~

Paris, January 2, 2004

Pat arrived at his hotel at a few minutes before noon, which gave him just enough time to put the roses into a vase with water and wash his face and hands before going down to the lobby to meet Officer Laurence. When he unwrapped the roses, a prayer card of some kind fell out; he put this in his pocket without thinking much about it. He told the desk clerk that he was expecting an Officer Laurence of the Paris police and pointed to a stuffed chair in a corner where he would be waiting for her. There he sat and began to ponder his strange meeting with the flower girl, but within seconds, or so it seemed, he was interrupted by a tall angular woman in her mid-thirties dressed in a chic dark blue suit over a white silk blouse. Her nose was on the large side and slightly bumpy, and would have dominated her face except that it was nicely in proportion to her high, wide cheekbones and full-lipped broad mouth. The eyes in this face, forthright eyes that met his squarely, were an arresting shade of gray-green that Pat had never seen before. Her gold bracelets jangled as she extended her hand to him and introduced herself with a half smile and a nod of her head.

"Do you speak French, Monsieur Nolan?"

"*Un peu.*"

"You prefer English?"

"Yes."

"*Mais oui.* Of course. You seem surprised, Monsieur. I am not dressed to chase criminals today."

"I was expecting someone in a uniform. Inspector Le-Grand said you were an officer."

"I am an officer of the judiciary police. In America I would be a detective."

Pat was surprised at Laurence's appearance, but it wasn't at the way she was dressed. Nor was it solely how lovely she was, although she was quite lovely to look at. It was, he realized, how interesting the look in her beautiful eyes was. There was no French arrogance in them, but its opposite, something akin to humility or a complicated, frustrating sadness not unlike his own. This look, whether imagined or real, and the thought it sparked in his overworked mind, took Pat for a moment—a very brief moment—out of himself, a process that on some wider level he observed with gratitude.

"Shall we go?" Laurence said softly, bringing him swiftly but gently back to the grim task at hand.

The ride to the hospital in Laurence's black Peugeot station wagon was short and quiet. Once there, Laurence spoke rapidly in French to a desk clerk, then shepherded Pat into an elevator which took them to the basement.

"Wait," she said when they exited the elevator; then, turning, she walked quickly down a long corridor, her high heels clicking on the tiled floor. She disappeared behind double swinging doors, reemerging a moment later and gesturing to Pat to come. It was a long walk for Pat, longer even than the one he had taken twenty-nine years ago to confirm for himself that his wife of eight months was dead. Laurence held open one of the swinging doors for him and he entered a squarish, harshly lit room with a wall of stainless steel body lockers at one end and an autopsy station at the other, where a lab technician in a white smock stood next to a gurney. Pat took this scene in for a moment and then felt Officer Laurence's hand on his left forearm. At the gurney, Laurence nodded to the technician, who pulled down gently on the pale green sheet. Pat's eyes went first to the shaved head, then to the crude sutures at the right temple, and then finally to the face, white and stony in death these last four days. It was not Megan. It was a woman generally of Megan's age and size and coloring, but it was not her.

"This is your daughter, Monsieur Nolan?"

Pat's mind had stopped working for a second, but it started again when he heard Officer Laurence's voice. Other voices then filled his head.

My birthday's coming up. You can bring me a present.

A quick cremation.

Have faith, Monsieur. *You will be led to her.*

Megan was alive but wanted the world to think she was dead. The world except for Pat and the flower girl on the Street of Flowers.

"Yes," he answered, nodding, and at the same time reaching out and placing his right hand over the body's left hand. He pressed through the sheet to feel for the heavy silver ring that he had bought for Lorrie on their honeymoon and then given to Megan when she turned sixteen. To the best of his knowledge, she had not taken it off since. He confirmed its absence, then stepped away from the gurney, keeping his eyes on the unknown woman who had visited Megan on December 30 and killed herself in furtherance of what dark and strange conspiracy—a conspiracy he had now joined—Pat could not fathom. *Why, Megan? And where are you?*

"She has lost weight from her cancer," said Laurence.

"Yes."

The detective nodded to the technician, who pulled the sheet up and began wheeling the gurney toward the lockers.

"Detective Laurence," Pat said.

"Yes."

"I would like to have my daughter cremated today if possible. Can you help me?"

"Yes. Upstairs we will sign papers to release the body. We will call a crematorium from my cell phone."

"And her personal effects?"

"I have them in my car. I will take you to her room if you like."

"Yes. I would."

"Perhaps you would like something to eat first, a drink?"

Yes, I could use a drink, a long night of drinking, Pat thought, realizing, as Laurence stared intently at him that the stunned look on his face was not what she thought it was, sorry that he had had to lie to her.

"No," he said, thanking her with his eyes for the sympathy in hers. "Let's get it over with."

~ 3 ~

Paris, January 3, 2004

"I have had a visit from Charles Raimondi from the Foreign Office. Do you know who he is?"

"One of de Poincare's boys."

"Yes, the inner circle."

Inspector LeGrand, apparently organizing her thoughts, remained silent for a second or two, drumming her fingers on her desk. As she did, Catherine Laurence recalled her one brush with Charles Raimondi. At a Europol conference in Brussels two years ago he had traced the back of her hand lightly with his fingertips and asked her to be his mistress. Handsome, but effete and arrogant, he seemed to guess that she was unhappy in her marriage, and, worse, to assume that she would be honored to receive the sexual favors of the man who was the Foreign Minister's liaison to the DST, France's very powerful equivalent of America's CIA. When she turned him down, the serpentine flash of anger that he could not—or would not—keep from his eyes told her all she needed to know about Raimondi.

"The Saudi government," LeGrand said, "is interested in Megan Nolan."

"But she is dead."

"They think not."

Catherine Laurence's distasteful memory of Charles Raimondi was immediately displaced by this startling piece of information. It was not every day that a father misidentified a dead child's body, or willfully participated in a faked suicide. Or that the Foreign Office and the Saudi government were at once interested in a case she was handling. "What is their interest?" she asked.

"The suicide bombings in Morocco in May."

Laurence and LeGrand were sitting in LeGrand's corner office the day after Laurence had accompanied Pat Nolan to the morgue. The Seine shone in the midday sunlight, and beyond it one could see a wide swath of the Right Bank in its staid and stately patterns. The sounds of traffic, muffled by the thick stone walls of the police building, seemed distant to Laurence, as if coming to them from another dimension, far away and not connected to Paris. Her husband, Jacques, had been killed in one of those bombings in Casablanca. She had not loved Jacques for several years before he was killed and had occasionally fantasized about his sudden and unexpected death. That part of her life seemed likewise to have occurred in another dimension, one not quite connected to her. She remained silent for a moment as she contemplated the deep irony of bringing to justice someone involved in the bombings that made her fantasies come true.

"The Saudis," LeGrand continued, "have someone they wish to view the body."

"The body was cremated this morning," Catherine replied.

"So quickly. Are you certain?"

"I drove Monsieur Nolan to the crematorium."

"*You* drove him?"

"Yes."

Again Inspector LeGrand was silent. Again she drummed her desktop with her fingers. *I have irritated her,* Catherine thought, *again,* recalling the puzzled look, the slight but insistent frown on her boss's face in the days after Jacques's death, when Catherine had quietly interred his remains—literally what was left of him—and returned immediately to the homicide she had been working on when she received the shocking news. Catherine knew what LeGrand and others in the department thought of her. Arrogant. Aloof. Whatever. She didn't care. Raised by old-school gendarmes—a cop's daughter and niece, and proud of it—she was very good at what she did, her closure rate and fearlessness on the street earning her a grudging respect. But her inner life she did not share, and this kept her from making lasting friends and from participating in the politics of police work that were a prerequisite to full acceptance and advancement. So be it.

"Have you befriended him?" LeGrand asked.

"No, but he has lost his daughter, his only child. I thought it right to offer to help."

"It is perhaps fortuitous that you did. We want you to continue to make contact with him. He may lead us to his daughter. And from her to others."

"Who is we?"

"The Foreign Office, the Saudis, me."

"Does DST know?"

"Yes."

"Then why are we handling it?"

"Because you have made contact with Nolan. He knows you. DST will shadow the investigation, but they want you to be at the point for now."

"What do the Saudis have?"

"They were watching an al-Qaeda cell in Casablanca. One of their agents was working them. Nolan was involved with a member of the cell. She was staying at the Farah Hotel, one of the targets, until the day before it was bombed. One of the bombers survived. His belt pack did not detonate. His car was hit by debris and he was knocked unconscious. He says that Nolan helped plan and coordinate the attacks. After the bombings, both Nolan and her boyfriend disappeared."

"Who is the boyfriend?"

"A Saudi national named Rahman al-Zahra."

"Is he supposed to be in France?"

"It is thought that he may be, that he traveled with Nolan, under a fraudulent passport of course. Just before the bombings in Casablanca, the Saudis picked up chatter that may have been about an operation in France. There was mention of St. Florentin, which as you know has a large Muslim community."

"What does he look like?"

"Unfortunately, there are no pictures. The agent was first put on to Nolan, and then, as soon as he discovered al-Zahra, the bombings occurred."

"There must be a description?"

"He's six-one, early forties, medium-to-slight build, dark hair, mustache, dark eyes, Arabic of course. No distinguishing features or marks."

"We are now down to one billion Arabic men. What about Nolan, the *real* Nolan?"

"Here. This was taken in May." LeGrand handed Catherine a manila folder containing an eight-by-ten color photograph of Megan shopping at an outdoor bazaar, presumably in Morocco. Despite the dust, the obvious heat, and the crowd around her, she looked coolly composed as she handed a trinket of some kind to the shopkeeper. Sunlight, diffused through the frayed awning overhead, cast her face and her long, reddish-blonde hair in a golden glow. She was a strikingly good-looking woman.

"Is that her?" LeGrand asked.

"It could be. The corpse I saw was emaciated, the head shaved." She shrugged, handing the picture back to LeGrand.

"She does not look ill in that picture."

"No."

"Monsieur Nolan was quite positive?"

"Yes. Why don't we ask him for blood or a tissue sample? We must have samples from the corpse to match them."

"We do not want to alert him to our interest."

"But he may be completely innocent and want to know that his daughter is alive."

"We cannot take the chance."

"What if he simply goes home?"

"We would like him to stay in France at least until you can get a DNA sample. Surreptitiously, of course."

"Shall I get a sperm sample?"

Catherine's question was not sarcastic, but there was an archness to it that she knew was her rogue nature asserting itself despite, or possibly because of, the extreme gravity of the idea of a major terrorist attack on French soil. Her husband had thought her sense of humor maddeningly inappropriate at best and macabre at worst. Attracted to it while courting, it repulsed him after only three years of marriage. Looking over at Inspector LeGrand and seeing the deadpan, slightly disapproving look on her face, Catherine felt sure her spinster boss and her late husband would have been sympatico at least on this one issue.

"His coffee cup will do."

"Yes, of course. How did the Saudis learn of the suicide?"

"Nolan's name was on a watch list. When I called about her diplomatic visa, the Moroccan Foreign Ministry notified their intelligence service, who notified the Saudis."

"And what is the basis of their doubts?"

"They believe al-Zahra tried to fake his own death by giving one of the Casa bombers his papers. It is a common ploy in the world of terrorism. He and Nolan disappeared at the same time. There was the chatter believed to concern a similar operation in France. Nolan does not appear to be the least bit ill in her photograph. She is a redheaded American. She would be undetectable as a terrorist until it was too late. They need confirmation of her death, or of her continuing to live."

"Are they sending anyone?"

"For the time being, no."

"Why the Saudis and not the Moroccans?"

"The Saudis feel they are better situated to track down al-Zahra. He is one of theirs. The Moroccans have agreed to let them take the lead. They will be busy enough interrogating and then executing the thirteen men they captured."

"And my assignment is, exactly?"

"Befriend Nolan. Find out if he is telling the truth. If his daughter is alive, he is our best hope of finding her. While you're at it, get a saliva sample. That should be easy enough to accomplish. Report directly to me. And only to me."

"Where does DST come in?"

"If you get a lead on Megan Nolan, they will take over the case. They want her, but they want al-Zahra more. He is a known terrorist. While you're working Nolan, they'll be checking out St. Florentin and the other Arab communities."

"What about my active cases?"

"You went on leave this morning. Delayed grief. I'll hand out your work to the others in your unit. If you need more time, I'll post somebody temporarily from the ranks, somebody senior."

"You've thought of everything."

"Yes, Raimondi was quite forceful. There is enough in this one case, he said, to make or break several careers."

~ ~ ~

Pat Nolan stood on his hotel room's balcony gazing absently down at the traffic on Avenue de Tourville. In his hand he held the prayer card that had fallen out of the roses the flower girl had given him. On the front was a haloed image of Saint Thérèse of Lisieux holding a spray of red and pink roses, her eyes sad and beautiful and looking right at him. On the back was a prayer to her in French. *O Little Flower of Jesus, ever consoling troubled souls ...* On his dresser was a white ceramic jar with a hinged top containing the ashes and small chunks of bone from the cremation of the body that was not Megan. He had spent the last two hours delivering the real Megan's clothes and jewelry to the Salvation Army headquarters in the suburb of Nanterre with the help of an Algerian taxi driver who turned off his meter when he realized the point of Pat's mission.

Laid out on his bed's pristine white counterpane were the items handed to him the day before by Detective Laurence: a photocopy of the suicide note; Megan's passport, (last stamped on May 16 in Tafira, Spain); her empty wallet; a transparent plastic picture holder containing a snapshot of Pat and Megan taken in Prague in 1992 and one of Lorrie taken on their wedding day in Las Vegas; a withdrawal receipt from a Montmartre bank for twenty thousand euros dated December 23; and a receipt for a round-trip rail ticket from Paris to Lisieux dated December 24. These last two items Pat had found in between the back-to-back snapshots in the picture holder.

Four stories below, across the street, the Christmas lights on the trees in a small park came on as a band began to set up on a concrete platform near the entrance. The weather had turned even nicer—it had reached sixty degrees today—and Paris was taking advantage. But Pat was not in Paris. He was in New Canaan, on the phone with eighteen-year-old Megan two weeks into her first semester at Bennington.

I hate it here. They're all elitist snobs. I'm going to Europe.

And then he was sitting with her at an outdoor café on the sunny side of Prague's Old Town Square, crowded with people enjoying a brilliant fall morning in November of 1992. The waiter had just taken their picture with Megan's Instamatic.

"I told you, I hated Bennington."

"There are other colleges."

"This is my college."

"Prague?"

"Europe."

"What about money?"

"I told you in my letters. I've got two jobs."

"That looks like a nice street you live on."

"It's cheap here."

"How long are you planning on staying?"

"I don't know. I'm having a good time."

Megan's strawberry-blond hair glinting in the bright sun. Her beautiful green eyes happy and determined. Very little sympathy in them.

"When will I see you again?"

"Let's meet somewhere at Christmas, It's only a few weeks away. How about Paris?"

"Sure, Paris sounds good."

Pat taking his wallet out of his jacket pocket, thumbing through the cash in the billfold and drawing out a crisp hundred dollar bill.

"*Your grandfather Connie was away a lot.*"

"*Your dad.*"

"*Yes. In the merchant marine. He'd be gone six, seven months at a time. He used to say that when people are separated, only two things will bring them together again: love or money. Every time he went away he'd tear two dollar bills in half and give half of one to me and half of the other to Frank. 'You know I love you laddies,' he'd say to us, but this is to make double certain I'll be back." He'd make a big show of sticking the two torn halves in his wallet. When we buried him, Frank and I tossed the last two halves he gave us into his grave. Here, take this.*"

Pat tearing the hundred dollar bill in half and handing one of the halves to Megan.

"*Inflation.*"

Megan smiling, putting the torn bill in her wallet.

On the street below, the band struck the first dreamy note of *Moonlight Serenade*. This sound, sad but insistent, reached Pat and pulled him back to the here and now, where he found himself staring down at his oversized hands as they gripped the balcony's ornate wrought iron railing. He released his death grip on the railing and was examining his hands—and thinking of Megan's empty wallet on the bed behind him, the same one she had had in Prague—when the phone rang in his room.

"Hello," he said as he picked it up.

"Monsieur Nolan?"

"Yes."

"*C'est moi*, Catherine Laurence."

"Hello."

"*Bonjour.*"

"What can I do for you?"

"I was wondering if you needed help delivering Megan's clothes to charity. You mentioned you wanted to do that."

"It's already done."

"Ah, I see. Will you be staying in Paris?"

"Yes."

"Then perhaps I can make you dinner."

"Make me dinner?"

"My father committed suicide when I was thirteen. He was a policeman. I thought we could talk."

"Sure."

"I live in Marais, on Rue St. Paul, number 221A."

"Is that in Paris?"

"Yes, the Fourth Arrondissement. You take the Château de Vincennes line—the purple line—and get off at St. Paul. Can you make it at eight tonight?"

"Yes," Pat answered, looking at his watch. It was four PM.

"*Bien.* Tonight then."

~ 4 ~

Morocco, January 3, 2003

Megan Nolan sat in a compartment on the left side of the train as it steamed south, arrow straight, from Casablanca to Marrakech. She had taken this ride before and knew that there was nothing much to see except the ocassional man and mule or tin hut breaking up an otherwise monotonously flat and dun-colored coastal plain. The sun, setting now to her right, cast an elongated shadow of the train. A shadow that, for all its fun-house shape, seemed to gently caress the parched and lonely landscape that it so swiftly passed over.

Lulled by the sound and movement of the train and the sight of its shadow double racing along with it, Megan fell to thinking of her father and of the Christmas-to-New-Year's week they had just spent together in Rome. Why was it that the holidays, with their insistent sentimentality, distorted and blurred relationships, like the racing shadow she had been watching distorted and blurred the shape of the train? She had dragged him to midnight mass on Christmas Eve at St. Peter's. It was a wondrous spectacle, but why had she done it? Why change their routine of fortune-teller and Chinese food on all the Christmas holidays they spent together in Europe? Afterward they had had champagne and exchanged gifts in their hotel's penthouse restaurant, Rome's seven hills gleaming below them. That scene came back to her now: the smile on her father's face as he opened his gift—a richly tooled wallet from Florence—and the awkward silences that followed.

These were and were not the same as the silences, awkward and sad, that she had experienced as a child, both when Pat was away and when he was home, which in the early years seemed only to be at holidays. One Christmas, when she was seven or eight, after Pat had bought them the little house in New Canaan and Megan allowed herself to believe that all was finally well in her world, Pat left abruptly on New Year's Eve for a job in Iran. She remembered watching him pack, wanting desperately to ask him to call her from this exotic place Iran, as she had heard from school-mates that their fathers did when away on business. But the words did not come, and Pat, in the short and brutal silence that followed, no doubt guilty and with a scotch or two under his belt, was soon dropping her off at Uncle Franks with a hurried kiss and barely a good-bye. She had turned the tables on him since then, but there was no great satisfaction in it after all. She hated New Year's to this day.

Six days later he was gone, relieved, she was sure, to be on his Alitalia flight to New York, scotch in hand. *Something's different,* he had said to her on their last night together, at dinner. *You seem quieter.* He probably thought she had been jilted by a man, gotten her just desserts at last. Poor Pat, she had left him to work his life out on his own, much as he had left her when she was a child to work out *her* life on her own. He had years ago stopped asking her when she was coming home, which was too bad, because if he had asked her this year she might have told him she was thinking about a return trip. A trip to *Connecticut*—the word itself was oddly comforting—might be just the respite she needed. How would he have reacted?

The sensation of the train gradually slowing interrupted this chain of thoughts. Megan first looked at her watch—they weren't due to arrive in Marrakech for another forty-five minutes—and then out the window. She saw ahead an old and crumbling concrete siding next to a signal stand with one of its paddle arms broken off at the base. As the train came to a stop at the concrete platform, she could hear voices, men's voices, jabbering in the corridor, and then, a moment later, a handsome, well-dressed Arab man slid open her compartment's door and told her in perfect English that they were clearing the track for another train to pass and would be delayed a half hour or so. Familiar with the ways of the Maghrib—the so-called western Muslim world—she shrugged and went out to the cracked concrete platform to smoke, sitting on the edge of the equally cracked signal stand with her large, all-purpose carry bag at her feet. These feet, shod in skimpy gold sandals, their toenails painted red, were lovely and, she knew perfectly well, shockingly naked for a Muslim culture. But she made no concessions to any culture. Neither her faded jeans nor her pale green silk blouse were form-fitting, but it was obvious that she was shapely.

The other passengers, all men, about a dozen in all, paced the platform or talked to one another in staccato Arabic or Berber. The handsome Arab went off toward a vendor who doubled as a taxi driver and who seemed to have arrived at the siding out of nowhere, which was what pretty much surrounded them in all directions. When he completed his transaction—talking and smiling as the vendor filled a paper cone with dates—the man turned and began walking toward Megan. The other passengers, in the frenetic style of the Muslim world, had accosted the conductor as soon as he stepped onto the platform. They stopped pestering him for a second to stare at the shockingly *outré* and discomfiting Megan and the totally Westernized and equally discomfiting Arab who was about to join her on the signal stand. Megan, who had seen the handsome Arab sitting in a private compartment aloofly reading the *Herald Tribune* as she made her way through the initially crowded train look-ing for a seat, was not certain that he would approach her. This was not, after all, a bar in a fancy hotel in Casablanca. This was *in country* so to speak, where there were no ho-tels or bars, and where the local Muslims took their code of conduct seriously, a code that abhorred fraternization with Western women in public or otherwise. But the man did ap-proach, casting a casual glance at his fellow male Muslims and a quick sly smile in Megan's direction as he crossed the platform.

He sat a few feet from Megan, crossing his long legs, smoothing his trousers, and then clasping his manicured hands on his lap before speaking. "Is this your first trip to Marrakech?"

"No."

"Where are you staying?"

"I don't know yet."

"May I suggest a place? I am there often."

"Of course. Where do you stay?"

"I have my own place. But I know several hotels where Westerners are welcome. If you give them my name it will help."

"And your name is?"

"Lahani. Abdel al-Lahani. My Western friends call me Del. And yours?"

"Megan Nolan."

"You are American." This was a statement, not a ques-tion. It was obvious that she was American and therefore it was not a very insightful statement. But something about the way he said it gave Megan pause. Could it actually be condescension? Or better yet, contempt? The tone of supe-riority in his deep and confident voice was barely detectable, but nevertheless there, and it sent a mild thrill through her heart. A thrill that stirred the demon anticipation that had been sleeping there for quite some time.

"American," she answered, her voice neutral, her eyes flat. She could tell by her new friend's New York or Parisian-cut suit and impeccable grooming that he had money and decent taste. These were two of her three prerequisites in a man she might take to bed. The third was harder to define. She often thought of it as unconscious superiority, the kind so obvious in royalty or celebrity or the bored children of the nouveau riche. Whatever it was, she knew it when she saw it, and if the Arab sitting next to her had it in the abundance she thought he did, then the dance might be on.

"And you?" she asked.

"I am Saudi Arabian."

"I see. A prince of the blood?"

"No, nothing of the sort. I am a businessman. That is all."

"What kind of business?"

"I sell influence."

"What kind of influence."

"The kind that gets people large government contracts—to explore for oil, to build factories, to rape the land."

"How is it that you have this influence to sell?"

"Such a good question, but one that would take time to answer. Perhaps we can have dinner in Marrakech. I will be there for five days. My home is in the medina. There is a small hotel on the same block, the Sultana, that you would like very much, I think."

Megan thought this offer over, seeing, dispassionately, all the phases of the relationship unfold before her mind's eye. *So sure of himself, this rich Saudi.*

"I leave for Zagora tomorrow," she answered.

"Zagora? In the mountains? What brings you to Morocco, Ms. Nolan, may I ask?"

"I'm a writer. I'm researching a story."

"What kind of story?"

"There is a blind family living outside of Zagora, in the foothills. Husband, wife, six children, five of them blind. I am going to interview them."

"And how did you hear about this family?"

"A friend of mine was in the Peace Corps there. He told me about them."

"And what will you write about them? That they are blind and poor?"

"Yes, the usual bullshit."

After she said this, Megan casually put her cigarette out in the dirt at her feet, turning away from Lahani for a second. When she turned back, her features composed, even tranquil, she looked for but saw no trace of a shadow in the businessman's dark, deep-set eyes. Indeed, he smiled and barked out a short laugh, throwing his head quickly back as he did.

"Such cynicism," he said. "And who will buy such a story?"

"If I understate it enough, The New Yorker, or Harper's."

"No drama."

"God forbid."

"*God forbid.* Do you believe in God, Ms. Nolan?"

"No, but it's faith that matters, not belief."

"A fine distinction."

"Not so fine. And you? Are you a believer?"

"I am Muslim. For me there is Allah and no other."

"You're not a terrorist, are you?" Megan asked. "A Wahabi madman?"

"Such direct questions," said Lahani, "are not asked in the Arab world." Megan watched his eyes as he spoke. She had meant to insult him and his culture. But again he seemed amused, not in the least angry or put off. Her intention was not to get a glimpse of what the real Abdel al-Lahani might look like beneath the highly civilized mask he wore, although that glimpse might be interesting, and useful. It was to set the pattern of their relationship early. But either he was very clever, very much in control, or the mask was real. Each of these alternatives intrigued her, as did the way his dark eyes flashed brightly when he smiled and laughed. He was handsome, she had to admit, and there was an intriguing hint of cruelty in his finely sculpted lips and mouth.

"Are they answered?" she said.

"Your question is a statement, is it not, Ms. Nolan? *I am in charge,* you are saying. *I am not afraid.* Statements do not require answers."

"I already know the answer."

"Are you sure?"

"Yes, you either are or you aren't." It was Megan's turn to smile. As she did, her face, which had shown no emotion throughout the conversation except perhaps mild curiosity, was suddenly transformed. Her austere beauty no longer a barrier, her smile became an invitation: to innocence and corruption, joy and pain. As smiles went it was pretty breathtaking, and she could see from Lahani's reaction, watching as he drank in his first taste of the most dangerous drink he would ever take, that he thought so, too.

"Good, then we can have dinner tonight."

"It will have to be late. I have to sleep, and make some calls."

"By all means. Say the lobby of the Sultana at ten?"

~ ~ ~

The Sultana was indeed an exquisite hotel—some twenty well-appointed rooms surrounding a hushed and verdant courtyard with a splashing fountain and reflecting pool at its center. While her tub was filling with hot water, Megan stood on her balcony looking down on the courtyard. The fountain was in the form of a lion's head spewing water from its flared nostrils. She watched the reds and yellows of the pool's tiled floor shimmer as the water moved in concentric waves over them toward the outer rim of the pool and then lapped back. Megan loved irony. She saw it as the ultimate cosmic hypocrisy, the final revenge of the gods of fate against humans who were too vain to know they were vain. It was therefore a matter of the most supreme irony to Megan that after ten years of tramping around Europe, caring for nothing except seducing rich men, accepting with thinly veiled disdain their gifts of cash and jewelry while letting them know that she was in charge of her own life *and* of theirs, she had succumbed to something outside of herself.

On September 11, 2001, she had been in bed with one of these men, a beautiful twenty-four-year-old graduate student in linguistics at the Sorbonne, whose father owned some fifteen high-brow jewelry stores throughout France. She had returned from the bathroom after their afternoon lovemaking to find Alain at the edge of the bed, glued to the television screen in their room at the Ritz, his eyes agog. A Noam Chomsky conspiratorialist, he was later to declare with confidence, his veneer of bored sophistication back in place, that it was the Jews who flew the planes into the buildings in New York and Washington. But that afternoon his face was unguarded as his child's brain absorbed the events transpiring across the Atlantic—several thousand Americans dead, the president and the Congress scurrying for safety, America in shock as it watched the repeated clips of the twin towers being hit and then collapsing. On that face Megan saw satisfaction and delight. And to her amazement she was angry. The smugness on the femininely beautiful face of America-hater Alain Tillinac had struck Megan Nolan dumb. To this day she summoned up that face, that look, with revulsion.

She sent Alain home and spent the rest of September 11 herself glued to the television. The next day she went to Paris's huge Bibliothèque Publique where she read all of the national and international papers. Then she saw a free computer, went to it, and typed *al-Qaeda* into its search engine. That click of her mouse had since led her down many paths in Europe and the Middle East. The latest had taken her to Morocco, where she was researching a story not about the blind family in Zagora but about its one sighted member, the eldest son, whom she had reason to believe was a member of an obscure terrorist group called the Al Haramain Brigade. And now there was another irony. There was a new rich man in her life, the first man, period, since the effete Alain Tillinac. This man had already been helpful. He had driven her in his Mercedes limousine from the train station to the Sultana, where he arranged for her to get a quite beautiful room overlooking the courtyard with its lovely fountain. He had also promised to find a competent and trustworthy driver/translator to take her to Zagora, a rugged drive across the Middle Atlas Mountains, nearly to the edge of the great Sahara. And he was a sophisticated Muslim, a Saudi who could perhaps help her gain insight into Wahabism, the most extreme form of Islamo-fascism, a "religion" that called for the murder of all infidels, including not only Christians and Jews, but all non-Wahabi Muslims as well. The ultimate in ethnic cleansing.

Abdel al-Lahani was handsome and sexy and exuded power, and she hadn't been with a man in over a year. He saw her, she was certain, as the next in a long line of sexual conquests. Perhaps she could pick his brain and his wallet *and* disabuse him of such thoughts all in one fell swoop. Smiling to herself, she turned and went into her room, where she would soak in her bath and reintroduce herself to the old Megan Nolan.

~ 5 ~

Paris, January 3, 2004

Catherine Laurence had called Pat Nolan on her cell phone from the lobby of his hotel. Afterward she crossed the street and found an empty park bench from which she could watch Le Tourville's elegant front entrance. She wore a suit similar to the one she had worn the day before. This one was a charcoal gray. Under it she wore a pleated tuxedo-style blouse with a black string tie and a silver choker at her neck. Underneath she had on the simple, barely-there black bra and panties that had driven her husband wild when they first met. Her half-heels were not stylish, but she walked a lot in her job and, at her height—close to five-ten—she really didn't need to accentuate legs that, though men clearly noticed and seemed to like, she felt were much too long. On bad days she felt like a giraffe, or a newborn colt.

The knot that she had felt in her stomach yesterday when she met Nolan had surprised and pleased her. Surprised because she had felt nothing like it for several years, and pleased because she could savor it without having to even think about an entanglement with Nolan, whom she had assumed until an hour ago she would never see again. It was likely the protection afforded by this thought that emboldened her to don her sexy underwear that morning, to go forth as a sexual being once again. She had pictured the tall and handsome American on an airplane, not sitting across from her at dinner in her apartment in Marais.

Catherine, her legs crossed, her black trench coat on her lap, listened idly to the band while reviewing the strange case now solely, it seemed, in her hands. She had been a policewoman long enough to know that she could believe anything of anybody. But the years had also taught her to trust her intuition, and her intuition told her that Pat Nolan was no aider and abettor of terrorism. There were, however, missing pieces to the Pat Nolan puzzle. Why the rush to cremation? Why the reaching and touching of his daughter"s left hand through the hospital sheet? And, most intriguing, why the sharp look, fleeting but discernible, in Pat Nolan's eyes when the sheet was pulled down to reveal Megan's face? A look that spoke not of anguish or of relief, but of something closer to surprise and possibly confusion. Nolan, who had been told to expect the worst, did not look like a man who would be surprised or confused by much.

It was also in Catherine Laurence's intuitive nature to question authority. Her periodic performance reviews made consistent reference to her "difficulty in adapting to situations," which in French politically correct newspeak meant she refused to follow orders to a T, to bow without dissent to the dictates of all superiors. Why, Catherine asked herself now, was the antiterrorism division of the Judicial Police not involved in the Nolan matter, a case with grave national security implications? Why the DST on its own? Why were the Moroccans not interested in pursuing a man who had killed thirty of their citizens? And why was LeGrand taking orders from Charles Raimondi? Perhaps he really was DST, but Catherine would have bet her pension—the sacred cow of all French statists—that he was not. Underneath that facade of glamour and smugness he was a coward, and no coward could last long in the DST, with its roots in *la Resistance* and its line of unsung but true heroes from then until the present.

With the band between songs, Catherine stopped her analysis, and in the last of the day's light, made her second careful sweep of the park, taking in the entrance at the corner of Avenue de la Mottes Picquets, where a middle-aged man in a tan trench coat was buying a bag of roasted chestnuts from a street vendor; the people walking on either side of a low wrought iron fence; the bandstand with a small group of jazz lovers standing nearby waiting for the next selection, and those sitting on benches situated, like hers, on the edge of a manicured lawn. On one of these were two young Arab men in jeans, athletic shoes, and down jackets, unzipped in the mild weather. When she first spotted these two, on entering the park, she thought she saw, briefly, a patch of dark brown leather tucked under the rib cage of the one nearest her. When she looked now she saw that his red jacket was pulled closely to his chest.

The endpoint of her sweep was Le Tourville's elegant entrance, with its Belgian block courtyard and tall glass doors under a stylishly undulating portico of stone and glass. Standing under the portico, in khakis and a weatherbeaten leather jacket, was Pat Nolan. He looked better-groomed than he had the day before, with his five o'lock shadow gone and his thick wavy hair parted and brushed away from his forehead. She could see the whites of his eyes as he, too, seemed to make a casual reconnaissance of the hotel's busy courtyard, as if contemplating whether or not to hail one of the cabs parked near its entrance. Catherine watched as Nolan instead put his hands—large and cleanly sculpted hands, masculine hands, she remembered—in his jacket pockets, made his way out of the courtyard, and then turned right, in the direction of the Métro station on the corner. The Arabs, she noted, rose and headed, not quite casually, in the same direction.

She made it to the platform in time to follow all three of them onto a train heading north across the river. She took a seat at the far left end of the car. The Arabs, perhaps in their mid-twenties and evenly matched in height and wiry build, one in red and the other in a blue jacket, stood a few meters away, holding on to the chrome poles that marked the car's center sliding doors. Beyond them by another meter or two, Nolan sat on a side bench. Settling into the gentle rocking motion of the train, Catherine wondered where they were going and what would happen when they got there.

~ 6 ~

Paris, January 3, 2004

Inspector LeGrand had asked Pat if he was aware of any friends or associates that Megan may have had in Paris, and he had answered no, which was the truth at the time. But the bank receipt in Megan's wallet had reminded him of one: a gypsy fortune-teller named Annabella Jeritza, whose storefront operation in Montmartre Megan made it a point to visit at least once a year, around the Christmas holidays if she could at all arrange it. Megan had spoken of Madame Jeritza over the years, but it was not until she dragged Pat with her in 1999 that he realized that an incongruous but genuine friendship had taken root between them. Megan had brought her a Christmas present that year, and though the old crone had charged them each the full fare for telling them their futures, afterward she had closed the shop and fed them tea from a samovar and flaky pastries dripping with honey. There had been a firm knocking at the front door and the telephone had rung several times, but Jeritza seemed oblivious as she concentrated on their small party, which ended when her son, a swarthy and swaggering little man in his forties, came home drunk and knocked over the whiskey bottle that Annabella had been using to fortify their tea. Pat, though more than a little drunk, did not miss the light that appeared in the old crone's eyes when she looked at Megan, whose hand she occasionally held and quietly stroked.

The Paris Métro was easy to navigate, but the labyrinthian streets of Montmartre were not. It was full dark by the time Pat walked through a bleak pocket park that looked familiar and spotted Madame Jeritzas sign in the middle of a crooked street lined with the detritus of Paris's retail world: a shabby pawn shop; a cobbler whose window was filled to the top with old shoes and boots of every size, shape and color; a wiccan bookstore; a used clothing shop with two naked and headless mannequins guarding the entrance. In the light spilling from the window and neon sign of a tobbaconist, Pat saw two young men on their knees working on the engine of a vintage motorcycle while a third sat in the sidecar and smoked.

Just beyond them was Madame Jeritza's storefront, its picture windows draped in dark brown from top to bottom, its solid wood doorway dark and unpromising. Pat knocked, not expecting an answer, and there was none. He knocked harder, and then after a moment of silent listening he walked toward the picture window to his right, where there was a slight opening in the drapes, to see if he could get a look inside. As he did this, one of the young men called to him, "*Monsieur, pardon. Madame Jeritza est fermé.*"

"*Parlez-vous Anglais?*"

"No".

A fair amount of Pat's high school French, drilled into his brain for four years by the Jesuits at Norwalk's St. Ignatius Academy, had surprisingly stuck and then been reinforced by his visits with Megan, who spoke it fluently and used it as her second language throughout Europe. He had all the guidebook phrases down and could speak in full sentences as long as he stuck with the present tense and a basic vocabulary. He was far from confident, but determined to make himself understood. After Annabella Jeritza there was the town of Lisieux, population forty thousand, where he knew of no one connected to Megan, and then he was out of leads.

"*Connaissez-vous Madame Jeritza?*"

"Oui."

"Je suis le père de Megan Nolan."

"Le père de Megan Nolan?"

"Oui. Il est très important que je parle avec Madame Jeritza ce soir. Immediatement."

"Immediatement?"

"Oui."

"Porquoi? Êtes-vous la police?"

"No. S'il vous plait. Ma fille ... ma fille est morte. Pouvez-vous dire Madame Jeritza?"

The neon light above the tobacconist's door described the outline, in bright yellow, of a cigarette, with dashes of smoke, flicking on and off, emerging from its glowing red tip. When the young man stood to talk to Pat, his face was washed by this eerie light. His shiny black hair was tied back in a ponytail. His eyes were like a cat's, dark and piercing. He held a wrench in his hand. Pat stared back at him, ready to throw the kid and his friends through the tobacconist's window if he had to. He had been an amateur boxer for three years after high school and had never lost the ability to throw a killer punch. Twice he had been arrested for assault for bloodying the faces of union goons who occasionally harassed the workers on his nonunion jobs. He was still very strong and agile, and in a way relished the idea of a brawl. It might release the frustration that had been building in him since the morning before, when he had discovered that Megan was not only not dead, but that she was in some sort of exotic, Meganlike trouble. And that he was expected to find her in a country of forty million people, none of whom he knew, and most of whom he assumed were antagonistic to Americans because they had chosen to *fight back* when attacked by terrorists.

"Attendez," the young man said, holding up the index finger of his right hand and breaking abruptly into Pat's overheated chain of thoughts. Turning, the youth spoke rapidly in French to his friends and then went into the tobacconist's shop. His companions watched him for a second, then kicked the motorcycle down from its stand and rolled it into an alley to the right of the shop, quickly disappearing into the darkness. The wooden wine crate they used as a toolbox remained on the sidewalk. Pat reached into it and picked out a spanner wrench with a heavy rolling head, which he put into the right front pocket of his leather jacket. A few minutes passed in which it occurred to Pat that he had been abandoned, but then the tobacconist's lights went out and ponytail appeared in the doorway motioning to Pat to come in. Pat did, following him through the darkened shop into a rear storeroom, and from there through a door that opened into a rear room of Madame Jeritza's quarters. The room was small and sparse, its floor covered by a stained and yellowed linoleum. On one wall stood a porcelain gas stove on lion's claw legs, on another a row of shelves containing a samovar, which Pat recognized, some china cups, and canisters of tea and spices. At a small formica-topped chrome-legged table sat Annabella Jeritza, in the same—or much the same—head scarf, hoop earrings, and multilayered silk gown that she had had on the last time he had seen her five years ago.

"S'asseoir," she said, "sit," motioning to the chair across from her.

Pat turned to see that ponytail had not followed, and then sat. The only light in the room came from a white candle in a brass holder on the table between them. Though the glow from the candle was soft, Pat could see that the intervening years had taken their toll on the gypsy fortune-teller who had befriended his daughter. The roughly applied rouge and eyeliner did nothing to hide the sallow and wrinkled flesh of her face. Her hair—what he could see of it—was dry and tangled, its original henna, whatever color it had once been, now a brassy orange. Only her eyes remained the same: calculating, intelligent, alert to the danger that gypsies expect to see on all sides. As Pat gazed into these eyes, he could also see that they were red and slightly swollen, as if the old woman had been crying.

"Thank you for seeing me," he said.

"*De rien.* You have brought bad news."

"No, Megan is alive."

"Alive? But my grandson said she was dead?"

"I had to get your attention. I had to see you."

"Where is Megan?"

"I don't know. I thought you could tell me."

"I can't."

"When did you last see her?"

"What has happened, Monsieur Nolan?"

Pat had had his hands in his jacket pockets, ready to wield the wrench, still half anticipating trouble. Now he took them out and placed them palms down on the table. Five years ago, Annabella Jeritza had taken his left hand before reading it and placed it against her heart. "That is the sound of a heartbeat," she had said. It had startled him, as had her next statement: "You feel you have been cheated. But perhaps you have been given a great gift." Her predictions—"I see two marriages. I see children"—made while gazing at his left palm, holding it gently but firmly in her slender, still-feminine hands, he had dismissed with a smile, relieved to know that she was just another hustler after all.

"The American consul called me to tell me that Megan had killed herself," Pat replied. "I came to Paris to identify the body. It was not her, but I said it was."

"Why?"

"She went to great lengths to fake her death. She must be in trouble. I have to find her. I believe she wants me to find her."

"Do you love your daughter, Monsieur Nolan?"

"Madame Jeritza ..."

"Do you know why she left home?"

Pat remained silent. This was a question he had asked himself for years, growing tired at last of the embarrassing triteness of the only answers he could think of. *She had no mother. She spent more time in day care than she did with him. She sensed that he blamed her for Lorrie's death, for the loss of the life he really wanted to live.* All true and all bullshit.

"Perhaps she has always been in trouble," Madame Jeritza said. "Perhaps she always wanted you to come looking for her."

"I'm looking for her now."

"Let us hope it is not too late."

"Madame Jeritza, have you seen her?"

"She came to see me on November 2, the day of All Souls. Do you know what that day signifies? *Le Jour des Morts?*"

"I've forgotten."

"The dead return to their homes that night, where it is warm and where supper is put out, so they can eat the food of the living. In Brittany, where I was born, the peasants go at nightfall to kneel at the graves of their loved ones, to pour water or milk into the hollows of their tombstones. Prayers are said for the souls in purgatory to hasten the day when they will see God."

"What does this have to do with Megan?"

"She came to pray for the souls of the three children she had aborted. To leave cakes and milk out for them."

"Christ."

"Yes, Christ."

Pat looked into Annabella Jeritza's eyes and then down at his hands. He had used these hands to do and fix many things. Move the earth with a giant machine, tear apart and rebuild a car engine, make a soda box wagon for Megan. He sometimes thought that whatever he was good for in life was contained in his hands. But now he had entered the territory of the broken heart, which hands could not repair.

"She also wanted the name of a midwife," Madame Jeritza said. "She was pregnant."

"Pregnant?"

"Yes, and she wanted no record of the child's birth."

"No abortion."

"No."

Pat was silent. Three abortions. He was not surprised or shocked. Megan's entire life, her inner life, the one that mattered, was a secret she kept from him. A weapon. But Megan giving birth, passing a child from her womb into the world, Megan a mother ... The feelings these images stirred in his heart did surprise him, so forcefully did they announce themselves.

"Where was she staying? Where did she go?" he asked.

"She was staying with gypsies here in Montmartre. I found her a midwife in that neighborhood."

"Did she have the child?"

"Yes, a boy. She brought him to me for a reading."

The candle between them had nearly burned down. Before it did, Annabella reached to the shelf behind her for a new one, which she lit from the old one's sputtering flame and then stuck into the melting wax in the bottom of the brass holder.

"Where did she go?"

"I don't know. She left a few days after the baby was born."

"The people she was staying with, do you know them?"

"Yes."

"Can I speak to them?"

"Yes, but I must speak to them first. They will not speak to a stranger. Come tomorrow, in the evening. Doro—my grandson—will take you to them."

~ ~ ~

Outside, Pat made his way to the small park, the only route he was certain would lead to a Métro station. Entering it, he was oblivious to the wind whistling softly through the naked branches of its trees or the chill that had descended on Paris. Against this chill he put his hands in the pockets of his leather jacket, finding in the right one the wrench he had lifted from Doro's toolbox. Its heft and rough metallic texture comforted him. It was a tool, something familiar that, unlike the souls of the dead and the murky world of gypsy fortune-tellers and midwives, he could put his hand around and know what to do with. Ahead, the path was lit by an ornate lamppost with only one of its cluster of three ball-shaped lamps working. In its dim light he saw two men in ski jackets walking slowly in his direction. As he neared them, he moved to his left, but they blocked his path and suddenly one of them had him by the arm and was sticking something hard and metallic into his ribs—a gun—and saying in thickly accented English, *Be silent, Mr. Patrick Nolan, and come with me or I will shoot you through the heart.*

Reflexively, Pat pushed the man away and in the same motion pulled the wrench from his pocket and swung it at his head, where it crunched against bone and knocked him flat onto his back on the park's cinder pathway. At the same time there were two gunshots. Pat whirled in the direction of the second one in time to see the other man falling to the ground clutching his chest and a woman in a black trench coat walking quickly toward him: Officer Laurence.

"Step away, Monsieur Nolan. Step away. *Vitement!*"

Pat took two steps back and watched as Laurence, whose long brown hair shone in the glow from the broken lamp, nudged the second man over onto his back with her foot. There was a large blotch of blood on the front of his gray sweater, still oozing. In his right hand he was gripping a small gun. She kicked the gun away, then knelt and placed two fingers against his carotid artery. She quickly turned to the man Pat had felled, who was lying on his side breathing heavily, moaning softly. Taking her makeup case out of her shoulder bag and flipping it open, she pressed two fingers of the man's right hand against its mirror. After a rapid search of his pockets, she tore open his sweater and found a leather neck pouch with a passport and other papers in it. These she leafed through quickly before slipping them into her trench coat pocket. She then went about the same process with the man with the chest wound. While she was occupied with him, the man Pat had felled rose slowly to one knee. Blood was streaming from a gash above his left eye. With his good eye he stared hard at Laurence kneeling over his partner and at Pat looming over him only a few feet away. Then suddenly he was on his feet and running toward the wooded area to his left. Pat, his adrenaline level in the red zone, spotted a gun on the grass a few meters away. He raced for it, but it was too late. The injured man had vanished into the pitch-black shadows of the woods. Pat took a step in that direction, but was stopped by Laurence's voice behind him.

"Let him go," she said. "We will never catch him in the dark."

"What about him?" Pat said, nodding toward the man on the path.

"He is dead."

"What are you doing here?"

"I was following you."

Pat took this in, remaining silent, trying to decide which of several logical questions to ask next. He was still holding the wrench, which was stained with blood on its business end. Seeing it, Pat recalled with a slight jolt the thud of metal against skin and bone as he whacked his assailant.

"Give that to me," Laurence said, extending her hand. Taking it, she wiped it clean on the front of the dead man's jacket and put it in her coat pocket.

"Following me?"

"Yes," Laurence replied, "but there is no time to talk. Help me."

Turning, she lifted the dead man under his arms and began dragging him off the path. Pat took hold of the man's legs and together they deposited him at the edge of some nearby bushes, but in plain sight.

"Let's go," Laurence said, "we will use the Métro."

"First tell me who they are."

"What is that on your hand?" She took hold of his sleeve to get a better look. A trickle of blood ran down to his fingers. There was a perfectly formed bullet hole in his leather jacket at his bicep, which was also oozing dark red.

"We will talk at my apartment."

"Who are they?" Pat asked again, pulling his hand away.

"They are *Mabahith*, Saudi Arabian Secret Police."

~ 7 ~

Morocco, February 5, 2003

"How was Zagora? Did you find your family?" Abdel al-Lahani asked.

"I did," Megan answered.

"And? Is there a story?"

"No."

"No? Why not? It seems perfect."

"I was hoping to find a terrorist, but I didn't."

"A terrorist. My God. Are you serious?"

"Yes, I am."

"But I thought you wanted to write a story about the natives. The blind family."

"I was told that the sighted son had terrorist ties. That was the story. His parents told me he was attending university in France. I turned up nothing to indicate otherwise."

"You did not tell me this. You did not trust me. You think because I am Muslim I am sympathetic to terrorists." Lahani smiled as he said this, modulating his deep, rich voice to a pitch somewhere between mock sternness and mock hurt, supremely self-assured, as Megan was learning he almost always was. What he did not know was that her confession was a tactical one, meant to stroke his already bloated ego, to dull his senses to her cunning if and when she decided to really use it.

"We had just met," she said, looking down as if embarrassed.

"But we are only meeting now for the second time."

"I know no one here, Abdel. I am hoping you can help me. You said you have influence. I would like you to introduce me to someone who knows the security situation in

Morocco. A scholar, perhaps, or someone with ties to the military or the police."

"But why? Morocco is a liberal country by Muslim standards. There have been no terrorist attacks here. You will find nothing."

"Then that will be the story."

This time Lahani's smile was one that Megan at first thought was meant to humor her. But her new friend had a way at times of smiling only with his mouth, as he did now, of keeping his eyes flat and emotionless, a trait much more attractive to her than mere expressiveness. In her experience, it took very little in the way of either time or prompting for most men to express their feelings, which usually centered around what they thought was love but was usually lust or the need for mothering.

"I have a friend at the university," Lahani said, his smile gone, his eyes meeting hers without a hint of humor or condescension. "An Islamic scholar. If I speak to him first, he may be willing to speak to you. I am going there tomorrow. I'll ask him."

"Thank you."

They were sitting at a wrought iron table in the tiled courtyard of Lahani's walled house in the heart of Marrakech's old city. A woman in a floor-length hooded djellaba, her veil down, her eyes averted and impassive, had served them a late afternoon dinner of couscous steamed with lamb and vegetables and a bottle of Bordeaux that Megan knew from her many adventures with rich Frenchmen was worth about two hundred dollars American. Afterward came dates, cheese, nuts, thick coffee, and conversation. Close at hand were tile-bordered gardens bearing lemon and acaccia trees and a small, gently splashing fountain whose pedestal and bowl bore mosaic images of Moorish Spain. Megan wore comfortable white linen pants and a white silk tunic with a diamond pattern embroidered at the cuffs and waist. At her neck was a thick eighteen-carat-gold chain given to her by Alain Tillinac in one of his futile efforts to win her back. Its burnished surface captured the late day sunlight to form a ring of fire around her smooth, perfectly modeled throat. On the Zagora trip she had pinned her hair up and worn a baseball cap, layered tee, and sweatshirts, but tonight she had on decent clothes and light makeup.

Lahani, who had been away himself in Europe, seemed delighted to receive Megan's call, and even more delighted to see her as she exited her taxi at the massive front gate of his house. She had used his first name and asked him for a favor, chips in a game of arousal and anticipation that she had played many times before. This one promised to be very exciting. There was, in Megan's experience of them, a feral look to the faces of many, if not most, Middle Eastern men, a facade painfully appropriate to their seemingly universal inner desire to subjugate their women. There was an elemental wildness, to be sure, about Lahani, with his chiseled face, thick black mustache, even thicker black hair, and burning, deep-set black eyes. And there was an undertone of power, even menace in his deep baritone voice. But there was also a refinement about him, what might almost be called a learned effeteness in his movements, as if in a deliberate attempt to conceal or suppress the rawness beneath the surface. This combination of power and grace had been rare in Megan's men, nonexistent actually until now. It was a heady combination, one that required her, in turn, to play her part carefully so that she could stay in control. In truth it was this very tension, the thrill of losing control—which to her amounted to subjugation—that so attracted her to Lahani, that made the game dangerous and worth playing.

Before either of them could speak again, the serving woman arrived and, still passive and withdrawn to the point of nonexistence, bent and whispered something in Lahani's ear. He nodded and the woman left.

"I have to take a phone call," Lahani said, rising and placing his linen napkin on the table. "It may be a while. The library is through the arcade just behind you. There are some paintings and sculptures there that may interest you." Before turning to go inside, he stepped toward Megan and, reaching quietly to her, stroked her cheek with the back of his hand, which he then ran through her hair, sifting strands of it through his fingers like the spun gold it was. "Where did you get this hair?" he asked.

"From my mother," Megan said.

"Is she beautiful like you?"

"She was. She died giving birth to me in a jungle hospital. I am a citizen of Uruguay as well as the United States."

"And your father?"

"He lived and raised me in Connecticut."

"You must tell me about all this."

"I will."

When Lahani disappeared into his house, Megan rose and wandered the courtyard for a moment, remembering the touch of his hand on her face, feeling the slight pressure of it as if it were still there. The sun was low, setting behind the house. Birds were beginning their evening singing in the lemon trees. Standing behind a stand of these trees, searching for a sight of the singing birds, Megan heard a noise and turned to see the serving woman clearing away the last of the dinner dishes. A man was helping her, and Megan was surprised to see that it was the same man who had driven her to Zagora and translated for her there and in the tiny unnamed kasbah a few miles away, where the blind family lived. The man—his name was Mohammed—was perhaps fifty and taciturn to the point of rudeness. But his English was good, as was his driving, and he had acquitted himself well, finding her clean and comfortable lodging, good meals, and putting the skittish natives at ease whenever they approached. Over two full days he had compliantly put Megan's questions concerning the blind family's sighted son to numerous people, until she grew tired of their uniform shoulder shrug and decided to head back to Marrakech. Stepping out from behind the trees, Megan waved to Mohammed, who, seeing her, stood motionless for a second before nodding solemnly in her direction. Then, lifting a tray of coffee and dessert plates, he turned and went into the house, followed by the woman.

Megan was good at withholding information and telling lies, big and small. She knew the protective value of secretiveness, of pretending to be surprised, or not surprised, upon hearing certain things. Mohammed knew that the focus of her visit to Zagora was not the blind family but their sighted son. Had he told Lahani? If he had then Lahani's reaction when she told him earlier of the true reason for her trip south was not candid. This thought did not bother Megan. She had lied to Lahani, after all, and she had no interest in having a moralist or a fool for a lover. Soon she would be in a position to ask Lahani why he had spied on her—if he had—and to use his answer, whatever it turned out to be, to gain an advantage in the game of hide-and-seek they had started playing almost the moment they met. Until then it would pay to be more careful, more observant.

This is what she was thinking when Lahani surprised her from behind, putting his hands gently on her hips and pulling her to him. She caught the scent of him—a blend of citrus and smoke and what she imagined was the coolness of the desert at night—as he lifted her hair and brushed her right ear with his lips. Megan stiffened at first, but then relaxed, welcoming his embrace and light kiss.

"You surprised me," she murmured.

"Something not so easy to do, I fear."

"I am more innocent than you think."

"And less, but a man wants both."

Megan turned and placed her hands palm down on Lahani's chest, feeling for his heartbeat, which was steady and strong. He wrapped his arms around her and again drew her to him, but she gently resisted so that she could face him, looking up, as at six feet or so he was taller than her by at least a head. Her last lover had been a boy of twenty-four. Here was a man in full, still only in his early forties, but with a hardness in his eyes that spoke of a disdain for life, for the mere years that are given men. No man, except for her father, had ever had or acquired the slightest power over Megan Nolan. The thought of ceding it to Lahani was suddenly quite erotic, causing her to involuntarily press against him, confused at first and then made slightly dizzy by the wave of desire that swept over her as she felt his very large erection against her abdomen. Pulling away, she smiled, regaining her composure, holding Lahani's hand but keeping him at arm's length.

"How long will you be in Marrakech?" she asked.

"Three or four days."

"Will you show me the sights?"

"The sights? You mean tourist attractions?"

"Whatever you think might be of interest."

"Leave it to me, Megan Nolan. You will not be disappointed."

~ 8 ~

Paris, January 3, 2004

"What were you doing in the tobacconist's shop?"

"I went to see the gypsy fortune-teller next door."

"I see. Why?"

"She was a friend of Megan's."

Nolan and Catherine were in the living room of Catherine's apartment on Rue St. Paul in Paris' upscale Marais District. On a plush sofa, Pat sat naked from the waist up, his left arm wrapped at the bicep in gauze pads and hospital tape. Catherine had just finished washing and bandaging his superficial but very bloody wound. On the elegant coffee table between them sat a snifter of cognac and two codeine-based pain pills she had left over from her previous life when her husband was alive and she was struck blind every couple of months by migraine headaches.

Two oversized armchairs faced the sofa. Catherine sat in one and Pat's flannel shirt and dark blue sweater—both with clean-as-a-whistle bullet holes surrounded by coagulated blood—lay on the other. These he reached over and plucked up, and then slowly fumbled into while Catherine watched. The beauty and obvious strength of his arms and chest, and even his abdomen, was enhanced rather than diminished by the awkwardness of his movements, evoking in the policewoman a strange feeling of despair. She studied the large American's chiseled face, his eyes giving away nothing, as he finished off his cognac in one long sip and returned the empty glass to the table. His hands, she realized—burnished like loved and well-used tools—were more revealing of his character. Though she did not have the legend, she was sure they were the road map to his soul.

At one time she had believed that the quest to access the soul was the journey that all human beings were on. But that was before she had killed her husband by wishing him dead. How odd that a pair of human hands, hands possibly belonging to a man who was acting in aid of a terrorist cell, would remind her that her despair was turning to self-pity.

"What are those pills?" Pat asked.

"Codeine, for your pain."

"I won't need them."

"What did the gypsy tell you, Monsieur Nolan?"

"Pat."

"Pat."

"Why did you leave that dead guy in the park? You're an officer of the law."

"I saw the one speak to you. What did he say?"

"Who were you following, them or me?"

Catherine watched as Pat rose abruptly, pulled off his sweater, threw it onto the sofa, and walked over to one of the three tall windows that took up most of the nearest living room wall. Opening it halfway, he stood still for a second or two, breathing, seeming to look at his reflection in the darkened window. Catherine felt the cool winter air as it wafted into the room in her direction. Did it bring Nolan's scent with it, his American scent—leather and aftershave bought at the corner drugstore—or was it her imagination? She watched in silence as Pat then loosened his belt and, working mostly with his good arm and hand, tucked his loose shirttails into his jeans. When he was done, he faced Catherine, who had kicked off her shoes and curled her long stockinged legs under her.

"You are now presentable," she said, unable to suppress a brief, wry smile. He returned her quasi-smile, shaking his head slowly. Was he blushing slightly? Or was it just the cold night air that had brought the color to his face? Catherine could not tell. But the smile and quizzical head shake were genuine. A man in his position *would* be wondering what in the world he had gotten himself into and what was going to happen next. He sat down in the armchair facing her. Catherine could feel the tension between them ease a bit. He poured himself another cognac and drank half of it down. The traditionally oversized glass looked small as he rested it in his grip on the chair's wide arm.

"One of us has to start telling the truth," he said.

"You have just made a start."

"As have you."

"Was that your daughter in the morgue?"

"No."

"Why did you say it was?"

"It wasn't something I thought through at the time."

"Yes, but afterward you continued the deception."

Pat finished his cognac, then looked down into the empty glass. The light from a nearby lamp cast a soft glow on his face, a somber face that, as it tilted downward in reflection, Catherine admitted was quite beautiful, with its thickly lashed, soft eyes and strong masculine features. Looking up, he said, "It was her note. She wanted to be dead to the world, but not to me."

"Why dead to the world?"

"I don't know."

"Can you guess?"

"She must be in danger."

"Perhaps she committed a crime."

Pat did not respond immediately. He tilted his snifter, seeming to concentrate on a last drop of cognac edging slowly toward the rim.

"I doubt it," he said finally.

"Why?"

"Do you know that Megan's mother died giving birth to her?"

"Yes. I read it in Inspector LeGrand's report."

Pat nodded and looked away for a second and then directly at Catherine. "I'll tell you something, Detective Laurence."

"Catherine."

"Catherine. It's something I've never told anybody. Megan's life these past twelve years has been one long act of revenge against me. I was twenty-one when she was born, left with a four-pound baby and no wife. It took me five years to start being a father to her, but I never fully got there. She doesn't need to commit a crime to hurt me anymore."

"She hates you?"

"She tolerates me, which is worse."

Catherine saw no anguish on Pat's face, no sign of emotion at all. Only the same quiet countenance with which he took all things in, assessed them, and stored them away in a heart that seemed remote and lonely.

"I am sorry," she said. "I did not mean to pry."

"You're trying to help. I can see that."

"Yes."

"Tell me about those Arabs. What are you going to do with those prints?"

"I am going to see if they match anyone in our data bank. When I get an answer, I will tell you more. In the meantime, you must trust me. What did the first man say to you?"

"He wanted me to go me with him. He stuck a gun in my ribs."

"Exactly what did he say?"

"'Be silent, Mr. Patrick Nolan, and come with me or I will shoot you through the heart.'"

"That's it?"

"Yes. Then I hit him with the wrench and you showed up."

"He knew who you were."

"Yes."

"Who knows you are in France?"

"My brother. I suppose he told his wife. That's it. I got a phone call and the next day I was on a plane."

"Have you met anyone here? Anyone who knows where you're staying, that is?"

"Just Inspector LeGrand and you."

"Your brother?"

"No. I told him I'd call him but I haven't gotten around to it."

"You are quite sure?"

"Yes. Only you and LeGrand know my hotel."

"*Bien.* You should stay here tonight. You are a large man, but that sofa is large as well."

"You mean there might be more Saudi Secret Police out there looking for me?"

"Yes, if they *were* Saudi Secret Police."

Catherine uncurled her legs, reached down to pick up her shoes, and rested them on her lap. "One last thing," she said.

"Yes."

"What did the gypsy have to say?"

"She told me Megan was pregnant. She delivered a baby boy in December."

"A child!"

"Yes."

"Who is the father?"

"I don't know. I didn't think to ask."

"We will ask tomorrow. Now you will sleep and I will work. There is bedding in that chest in the corner. *Bonne nuit,* Monsieur Nolan."

"It's Pat. Remember?"

"Yes, of course. Good night, Pat."

~ ~ ~

In her study, which she had transformed from an old walk-in closet across the hallway from her bedroom, Catherine dusted and lifted the fingerprints on her makeup mirror, then scanned them into her computer. She stared at them on the screen for a long moment, mesmerized, as though she might find the secret to evil in the world hidden in their delicate whorls and loops. Then she sent them to her uncle, Daniel Peletier, a retired Gendarmerie forensics expert, hoping he would be awake and at his computer in Normandy, in his stone-and-timber farm house on Cap de la Hague overlooking the English Channel, winter-mad with storms and gales this time of year. *Call me,* her e-mail said. While her bath was running, she made a pot of hot chocolate and put slabs of fresh butter on several chunks of bread leftover from her breakfast. These she took—along with her cell phone—into her bathroom with her, eating and drinking while she slowly undressed. Unhappy before and then guilty after Jacques's death, she had ignored her body for long stretches. Tonight, with a strange and handsome man in the house, she looked at it. Acknowledged it. Her tiny black bra and panties punctuated this acknowledgement as she dropped them to the white tile floor. Crossing past the living room with her food and phone, she had slowed for a second to see Patrick Nolan asleep on his back on her sofa, his bandaged arm across his chest, his good arm hanging straight down, the hand resting with curled fingers on her Persian carpet. A band of yellow light no wider than an inch or two, spilling from the half-closed kitchen door, lay diagonally across Nolan's face, illuminating his lustrous dark brown eyelashes and a brow furrowed more in sleep than when he was awake.

She finished her bread and chocolate while soaking, and then afterward she put on silk pajamas and a robe and sat at her desk to read the flimsy file entitled *In the Matter of M. Nolan*. It contained the responding officer's report, a statement from the concierge at the Hotel Lorraine, the autopsy report, Megan Nolan's passport and Moroccan visa, and Catherine's half-page report of Pat Nolan's positive ID at the All Souls morgue. Attached to the visa was a note dated January 1 in Inspector LeGrand's hand of her call to Rabat to inquire about the visa's provenance. There was no note indicating that her call had been returned. She saw at the bottom of the autopsy report that copies had been sent to *Insp. LeGrand, etc.* She made some notes of her own, questions to ask Uncle Daniel, and then leaned back in her leather chair to stare up at the painted tin ceiling of her hundred-year-old apartment. When she and Pat exited the Metro near Rue St. Paul, she had stopped at a pay phone and called the police precinct in Montmartre to report, anonymously, that she had been out walking her dog and had heard gunshots and then seen a man running from the area of the small park near Rue Volney. She knew they were gunshots, she said, because her husband was a hunter and had taken her along on several trips to shoot quail in Normandy. She did not know if quail were to be found in Normandy, and if they were if they could be shot there, and now she smiled to herself at this thought. By now the police would have found the body.

The ringing of her cell phone interrupted this chain of thoughts.

She picked it up and flipped it open. "Hello."

"Catherine, *c'est moi*, Daniel."

"Uncle."

"How are you, *ma petite niece?*"

"I am well, *mon petit oncle*."

"I have received your prints."

Daniel Peletier, now seventy-two, and his brother, Jean-Paul—Catherine's father—five years younger, had both had long and respectable careers in French law enforcement. Daniel as a forensic scientist and Jean-Paul as a gendarmerie detective in St. Lô, their home city in northwestern France's Manche province. They were uneventful, unspectacular, plodding careers in the old-fashioned practical way of the mid-twentieth-century French middle class. So plodding, so evenly paced, that unless you observed them periodically and with a skilled eye, you would not know that from one year to the next they accomplished all that they had set out to do in their lives: perform honorably at their jobs and raise their families in as much security and comfort as they could. It was her father's sudden death in his sleep in 2001—she had lied to Pat earlier in order to get him to have dinner with her—that unmoored Catherine and left her stranded, with only a desolate marriage. Her mother, suffering from multiple sclerosis for twenty years, had died a year earlier, but even then it had never occurred to Catherine that Jean-Paul, only sixty-four, her childhood hero in his stylish uniform and hallmark gendarme's hat, could conceivably leave her. She had no siblings. Uncle Daniel, retired these past two years, childless, also a widower, was all she had left.

"What is it?" he asked. "What are you working on?"

This question aroused Catherine from her brief reverie. She did not know at the moment exactly what it was she was working on. *The Saudis would not be involved,* Inspector LeGrand had said. The impact of the risk she was taking by leaving a dead body in the park and letting the injured man get away without pursuit hit her fully now. A simple call to the local precinct would have kept her career on its so far straight and narrow course.

"I cannot say at the moment," she replied.

"Have you been promoted?"

"No."

"You want these prints run, I take it?"

"Yes."

"Whatever I do will leave a trail."

"Give me your password. I will do it from my computer."

"Impossible. The software includes voice recognition."

"Forget it then."

"Too late. I have already run the prints through."

"I told you to call me first, Uncle."

Catherine took a deep breath, her lips tightly set. She had put Uncle Daniel in danger. Tomorrow, or later tonight, she would make up a story to explain the whole thing to LeGrand.

"And the results?" she asked.

"I do not have them yet."

"How long will it take?"

"An hour or so."

"Let me ask you."

"Yes."

"You have read autopsy reports?"

"Thousands."

"If a woman had delivered a child, say within two weeks of death, would there be signs?"

"Yes, of course."

"Would a woman in the last stages of ovarian cancer have been likely to have been pregnant and delivered a baby two weeks before she died?"

"You must tell me more, my dear. What does this relate to?"

"A faked suicide."

"Is there DNA available?"

"No, but the thing is, we know it's a fake. I just want to know who else might know."

"Ah, someone who has read the autopsy for example."

"Yes."

"All autopsies on women will note certain conditions regarding pregnancies and childbirth. For example, *nulligravida* means 'never pregnant,' *nulliparous* means 'never given birth,' and so on."

"It's that simple?"

"Yes."

"Call me on my cell when you have the prints results, and use yours."

"Catherine, I am worried, of course."

"Yes, I know."

"In France, the world's greatest and most arrogant bureaucracy, it is anathema to go around the system."

"Yes, I know."

"And you will not tell me more?"

"No."

"On the other hand, there is something in your voice. Have you returned to us? Is there a man involved?"

"There's a man sleeping on my couch right now, but it's not what you think."

"I see. Promise me something."

"Yes."

"Whatever is happening, don't try to do it alone. Call on me. I am old and tired of feeling useless. Your word, *ma petite.*"

"Yes, you have my word, Uncle."

Catherine hung up the phone and leaned back in her chair. She removed the towel from her wet hair and let it fall to the floor. In the pocket of her thick terrycloth robe was a pack of Galloises and a disposable lighter. Before Jacques died, she had struggled unsuccessfully to quit smoking, making of it unconsciously a metaphor for what she saw as her cowardly inability to end her marriage. After his death she lost her taste for cigarettes—except for when it returned at moments she least expected—while bathing, for example, or while standing on one of Paris's bridges watching a barge emerge like a sea monster from the morning mist on the Seine. She was free now, free to smoke and free to live, but her conscious mind would not let her assimilate this fact. She lit a Gallois and stepped to the large mullioned door that led to a balcony overlooking Rue St. Paul. Across the street a young man—no more than twenty or twenty-one, with beautiful long black hair—was standing under the cone of light of a street lamp, also lighting a cigarette. Catherine stepped back into a deep shadow and watched as the man smoked for a second or two and then moved slowly on without looking up. She smiled as she remembered that both her father and Uncle Daniel had reminded her often that paranoia was a good detective's radar. The blips on its screen should always be tracked.

Both *nulligravida* and *nulliparous* were noted on the Megan Nolan autopsy report. Whoever knew that the real Megan Nolan was pregnant and had seen the autopsy report would know irrefutably that she was alive and had gone to great trouble to fake her suicide. Five people—not counting

Catherine—knew about the "suicide" of Megan Nolan: Patrick Nolan, his brother, Inspector LeGrand, Charles Raimondi, and an unknown person in the Moroccan diplomatic service in Rabat. An Arab. And then two Arab men, professionals on one side or the other of the law, or perhaps both, appear in Paris to abduct Nolan *père* at gunpoint. How did they know how to pick up his trail? Catherine finished her cigarette, sucking in the last drag like the narcotic it was. As she was stubbing it out in a thick glass art deco ashtray on her desk, her cell phone rang.

"Here are your prints," said Daniel without preface. "The first set matches to Ahmed bin-Shalib, twenty-five, Pakistani, wanted on a terrorist warrant issued by the US."

"Anything else on him?"

"They are associating him with the death of the American journalist in Karachi, the beheading."

"Michael Cohen."

"Yes."

The two paused to assimilate this information. Catherine could hear her uncle breathing softly through her phone's high tech receiver.

Daniel was the first to speak. "Where is he now, Catherine?"

"Somewhere in Paris. And the other?"

"No match. Where is be?"

"Probably in a morgue."

"Is that a good thing?"

"Yes."

"You do not sound—how shall I say it—elated."

"Bin-Shalib got a good look at me, and I him."

"I see. Why don't you take a ride up to see me? We can talk. It is lonely up here at the end of the world."

"I will, Uncle, and maybe sooner than you think."

"Don't fret, *ma petite,* I will make it all well."

"Yes, just like Papa."

"Just like Papa."

~ 9 ~

Paris / Courbevoie, January 4, 2004

The next morning, while Pat was still sleeping, Catherine went out to pick up a copy of *Le Monde,* which she skimmed through quickly at an outdoor table of a patisserie. She found no mention of a shooting in Volney Park or the discovery of a dead Arab anywhere in Montmartre, or Paris for that matter. She bought croissants and, once at home, placed them on a white china plate that she covered with a fresh cotton napkin and placed on the center of her small kitchen table. Outside, the early sunlight was fading as storm clouds gathered. She turned up the heat in the apartment and, while putting on a pot of coffee, heard the comforting hiss of her steam radiators responding. Pat still slept. In her study she made a series of calls. The first was to the police precinct in Montmartre, the last to Charles Raimondi. When she was done, she returned to the kitchen to find Pat splashing water onto his face and running it through his thick wavy hair with his hands. She took a dish towel from a drawer and handed it to him as he finished. It looked more like a handkerchief in his hands as he dried his face and used it to try to pacify his unruly black mane. He was still wearing the clothes he had slept in. He had even put on and laced up his sturdy and severely unfashionable American walking shoes.

"How did you sleep?" she asked.

"Well. Thank you."

"And the arm?"

"It's fine. A little sore."

"Are you hungry? I have bought croissants."

"I'm very hungry

"*Moi aussi.* Sit."

In a few minutes the half dozen pastries were gone and they were each sipping their second cup of Catherine's strong African coffee.

"This coffee is good," said Pat.

"It's the last of my husband's."

"Oh ... where is he now?"

"He is dead. He was killed in a terrorist bombing in Casablanca last May. He was a consultant to importers and exporters. Coffee was one of his specialties."

"What was his name?"

"Jacques."

"I'm sorry."

"Yes, I am too ..."

As she was finishing this sentence, the phone rang in Catherine's study. She rose quickly to get it.

"I am going out to meet a colleague," Catherine said, reappearing in the kitchen five minutes later. She had put on lipstick and was standing before Pat in a stylish black overcoat with a dark green, yellow-bordered silk scarf around her neck.

"You look beautiful," Pat said.

Catherine frowned, and her heart sank a little, though she wasn't sure why. Many men had told her she was beautiful. Charles Raimondi, for example, whom she was meeting for coffee in fifteen minutes. Could there, however, be two men more opposite than Charles Raimondi and Pat Nolan? This thought raised her spirits, though again she wasn't sure why. Unless she was attracted to Nolan. It had been so long, she had forgotten how it happened, real attraction to a man. Confused, she did not reply, only nodded and turned to leave.

"We need to talk," Pat said.

"If you are here when I return, we will talk," Catherine answered, turning back to face Pat.

"Where would I go?"

"I don't know To continue your search for your daughter."

"It's a matter for the police now, isn't it?"

"That's what I"m trying to find out."

"I don't understand."

"The dead man was not found in the park. According to the police in Montmartre there was no shooting, no dead body."

Yes, Patrick, Catherine thought. You heard me correctly. The police may not be the good guys in this case. In which event you, your daughter and I are in a lot of trouble.

"I'll be here," Pat said.

"Good. I won't be long."

~ ~ ~

"I have found Megan Nolan."

"Excellent."

Catherine had come almost immediately to the point, as, she noted, had Charles Raimondi. They were seated at a window table at a small café just around the corner from Catherine's apartment. She had arrived early and watched as Raimondi pulled up in front, parking his diplomat-tagged black Citroën in a clearly marked no-parking/loading zone. As he stepped out of the car, his black hair perfectly groomed, his movements graceful and erect, in a cashmere overcoat and soft wool Burberry scarf, he seemed as elegant—and haughty—as a swan. Watching him coolly survey the street before entering the café, she was reminded of their last meeting, when she had been repelled as much by his unselfconscious arrogance as by the transparency of his motives in attempting to befriend her.

"How did you know she wasn't dead?" she asked. "Inspector LeGrand said something about faked suicide as a terrorist MO, but that seemed too vague to me. Was it something in the autopsy report?"

Raimondi was lifting his espresso cup to his lips as Catherine asked this question. His arm paused in midair for a fraction of a second before he completed the movement—sipping and gently replacing the cup on its small saucer. He remained silent, assessing Catherine Laurence perhaps for the first time as a detective.

"You were copied on it," Catherine said. One of her calls earlier that morning had been to the pathologist who performed the postmortem and dictated the report. He recalled that the etc. at the bottom of the last page was meant to indicate that a copy had been sent to the Foreign Office, to a Florence Natale, whom another call revealed was Raimondi's administrative assistant, French-speak for secretary. The pathologist had been requested to leave no trace of the Foreign Office on the report, but his cover-your-ass bureaucratic instincts had insisted on some record of the transaction.

"I did get the autopsy," said Raimondi, like any good poker player knowing when to fold and on which issues, "but it was the Moroccans' idea—the possibility of a faked suicide. I just passed it along. Where is she? Nolan."

"In a house in Courbevoie."

"Have you told LeGrand?"

"No."

"Why not? This is highly unusual."

"I wanted an excuse to see you again. I feel I behaved badly the last time we spoke." This statement fell more easily from Catherine's lips than she thought it would. She had been prepared, for one thing, and for another she was beginning to look at Charles Raimondi with professional suspicion. Her instincts as a detective overrode all personal qualms. Raimondi could easily have faxed a copy of the autopsy to his counterpart at the Moroccan Foreign Office, someone who knew that the real Megan Nolan had been pregnant. How else to explain the two Arabs following Pat Nolan? She had no doubt that Raimondi would take the bait, his sex appeal and charisma, in his own mind, too much for any healthy young woman to resist for very long.

"Well," Raimondi replied, a slight smile crossing his lips," in that case I will square it with Inspector LeGrand."

"Thank you."

"Is Nolan alone?"

"I believe so."

"Have you told anyone else?"

"No, I came right to you. What about Europol? Shall I notify them?"

"No. I will take care of it."

Catherine glanced out the window to see if Raimondi had brought along his bodyguard or any kind of backup. It seemed almost certain that he had not. His black sedan sat silently at the curb, empty. No plainclothes police or Foreign Office security types were to be seen within a hundred meters of the café's entrance. One of Catherine's calls this morning had been to Pierre Torrance, a colleague from her police academy days, now assigned to Europol's antiterrorist unit in The Hague. He had assured her that no investigation involving a terrorist named Rahman al-Zahra was underway in France, as by law his task force was required to be notified if it were.

"I am beginning to wonder, Charles," she said, "are you DST yourself? Is the Foreign Office your cover?"

"My dear Catherine," Raimondi replied, affecting an innocent smile and raising his eyebrows in mock astonishment, "you are too smart for your own good, but I am afraid I must disappoint you. I am a liaison, that is all. Now tell me, how did you find our Megan Nolan?"

"The father led me there."

"I see. Is he still at Le Tourville?"

"As far as I know."

"Tell me about the house and the neighborhood."

"It looks shuttered, possibly abandoned. The neighborhood is quiet, working class."

"Is she there now?"

"I saw her go in this morning carrying groceries. She was walking."

"No car?"

"No, I believe not."

"The address?"

"121 Avenue des Ormes. Shall I pick her up myself, or shall I coordinate with DST? I will need help in any event."

"I will take care of it."

Catherine feigned confusion, hesitating a second before speaking. "What will be my role?"

"None, I'm afraid."

"But Charles, I found her. It would be good for my career." These words did not come so easily to Catherine. They smacked of begging, of prostration before the superior male. But she needed to be convincing, to dull Raimondi's already dull senses.

"You will get credit internally, my dear. I will see to that. But this is from on high. When it is done, I will buy you dinner. Perhaps we can get away."

"Oh, Charles ..."

"Tut, I must go."

Catherine, confident that her *Oh, Charles* had conveyed the right mix of disappointment, sycophancy, and sexual coyness, watched as Raimondi pulled his cell phone from his coat pocket before even getting into his car. He spoke hurriedly into it, then got in, started up the engine, and drove away.

Twenty minutes later, Catherine and Pat Nolan were sitting in Catherine's unmarked Peugeot, parked diagonally across the street from 121 Avenue des Ormes, in a neighborhood that was neither quiet nor quite working class. Bounded on one end by a small public housing complex and the other by an electrical transfer station, it had an air of hopelessness about it. Even the old elm trees that lined it, their branches bare under an increasingly lowering sky, seemed resigned to the litter swirling on the street and the dead-end poverty of the housing project. A group of boys kicked a soccer ball around in a chain-link-fenced enclosure while three older men watched and smoked.

Catherine had hurried Pat out of the apartment and into her car, making the five-mile trip through morning traffic to Courbevoie in fifteen minutes. On the way, she had remained silent, except to tell Pat that they would soon find out whether or not the investigation into the whereabouts of his daughter was as straightforward a matter as Inspector LeGrand said it was. She had last visited the house she had selected for the DST to raid right after her husband's death in May. Her first real boyfriend had lived in it while waiting tables and writing a novel. She had lost her virginity in its loft bedroom and thought at the time that life—and the future—were full of romance. When Jacques was killed, it was the loss of her girlhood that struck her out of the blue, like a sharp blow. His death, sad enough on its own no matter how she felt about him, echoed all of her losses—of her parents, especially her father, and of innocent love in her life. Her grief had brought her to 121 Avenue des Ormes, which she stared at for a long moment, sobbing at the sight of its boarded windows, peeling paint, and tiny lawn of knee-high weeds.

Patrick Nolan had not pressed her for additional information, intuiting perhaps that Catherine's professional life hung in a balance that required silence in order to be accurately measured. Jacques's quiet interludes were rare, his questions seemingly unending. She had learned from living with him that it required a certain self-possession to simply keep quiet, a trusting nature to let questions go unasked. Neither of which he had possessed. She could see from Nolan's eyes and his body language that he was thinking, thinking intently, and that he would soon want answers. But meanwhile he was still, occasionally glancing at Catherine but otherwise watching her old lover's house with a calmness that belied any curiosity. Their silence did not last long. Within five minutes, a dark blue BMW sedan pulled up in front of 121 Avenue des Ormes. From it emerged four men, all Arabs in their mid-to-late twenties. One of them had a bandage above his left eye.

"Our friend," said Pat.

"What?"

"From last night."

Now Catherine took a closer look at the man with the bandage. It was indeed Ahmed bin-Shalib, the man who had accosted Pat, whom Pat had struck with the wrench, who had run off into the night. The man who had beheaded Michael Cohen in Karachi.

"Yes," she said. "Our friend."

The four men split into teams of two, one team going around back of the house, the other to the front. The two at the front drew nine-millimeter pistols from their jackets before kicking in the door and entering with the swift and sure movements of a professional SWAT team. A few minutes later all four men emerged through the narrow side yard, entered the BMW, and drove off. The front door of 121 Avenue des Ormes swung askew on one hinge. The boys at the end of the block were still playing soccer, the men still smoking and talking, and the litter on the street still swirling as the first heavy flakes of wet snow began to fall.

~ 10 ~

Morocco, March 3, 2003

Megan and Abdel al-Lahani sat sipping coffee in the bright morning sunlight on the balcony of Lahani's fourth-floor penthouse in Casablanca's old city. Below them was a small courtyard used by local housewives to hang laundry. The courtyard was surrounded on all sides by buildings similar to Lahani's. One of these was smaller, which afforded a view from Lahani's balcony over a series of jumbled rooftops to the tall buildings—hotels and office towers—that surrounded Casablanca's main square, from which all of the city's major avenues radiated. In the distance beyond the square was the airport where jets had been landing and taking off all morning. Lahani had returned the day before and Megan had spent the night with him. Breakfast had been served by the same grim-faced native woman, wearing the same dark blue hooded djellaba, who had served them dinner at Lahani's house in Marrakech a month ago. Megan had been in the bathroom earlier, the door half open, peeing, and had seen the woman—Lalla, she remembered was her name—silently enter the apartment using her own key, and just as silently enter the galley kitchen and begin making breakfast.

"So you have turned up nothing on your terrorist groups?" Abdel al-Lahani asked.

"No, I haven't," Megan replied.

"What were they called again?"

"Al Haramain and Salafist Jihad."

"Yes, I remember now. And Professor Madani was of no help?"

"No. He was very nice, but these groups were completely unknown to him."

"And the Falcon of Andalus?"

Megan smiled wryly, her thoughts rapidly going over the ground she had covered in the last two years of her life. Her last article prior to 9/11, for *Cosmopolitan,* was entitled, "Octopussy: The Search For Your Eight Ultrasecret Erogenous Zones." Now she was writing about Muslim hegemony in Europe and looking for a terrorist mastermind who called himself the Falcon of Andalus. Which search, she wondered, was more delusional?

"Of course he knew of him as a historical figure," she replied, "but he knew of no myth of his returning to reconquer Spain."

"Did he take you seriously? He is a good friend, but his scholarship comes before all else."

"Yes, he had read my work and spoke well of it."

Since 9/11, Megan had published four lengthy, well-researched pieces in respected online political journals, in which she had explored the threat posed by the densely packed Muslim communities that had sprung up over the past decade in Europe's major cities. It was in and around Madrid's Moroccan-dominated Lavapies neighborhood that she first heard of the mysterious Al Haramain Brigade and the even murkier Salafist Jihad movement, both, it was said, based in Morocco and both dedicated to the reestablishment, by force, of Muslim authority on the Iberian Peninsula. It was a matter of faith, she was told, among Madrid's emigrant Muslim proletariat, that Abdur-Rahman al-Zahra, the Falcon of Andalus—the greatest of all Muslim caliphs in Spain, dead some twelve hundred years—would soon return to lead a Muslim army in the retaking not only of Spain but of Portugal and parts of southern France as well.

"I don't think they exist, these groups. Not in Morocco," Lahani said.

"You mean these specific groups or terrorist cells in general?"

"Terrorist cells in general."

"That's absurd, Abdel. I've been through Sidi Moumin. There's enough hate there to move Mount Everest."

Megan could see that her last comment did not sit well with her new lover. He did not like to be contradicted, his opinions dismissed out of hand as she had just done. It was an old story to Megan, and to humans in general. First we make love with someone, then we learn about them.

"I am not Moroccan, Megan," Lahani said, "but I have two homes here and I know it well. It is a liberal country. The parliament has some power. King Mohammed is benign. There may be some anger in the slums, but not *jihadist* anger, believe me. To attack this government would be an act of insanity."

"But they would attack in Spain, not here."

"Yes, but there would be brutal reprisals by the palace and the national police once it was discovered that Morocco was their home base. The country would become more secular, more repressive of fundamentalist Islam."

"Aren't all terrorists insane though, not rational by definition?"

"I doubt that even the best experts would say it was that simple." The icy look that had appeared briefly in Lahani's dark eyes had vanished. He was smiling again. A very handsome smile indeed, meant, Megan felt, not so much to charm as to pacify her. He *will not be so easy to figure out, or control,* she thought, and she smiled to herself at this thought, anticipating the contest ahead and the great love-making it would engender, like last night's.

"There is a neighborhood called Carrières Thomas," Megan said, "where no one would speak to me. Will you come there with me? Someone might be willing to talk if you are with me."

"Yes, I will. There's an extraordinary market there—dangerous but extraordinary—where I know some of the merchants."

"Good, you can introduce me. When can we go?"

"Today, this morning if you like. But do not expect to discover any terrorists."

"You mean they won't be wearing jihadist garb?"

"Megan, I too have read your articles. I know you are a serious writer. I do not doubt that terrorists are incubating in Paris and Madrid. But this is an Arab country. Nothing is as it appears. Secrets here are the most valuable of currencies. The Arabs in Europe are *outré*. They will talk because they are isolated and perhaps desperate. Here you will get only polite nonsense."

"I understand. I appreciate your taking me. It's a start."

As Megan was speaking, a phone in the depths of the apartment began to ring. When she finished, Lahani excused himself and left the balcony to answer it. Lalla had let herself out after serving breakfast. Thus far, not a word had been exchanged between the two of them. Megan rose after a bit to stand at the balcony's railing. At the airport, the morning rush of jet traffic had slowed. Below, two women, their hoods draped around their shoulders like Lalla's, were at opposite windows of the courtyard hanging clothes and talking to each other in Berber across the open space. Megan was not surprised to learn that Lahani had read her articles. She had expected him to look into her background as she had done his, finding on her laptop screen the home page of a Lahani Construction Company in Saudi Arabia, in business for more than fifty years, but containing no mention of a member of the firm named Abdel.

Megan was happy that the old game was on. And she was sure that she would win, even though Abdel al-Lahani was obviously very powerful and used to getting his way. She might not get Lahani to grovel, as she had other dominant males, but he was in for several surprises. She would take his money if he offered it, though she didn't need it—the nearly half million dollars she had in a Swiss bank would last a long time, and there were plenty of rich fools out there as sources of replenishment. No, more important—and more gratifying—she would use Lahani to help her track down and write about the Al Haramain Brigade and the Salafist Jihad. Perhaps the trail would lead to someone calling himself the Falcon of Andalus, who actually fancied himself the infidel-killing hero who would return the Moors to their days of glory in the West. Now that would be a hell of a story.

Megan's thoughts were interrupted by the sound of Lahani's footsteps crossing the tiled floor of the large living room that led out to the balcony. She was wearing a deceptively simple pale green silk robe with nothing underneath. She untied its sash and was about to turn to greet Lahani, the beginning of a demure smile on her face, when a movement, or rather a sudden stillness below, caught her attention. Looking down, she saw that the woman at the window on the right was Lalla, who was now staring up at Megan, her face wearing its usual stolid, impassive mask. Megan pressed her body against the balcony's wrought iron railing, as if to emphasize her sensuality, and nodded dismissively toward the servant. She did not like being stared at. Lalla nodded as well, ever so slightly, and withdrew. Before she could turn, or consider Lalla's behavior, Megan felt Lahani's large brown hands on her breasts as he embraced her from behind. Her breath caught in her throat at his touch, and all thoughts of mythical falcons and sphinx-like servants vanished, replaced by a rush of desire.

~ 11 ~

Paris / Rambouillet, January 4, 2004

"Geneviève, Charles Raimondi."

"Yes, Charles."

"I would like to speak to Catherine Laurence. Can you patch her in, or have her call me?"

"She has taken a leave of absence, Charles."

"A leave of absence? When did this happen?"

"Just a few minutes ago. I put her on leave status while she was handling your case. You and I discussed it, if you recall. She asked that it be made official. I authorized it, of course. She actually never did take any time after her husband's death."

"Yes, I see, but it is imperative that I speak to her. Is she traveling?"

"She didn't say. She told me she located the girl and that you advised her that you would handle the arrest. She felt she was free to get away. Is there a problem? Can I assign someone else?"

"No, that won't be necessary. Can you give me her cell phone number?"

"Of course. Hold on."

While he was on hold, Charles Raimondi swiveled in his chair to look out the sealed window behind his desk. From his thirty-fifth-floor perch, he could see the Arch de Triomphe below him to his right and the Eiffel Tower in the distance across the winter-brown Seine. Though it was only three PM, the street lamps lining the Avenue des Champs-Elysées were on. Snow was spitting from a leaden sky. *Dirty weather, dirty business,* he thought, wondering where Catherine Laurence had gone off to and whether he might surprise her there when his dirty business was done. Ms. Nolan had given him the slip, as they said in American gangster movies, but surely someone in the neighborhood had seen her.

It was a pity Nolan was wanted so badly. She was strikingly beautiful, with her long reddish-blond hair and exotic eyes. And her unmistakable air of superiority. It would have been interesting to have met her under different circumstances. Catherine Laurence, however, was in the same category of beauty. Her provincial Frenchness worked against her, but after all he would not be marrying her. He was sure that there would be logical answers to the panicky questions raised by his Saudi Arabian contact. It would give him another excuse to speak with Catherine, perhaps catch her in her apartment as she was packing or getting out of the shower.

"Here is the number, Charles."

"Yes, go ahead." Raimondi wrote the number down. "And her home address?" He listened and wrote again.

"Will you be needing anything else?"

"No, DST will handle this from now on."

"I would have liked to stay on the case. A *terrorist* cell ... Good luck."

"Thank you, Geneviève, By the way—no one will approach you about this case, but if someone does, you must say nothing and call me immediately."

"Yes, of course, Charles. I understand."

No *you don't,* Raimondi thought, smiling. Then he picked up one of his untraceable, throwaway cell phones—which he kept handy for purposes of liaison-making with the wives of fellow diplomats—and dialed Catherine Laurence's number.

~ ~ ~

"Are you going to answer that?" Pat asked.

"No," Catherine answered, reaching into her shoulder bag on the console between them, extracting her tiny silver cell phone, and pushing the off switch.

"Where are we going?"

"To a house that my husband owns—owned—in Rambouillet."

"*Rambouillet.*" Pat repeated the word, attempting, not entirely unsuccessfully, to duplicate Catherine's pronunciation.

"It's not far, forty-five minutes."

"What's going on?"

"Let's get there first. Then we can talk."

"No, Catherine. I want answers now. I want my own options."

"You have none."

"I'll decide that."

They had approached the entrance to a highway marked A10 and Catherine slowed down and concentrated on slipping into its stream of traffic. When they were safely on, Pat said, "What about my hotel?"

"You cannot return to your hotel."

"Why not?"

"Because the men we just saw will come for you there."

"Good. I'd like to talk to them."

"No, Patrick, you would not. The one with the bandage is a wanted terrorist. He beheaded the *Newsweek* journalist in Karachi last summer."

"What?"

"Yes, and now, for reasons I cannot understand, he is looking for your daughter. And I am not sure of this, but I believe he has the help of the French Foreign Office, and quite possibly the DST, which is our equivalent of your CIA."

"Why do you think that?"

"I set up the raid in Courbevoie by telling the only DST man I know, the one who ordered me to follow *you,* a man named Raimondi, Charles Raimondi. The men who showed up were not DST, could not have been."

Catherine glanced over at Pat to see his reaction to this information. If he was shocked, or even mildly surprised, he did not show it. The wearily grave cast of his handsome features seemed merely to intensify.

"And they think I will lead them to her?" Pat said.

"Or that you are in league with her and know where she is."

"Unbelievable. I should have hit him again with the wrench last night. I should have killed the motherfucker."

Catherine did not respond. She had fired her police pistol several times in the line of duty. Accurately and without fear. For her, using a firearm was not related to gender. But perhaps striking another human being with a fist or a blunt object like a wrench was. She herself had never done it. There was, she admitted, something exciting, viscerally exciting, about the visual of Pat Nolan swinging that wrench against the side of Ahmed bin-Shalib's face. It set him apart from her. She flushed, though she did not know why, at this thought, keeping her eyes on the road ahead.

"What's his name?" Pat asked.

"Ahmed bin-Shalib."

"I've heard of him. The Pakistani."

"Yes."

"Why do you think your DST is involved?"

Catherine did not answer immediately. The enormity of what they were discussing had not escaped her, nor had it Nolan, she assumed from his startled *what?* and the fierceness in his voice as he recalled his encounter with bin-Shalib. But neither had it fully penetrated. It was too big, flowing around them like a torrent that they refused to admit might sweep them to their deaths.

"Have you told me everything, Patrick?" she asked finally.

"Yes."

"Will you tell me about your daughter, her life, her values, her interests, her lovers?"

"It's not a simple story, but yes, I'll try."

"She has an interesting array of people pursuing her."

"I heard you on the phone at the apartment. Why did you take a leave of absence?"

"Because I may want to join the hunt in an unofficial capacity."

"Why? What about the DST?"

"I will tell you once we're safely inside."

The road was like any to be found in America or elsewhere in the world: paved, divided, shouldered, designed with safety, convenience, and even beauty in mind. The falling snow—rare but not unheard of in the usually temperate Paris winters—seemed to be keeping traffic to a minimum, making it easier for Catherine, using her rear and sideview mirrors, to do three-sixty scans as she drove at the highway's speed limit. Off the A10, they took a secondary road through a heavily wooded landscape of tall live oaks and beeches. Every mile or so these thick woods were interrupted by gatherings of giant evergreens reaching to the gray sky and imposing themselves over the forest with the silent power of ancient stone monoliths. Driving in silence, the car hermetically sealed against the winter wet and cold, they were soon on a tertiary road that followed a sharply winding river—the Eure, Catherine said, noticing Pat gazing at the now-diminishing snow melting on the river's slate-colored surface. After some braking and slowing, Catherine found a landmark she was looking for and turned down a dirt road that ended, after a hundred meters or so, at a small clearing, on the opposite end of which stood the house—a tired old stone-and-timber affair sitting on a na-ked spit of land that formed one of the Eure's many bends.

Catherine turned the car off and began searching, head down, for the house keys in her bag. She stopped suddenly, a puzzled look on her face, and then, the puzzle solved, her head flew up at the sound of a car rushing up and coming to an abrupt stop behind her. She made an aborted attempt to replace the car key in the ignition, aborted because in an instant her car was surrounded by three men, all grim-faced and dark-eyed, all hooded against the snow that had now turned to a light rain. All pointing guns at her and Pat.

~ ~ ~

Pat rolled his window down and was looking into the face of someone surprisingly young, and more surprising, vaguely familiar. It wasn't Ahmed bin-Shalib, the man he wished he had killed last night. And then it came to him.

"Exit the car, please Monsieur Nolan, with your hands on your head," said the young man. "Quickly."

"You are Madame Jeritza's grandson," said Pat, who had not moved.

"Yes, I am Doro. My grandmother is dead. And I will kill you if you do not do as I say."

"Dead ..." Pat said, and then, moving slowly, he unfold-ed his large body from the car, placed his hands on his head, and stood before Doro, all of nineteen but with a serpent's coldness in his eyes. Catherine had exited on her side, and was standing quietly, calmly, her hands on her head while the man behind the car, also no more than nineteen or twenty, walked over and frisked her, not professionally but thoroughly nevertheless, extracting her police revolver from her arm holster and her Judicial Police badge and ID from her shoulder bag. The gun he put into his jacket pocket. The badge and ID he stared hard at before handing them to Doro. The man also frisked Pat and then led them inside.

"Sit down," Doro said once they were in the house. Pat and Catherine complied, sitting next to each other on one of several small couches that faced a wood-burning stove at one end of a long room. At the other end stood a rough-hewn trestle table surrounded by eight straight-backed chairs. Off to the right of the dining area, they could see into a kitchen. Above the living area the brass railing of a loft bedroom was visible.

"Ephrem will make a fire," said Doro. Ephrem, the youngest of the three at seventeen or maybe even younger, put his gun into a front pocket of his black leather jacket and went out through the door they had all come in.

"How did you find us?" Catherine asked.

"We have been following you since last night," Doro replied. "We saw you in the park. The man that got away, he killed Annabella today."

"Are you sure?"

"Yes. I saw him leaving her store. When I went in, she was dead, her head crushed. Three of her fingers had been cut off."

Catherine did not reply immediately. "What do you want with us?" she asked finally.

"I want to find the man who killed and tortured my grandmother. I think you know who he is. I do not want to hurt you, but I will do whatever is necessary to avenge my family's blood."

"Why did you follow us last night?" Pat asked.

"We saw the two Arabs following you. We were curious. We did not see mademoiselle until the shooting." Doro nodded toward Catherine. "Afterward we were thinking of blackmail."

"Blackmail?"

"Yes. You killed a man. You removed something from his body. You left him in the park."

"So you followed us from the park."

"Yes."

"And this morning."

"Yes."

Ephrem had returned with an armful of wood, which he loaded into the stove. Then he struck a match to its tinder box. While this was happening, Pat looked down and realized that he had taken Catherine's hand. He let it go, gently, slightly embarrassed. Doro and his other partner were still facing them, their pistols, deadly-looking stainless steel affairs, pointing at Pat and Catherine.

"You don't need the guns," said Catherine.

"Who were those men?"

"One was a known terrorist, the one that got away. He and the dead one were carrying the credentials of the Saudi Arabian Secret Police. Maybe stolen or forged, maybe not. Did you see the raid on the house in Courbevoie?"

"Yes. He was there, the one with the bandage. He killed Annabella."

"Were there others?"

"One other. What is his name, the killer?"

"Bin-Shalib, Ahmed bin-Shalib."

"How can I find him?"

"Put the guns down," said Pat. "We'll tell you all we know, but not with guns in our faces."

Doro stared at Pat, then at Catherine. The fire was now crackling, its pungent heat beginning to fill the room.

"You are a policewoman," he said to Catherine, keeping his gun pointed at her.

"Yes, but not in this matter. I am a private citizen helping Monsieur Nolan find his daughter. It is she the terrorists are looking for."

"And they think you know where she is," Doro said, turning to face Pat.

"Yes."

"You can destroy me with a phone call, Doro," Catherine said. "I killed a man last night and did not report it."

Doro put his gun into his jacket and nodded to his colleague, who did the same. Ephrem was sitting on a nearby couch, leaning forward attentively, his weapon still in his pocket. Neither he nor the third young gypsy had spoken. Outside, the rain was coming down harder, pelting the house's ancient tin roof. Doro walked over to the stove to warm his hands, turning his back to Pat and Catherine. When he was done, he turned to face them again.

"Your daughter stayed for several months with gypsies, tribesmen of ours, in Montmartre," he said to Pat. "After I found Annabella's body, I sent Ephrem to warn them, but they were gone. Annabella must have warned them."

"I was supposed to see Anabella tonight," said Pat. "She was going to put me in touch with those people. Where are they?"

"I don't know."

"Is Megan with them?"

"I don't know."

"Do you know about the child?"

"Yes, it was delivered by a gypsy midwife. She is gone, too."

"Is the baby with Megan?"

"No, your daughter delivered the child to the Carmelite nuns in Lisieux. To the orphanage there."

Pat shook his head. That explained the train ticket in Megan's wallet. But it did not explain why the exquisitely selfish Megan Nolan would, after three abortions, go through the trouble of a full-term pregnancy—while in hiding from some obviously grave danger—only to give the child up almost immediately after it was born.

"Who is the leader of your tribe, Doro?" Catherine asked.

"My uncle, Corozzo."

"Ah, Corozzo, with the eye patch and the gold tooth."

"Yes."

"And the black heart."

If Doro was surprised by the fact that Catherine knew who Corozzo was, he did not show it. Gypsies and police all over the world danced perpetually to the music of mutual suspicion and often deep hatred.

"Will he know where these people are?"

"He knows everything about his tribe."

"Where is he?"

"The last I heard in the Czech Republic."

"Can we contact him?"

"He would never speak to you. I will contact him."

"And if he knows where Megan is?" Pat asked. He had gotten up from the couch and was now standing behind it, his hands resting on the carved wooden edge of its backrest. "She will not help you," he continued, "unless I am involved." This was a bluff, but he doubted Doro had any knowledge of his tortured relationship with his daughter.

"You cannot come with us," Doro answered.

"You can reach us at this number," said Catherine, reaching into her bag for a scrap of paper and and a pen, and then writing quickly. "Ask for *mon petit oncle*. Speak only to him. He will reach me." She handed Doro the paper, which he looked at carefully before handing it to Ephrem.

"I make no promises. Your daughter may not be with the same people. She may have gone off on her own."

"Doro," said Catherine, "bin-Shalib—or whoever is behind him—wants Megan dead. They will stop at nothing. They will kill anyone who gets in their way."

"Yes, Mademoiselle Detective, I understand. But I am a gypsy. I am cunning by birth. I will draw Monsieur bin-Shalib to me and I will cut off his fingers and crush his head as he did to Annabella."

"*Bien. Bonne chance.*"

"*Merci,* and what will you do?"

"I believe Monsieur Nolan will want to go to Lisieux, to see his grandson."

"Yes," Pat said, "that will be our first stop."

~ ~ ~

After the boys left, Catherine went out to get food for dinner. While she was gone, Pat brought in more wood and used it to feed the stove in the living room and to build a fire in the large and deep fireplace in the kitchen. He tried to take a shower, but there was no hot water. He searched the house until he found the electric hot water heater in a back closet and saw that its temperature gauge was set too low and that its connections to the main circuit box were loose and covered with dust, mouse droppings, and spiderwebs. He cleaned and reconnected them and set the temperature to 110 degrees Fahrenheit. While waiting for the tank to heat, he poured himself a half glass of bourbon from a bottle he had found earlier and sat before the wide brick hearth in the kitchen to drink it. He gulped half of it down before permitting himself, for the first time since hearing the jarring news of her death, to recall the wrinkled, incongruously kind face of Annabella Jeritza, who had been so brutally killed because she had made room in her heart for Megan. He did not know just how anxious he had been until the whiskey, strong and hot in his throat and stomach, brought some relief. Death, dead bodies, and now a birth. A child of Megan's. Blood of his blood. Thank God for Catherine, who had convinced him that, once he had seen his grandson tomorrow, it would be best to leave him with the nuns in Lisieux. *He will be safe there, she said, until this danger you are in has passed and you, or Megan, can claim him.* He had fought her, but she had been right. How could they track down Megan with an infant on their hands? *It is likely that you will be dead soon in any event, that we both will.* She had not said this, but it really didn't need saying.

He brought another half tumbler of bourbon upstairs with him and sipped from it before, during, and after his shower, which was hot and steamy and which, along with the whiskey, helped put him in a comfort zone that, though he knew to be temporary, was nevertheless very welcome. He had dressed and was standing at the railing of the loft bedroom, drying his hair, when Catherine, carrying two sacks of food, swung open the front door, bringing some of the rain and wind in with her. Her hair was in some kind of transparent kerchief that she must have bought when she was out. She stopped on her way to the kitchen as if she had been struck by a sudden thought or heard something that didn't sound right. Rain water glistened on her kerchief and on the strands of hair around it.

"I'm up here," Pat said, not loudly, not wanting to frighten her. She turned and looked up and smiled. "I took a shower," he said.

Catherine took off her head cover before answering, shaking it out and throwing it on a nearby end table. "You have made hot water?" she said.

"Yes."

"It has not worked for months."

"American know-how."

"Come down. You can start dinner while I shower."

In the kitchen, Pat flipped on a small shortwave radio on a shelf above the sink and turned the dial through a lot of static until he heard a woman singing something operatic. He turned the volume up a notch and began cutting and chopping the vegetables that Catherine had bought. Peppers, eggplant, onions, carrots, and more from a pile she had made on the hardwood countertop after rinsing them thoroughly in the deep enameled sink. He chopped, sipping his bourbon and listening to the radio and to the thrum of the shower in the upstairs bathroom. When Catherine came down, she was wearing a pair of worn corduroy pants and an oversized denim shirt with its cuffs rolled up to her elbows. She poured herself a glass of wine from one of the two bottles she had bought and stood next to Pat, watching his hands as he finished the job of cutting up the vegetables.

"Her lover will not return," Catherine said.

"Whose lover?" Pat asked, holding the fat old knife in midchop for a second, puzzled by this statement.

"Madame Butterfly. Maria Callas. You have picked a very sad moment in her story for us to listen to. And very beautiful."

"I didn't know what it was," Pat answered, "but you're right, it is very sad and very beautiful." He had been absorbing the music without thinking too much about it while working. They listened for a moment, side by side, to Callas's unbelievable voice, filled with the courage and pathos of every woman who refuses to believe that she has been wronged, that her heart will be broken. *You can start dinner,* Catherine had said. Such a simple, domestic, *intimate* thing to say, as if they had been friends or lovers or both for many years. The warmth of the fire spread over them, as if to confirm Pat's thought, which didn't need confirming. *You look lovely,* he wanted to say, but didn't, remembering this morning and Catherine's nonresponse, the odd look on her face, that sadness again when he told her she looked beautiful. Tonight, without makeup, her face flushed from the hot shower, her long brown hair still damp and glistening, she looked even more beautiful. *I won't say* it, he thought, and then she touched his hand as it rested on the worn wooden counter and he smiled without looking up.

They ate their ratatouille with French bread and drank the bottle of wine that Catherine had opened at the small kitchen table near the fireplace. Pat did not realize how hungry he was and thought the hole in his stomach could not be filled. The ratatouille with its al dente vegetables and savory sauce and the delicious hearth-made bread finally did the job. They brought the second bottle of wine into the living room, where they spread a blanket on the floor and sat in front of the stove, which was glowing and which by now had heated virtually the entire house. Pat could easily have slept, but there were questions on his mind and he could still feel the spot on the back of his hand that Catherine had touched in the kitchen.

"I am not your enemy," Catherine said, preempting him.

"How can I be sure of that?"

"I see your point. There could be double-dealing within double-dealing. I could be a master of deceit."

"You could be."

"My father used to tell me to listen to my heart. It will not lie to you," he said."

"Is that your husband's shirt you have on?" Pat had not meant to ask this question, but there it was.

"Yes, why?"

"No reason. Tell me about him."

They were both sitting against the couch that faced the stove, their legs extended, the bottle of wine between them. Catherine drew her legs to her chest and rocked slowly for a moment or two on her haunches, looking away from Pat. Then she got to her knees and reached over to the woodpile Pat had made, picked out a small log, and put it into the stove, pushing the door shut with another log. Still kneeling, she faced Pat.

"I hated him," she said.

Pat took this in, suspended in that place where there are no thoughts and certainly no spoken words.

"I'm not in mourning," Catherine continued.

"Why did you hate him?" Pat asked, finding his tongue.

"Because I didn't love him and he refused to see it, refused to let me go. I hated his obtuseness, his incessant desire for me."

"And now you're guilty?"

"Yes."

"So this is really happening?"

"Yes."

Outside, the rain was finally stopping, the patter on the tin roof slowing to a few isolated pings. The wind, which had been rushing against the house with force, was now only sighing. In the sudden quiet, Pat could hear his heart, his wordless inner voice. The course of his life, it told him, would turn, pivot on his decision to trust the handsome, despairing woman sitting next to him. *Let it,* he thought. *If her vulnerability is false then she is the loser, not you. But it isn't. Yes, this—and more—is really happening.* Catherine had let go of her knees but not fully reextended her legs. He watched her, tracing her profile with his eyes as she leaned back against the sofa and stared at the fire burning in the stove, giving him space and time to think his thoughts, which now turned from the profound to the practical.

"There must be someone you can go to," Pat said. "Someone in law enforcement or the government that you can trust."

"That sounds logical, except that Charles Raimondi is in the top echelon of our government, high in the Foreign Office and very close to the DST if not DST himself. And he is the one who brought a known terrorist, a beheader, down on you. No, we will go to Cap de la Hague tomorrow, after Lisieux. Uncle Daniel will advise us." She had told him of Daniel Peletier over dinner, that he was the one who had run the prints taken from the Arabs in Volney Park. Uncle Daniel whom she loved and trusted.

"I was jealous," he said.

"Jealous?"

"Of your husband. That's why I asked about the shirt." Pat let his eyes drift over Catherine's chest as he said this. Though the shirt was loose-fitting, he could easily see the outline of her large breasts and had no trouble imagining that they would be soft and touchable and perfectly formed. He had decided when he first met Catherine—he could not believe it was only two days ago—that he would not look too closely at or think too much about her beauty.

But that decision was made long ago, by another Pat Nolan in another life, the Pat Nolan who thought his daughter had killed herself to spite him, who had looked into the face of despair and saw that it was his. That decision could now be rescinded. Looking up, he saw that Catherine was smiling.

"Shall I take it off?" she said, and, after a slight pause, continued, "and put something else on?"

"No," Pat said, shaking his head and smiling in turn. "I'm not so jealous now that I know ..."

"That I hated him?"

"Yes."

"It sounds awful, doesn't it?"

"No."

"He was a quite ordinary man. A little arrogant, a little insecure, that's all. Not someone to be hated. It was myself I hated."

"And you still do."

"Yes, at times I do."

"I hate myself, too."

"Why?"

"For dragging my young wife to the jungles of South America where she died in childbirth."

Catherine remained silent, sipping her wine.

"And for leaving Megan with my brother and sister-in-law while I traveled around the world working on project after project. Drinking too much, using my bitterness as an excuse for my bad behavior, for hurting people."

"Like Megan."

"Yes."

"You did not raise her?"

"When she was six, I bought a house and stopped running away. But Frank had to shame me into it. Be a man; he said. 'Be a father. Raise your daughter.'"

"So we have some things in common."

"What?"

"I killed my husband by fantasizing about his death. We're spouse killers. Outcasts."

Pat did not immediately respond. Behind him were a series of surface relationships that had failed because of his refusal to commit, a refusal born of loyalty to his dead wife, a proud, stubborn loyalty that quickly became a fetish. It was, he had told himself with deadly seriousness, the least he could do for the girl he had killed—and to punish himself—to never fall in love again. Ahead was a world he could never have imagined would exist up until a few days ago: Megan running, desperate, turning to Pat for help; a grandchild. And Catherine.

"We can build on these things, I suppose," he said finally, smiling, shaking off the somberness of his thoughts.

Catherine smiled as well on hearing this, and Pat, seeing how beautiful her smile was, took her hand and held it in his. Her skin was soft, feminine, her fingers delicately tapered. Pat felt that Catherine's hand, unadorned, the fingernails cut short and unpolished, like a young girl's, contained the story of her whole life, that if he stared at it long enough he would see her future. And his. Smiling at this thought, he touched the same spot on the back of Catherine's hand that she had touched on his earlier, then returned it to her lap.

"You were very brave with Doro," Catherine said.

"No, not really," Pat answered. "He's just a kid."

"Gypsy boys grow up very fast."

"Do you think he meant what he said?"

"I do. If Megan is with gypsies, Doro will find her."

"And the revenge he's seeking? Is he serious?"

"I believe he is."

"The other two were mute."

"Yes, they were quiet. I believe all three of them know how to kill."

"So that's our team. You and me and three gypsy boys."

"And Uncle Daniel."

"And Uncle Daniel."

"And tomorrow you will see what your future looks like."

"My future?"

"Yes, your grandson. You must live for him, Patrick. No matter what, you must live for him."

And for Megan, Pat thought. And for you. Not least of all for you, Catherine.

~ 12 ~

Morocco, April 4, 2003

Throughout the winter and early spring of 2003, Megan went back to Sidi Moumim, Casablanca's vast slum, many times. At first Lahani accompanied her. When he wasn't in town, he sent Mohammed. Sidi Moumim was not the place for a Western woman of a certain age, however modestly dressed, to be walking around alone. She discovered early on, however, that no one would engage in anything but polite and meaningless conversation with her in the presence of either man. So, despite the danger, in mid-March she started going on her own, primarily to the Carrières Thomas neighborhood, whose souk Lahani had introduced her to a week or so earlier. Her strategy was simple: go frequently to the open-air, and therefore safe, market square; befriend a respected, English-speaking merchant—preferably an older man—although *respected* was the operative word; be seen as being under his protection; use that friendship and the perception it generated to get the natives, preferably the angry young male natives, to open up. This strategy had worked before, in Muslim enclaves in London, Paris, Madrid, and Berlin. But here in Morocco it was different. Casablanca, Sidi Moumim, Carrières Thomas: these were Arab enclaves within Arab enclaves, concentric circles enclosing ever denser, more secretive, and more suspicious communities.

Her break came one afternoon in early April. She had been to a dress-maker's shop in the Carrières Thomas market to pick up the four djellabas, two silk and two spun cotton, that she had been fitted for a few weeks earlier. In the interim, she had dropped by several times to speak to the wife of the shop's owner, Yasmine, a plain-looking but highly intelligent woman of Lebanese descent who was vastly curious about America and who stopped whatever she was doing whenever Megan arrived to sit, sip mint tea, and talk. Yasmine had not been in the shop when Megan picked up her djellabas, so she decided to have tea by herself in the café in the square, edged in between a dentist's and a brass worker's stall. She had been feeling nauseous on and off since the day before and thought the tea might settle her stomach. From where she was sitting, in the shade of a frayed but serviceable awning, she could see a snake charmer squatting before a cobra, playing hypnotically on his wooden flute, the crowd of natives looking on in hushed silence, as if the slightest noise would break the spell the snake had been put under. Megan was mesmerized as well, and was therefore startled when she felt someone insistently tugging on the sleeve of the cotton blouse she had put on that morning over a silk T-shirt to go with her jeans and sandals. Looking up, she saw that it was Hakim, Yasmine's twelve-year-old son, who was pulling on her sleeve.

"Miss America, Miss America," he was saying, "you come for medicine, you come for medicine."

Megan followed Hakim back to the dressmaker's, where Yasmine greeted her with a hug and immediately poured out the thick, sweet mint tea that would be among the few contenders to be named Morocco's national drink.

"You are ill," Yasmine said.

"Yes," Megan replied, remembering that she had mentioned her upset stomach to Yasmine's husband when she picked up her djellabas.

"My brother-in-law Abdullah is a *pharmacien*, a chemist. He has a shop in the souk. If you like, Hakim will take you there. Abdullah will prescribe something for your stomach."

"Thank you, yes," Megan replied. "When I return we will talk."

Physically, the Carrières Thomas souk, though much smaller and not nearly as clean, was not unlike its more famous counterpart in Marrakech. Both were accessible from a public square, and both consisted of a rabbit-warren of winding streets and alleys—many of them dead-ends— and permanently tented minimarkets that were often as dark during the day as they were at night. In both souks, the street-front shops and the stalls in the markets sold everything from freshly slaughtered lamb to love potions. Unlike in Marrakech, however, in Carrières Thomas there were no tourists, but more to the point, no foreigners at all. Not the adventurer looking for sex or drugs; not even the stereotypical ex-pat—stoned or drunk or both—that Megan had spotted with depressing consistency slumped at a café table deep in the bowels of other Arab cities. Did they enter and disappear, or did they sense the hatred in the air and stay away? The same hatred, for example, that she saw on the faces of the small group of Arab men—all young, all bearded—standing in front of a coffee shop, who turned to stare at her as she and Hakim passed. Once, when she and Hakim stopped to let a man leading a basket-laden donkey pass, she looked back along the narrow alley they were in and realized that not only would she have a hard time getting back on her own, but that she would not want to try. She said as much to Hakim, who assured her that he was under strict instructions from his mother to wait in his uncle's shop for Megan to make her purchase and then lead her back.

Abdullah turned out to be not just a pharmacist, but a former chemistry instructor at the American University in Beirut. In his early sixties, of medium height and build, his liquid brown eyes shone brightly from a deeply lined sunburned face: intelligent eyes that looked out above a prominent, aquiline nose and a neatly cropped black beard shot through with streaks of white and gray. His shop was spacious by souk standards, perhaps fifteen feet by fifteen feet, its walls covered with shelves lined with apothecary jars filled with powders, crushed herbs, barks, twigs, and teas of all kinds, each jar bearing a white label on which its contents were neatly written in Arabic and English. In the corner near a back door was a small table with a chess board on it, its pieces arrayed in mid-game. Megan turned to study the board when Abdullah went into a back room to mix a remedy for her nausea.

"Do you play?" he asked, seeing her scrutinizing the board when he came out of his small lab.

"My uncle taught me when I was a girl," Megan replied, "but I haven't played in years. Are you in the middle of a game here?"

"Yes, I am."

"Did I interrupt you?"

"No, I am playing with a former student via e-mail. I can see the board on my screen, but I like to feel the pieces and to look at the board as I work. Would you like to play? I can easily play two games at once."

"You mean now?"

"We can set a board up now, and then you will have to stop back so we can continue. I am busy with my shop, and so a move every few days is a good pace for me."

"I won't be much of an opponent."

"Do you remember the basic moves?"

"I think so."

"Then I will refresh your memory and we will proceed from there."

Megan smiled. The man in the gray djellaba and thick sandals standing before her was her entree into the real life of Sidi Moumim. She had in fact turned on the tape recorder hidden in her bag the moment she entered the shop. But perhaps courtly Abdullah, with his old-world ways, was something else. Perhaps he would turn out to be a friend, as Abdel al-Lahani had turned out not to be. It struck Megan that she was lonely, something she could not remember feeling since she was a child and her father was away, always away, for months that seemed like years, like eternities at the time.

"How shall I address you?" she asked, meeting and holding his gaze, telling him with her eyes that she respected him and was grateful for his offer.

"Abdullah will be fine."

"Not Professor?"

"No."

"May I ask, Abdullah, are you Muslim?" Through a small window behind the chess table, Megan had seen three men kneeling on faded wool mats in a dusty courtyard, praying, their foreheads touching the ground." I thought I heard the call to prayer."

"I am a Coptic Christian."

"Ah. Iraqi?"

"No, Syrian."

"Can you worship here?"

"You cannot stop a man from worshiping, even if there are no churches."

"Yes, I will play," Megan said. *And we will talk.*

~ 13 ~

Lisieux, January 5, 2004

Pale winter sunlight slanted down on Pat and Catherine as they walked under the striped awnings of a row of shops and cafes on the perimeter of Lisieux's main plaza. To the east, in the direction of the rising sun, was a series of low hills. On the nearest of these hills stood the Basilica of St. Thérèse, its oddly pointed white domes still in shadow as they reached heavenward. Next to it was the Carmelite convent that housed a group of cloistered nuns and a grandchild whose existence Pat could not quite grasp as real. It was a Sunday morning and, other than townspeople making their way in twos and threes to early mass, the plaza was empty. Ahead, near one of the small fountains that marked the corners of the square, Pat saw a girl selling flowers. Her raven-black hair shining in the sun, the girl stood placidly as the churchgoers passed her without a glance. His prior encounter with the pale and exotic flower girl on the Rue des Fleurs came back to Pat—*she told me you would come. You must go to her*—as he took Catherine's arm with a sudden urgency and led her toward the fountain.

"*Bonjour, Monsieur, Madame,*" the girl said as they approached.

"*Bonjour,*" Pat replied. "*Comment allez-vous...* how are you?"

"I am well. Peaceful."

"Peaceful?"

"Yes, Sunday mornings are very peaceful. When the bells ring the doves leave the church spires and come down here for me to feed them."

Turning to Catherine, Pat said, "This young lady sold flowers to Megan last week. I met her the other day, just before you and I met, actually." And then to the girl: "Do you remember me?"

"Yes, Monsieur. I knew you would come to Lisieux."

Pat did not answer. He stared at the girl. She was very young and yet seemed as composed as a saint. Indeed, it struck Pat that her eyes, deep-set, dark, and glowing, were very much like the eyes of the image of St. Thérèse—the Little Flower—on the prayer card that the girl had given him in Paris.

"Your daughter is in danger, Monsieur," said the girl.

"How do you know this?" Catherine asked, the sharpness in her voice jolting Pat out of his small reverie.

"And the child, too," the girl said.

"Where is my daughter?" Pat asked.

"You must ask the Little Flower, Monsieur. She will lead you to her."

"My child," said Catherine, her voice now under control, "how do you know Monsieur's daughter is in danger?"

"I must go, Madame, Monsieur," said the girl, turning and bending to gather the half dozen bouquets of red, pink, and yellow roses laid out on the fountain's sandstone ledge. "Please do not follow me, I beg of you." The bouquets clutched to her chest, she turned and walked away, stepping softly but purposefully, turning out of sight onto a winding street that led from the plaza up the hill in the direction of the basilica and the convent.

They did follow, Catherine pulling Pat by the arm this time, but when they reached the winding street, a cobblestone alley, really, with precarious-looking balconies hanging on either side, the girl was out of sight—around a bend or into one of the yellow brick three-story apartment buildings that lined the street. They continued, stopping to gaze around a small plaza midway up the hill. At the top, the alley gave way to a brick sidewalk that bordered a half stone/half wrought-iron fence that enclosed a long, school-like building dominated at its midpoint by an ornate stone cupola standing on four columns. In an enclosure in the cupola stood a statue of the Virgin Mary, her arms slightly akimbo, beseeching those below to come to her. On the stone lintel above the front door were etched the words *Carmel Lisieux*.

"We're here," said Pat.

"Yes, so we are, and right on time," Catherine replied, glancing at her watch. "We will search for the girl afterward. Perhaps she is known in the convent."

Their appointment with Mother Marie de Ganzague, the prioress of the convent, was for ten o'clock, which was announced by the first notes of the *Angelis* coming from the bell tower of the basilica looming above them to their right. Catherine had called in her official capacity the evening before to arrange for the meeting. They had slept at the house in Rambouillet, leaving at eight for the hundred-mile drive to Lisieux, a town of some forty thousand people located in Normandy, not far from the famous beaches of D-day.

Mother Marie's office on the first floor was small, simple, and without decoration except for a wood-and-bronze crucifix on one wall, a picture of St. Thérèse on another, and a liturgical calendar on another. Light entered from the window behind the prioress's desk, a window that gave a view into what appeared to Pat to be a shaded and very quiet courtyard. Mother Marie, seventy or so, wore the same flowing and hooded black habit and snowy white square neckpiece as the other nuns Pat and Catherine had seen going about their business on their way in. On the desk in front of the prioress was a white, business-sized envelope, which she fingered as introductions were made and Catherine's credentials displayed.

"Mother," said Catherine when they were all seated, she and Pat facing the aged nun in straight-backed wooden chairs, "as I told you yesterday on the phone, we are searching for a child that we think was brought here on December 24—and for his mother as well. Monsieur is the child"s grandfather. His daughter is the mother. Was there such a child? Is he here?"

The prioress did not answer at first, but continued to lightly lift and replace the envelope, tapping it once or twice on her wooden desktop. Her slender hands had retained some of the feminine delicacy of her youth despite the redness and roughness that were the inevitable consequence of many years of manual labor. Her lined face was dominated by a bumpy and pronounced nose, but Pat could see kindness in her eyes—and something that looked like sadness—as she glanced from the envelope to him.

"We found an infant on our front doorstep on Christmas morning, Monsieur, a boy. It was dead, Monsieur, I am sorry to have to tell you."

"Dead?"

"Yes, Monsieur."

She left it outside overnight, Pat thought. After all the trouble of delivering the baby by a strange midwife, caring for it, taking it on the train to Lisieux, she leaves it outside to freeze to death! He thought he was inured to Megan's habit of giving and then taking away, but here it was again, more painful than ever before.

"Was it from the cold?" Catherine asked."Exposure?"

"Yes, that appears to be the case."

"Were the police called?"

"Yes. They were here. The coroner found no foul play. He issued a death certificate the next day. We named the child Louis after the father of St. Thérèse, He is buried in our cemetery."

"How old was the child?" Catherine asked.

"It appeared to be newborn, perhaps a day or two days old."

"What's in the envelope?" Pat asked.

Slipping her fingers into the envelope, Mother Marie extracted a worn silver ring, its outer edges beveled and etched with a delicate filigree, and placed it on the desk. Pat picked it up, looked at it for a moment, and then put it back down.

"That's the ring I gave my wife when we were married," he said. "I gave it to Megan—my daughter—on her sixteenth birthday. She never took it off."

After saying this, Pat looked down at the ringless second finger of his left hand. He showed no emotion, keeping his hand steady as images of his youth and lost love—his prior life, never very deep beneath the surface—flashed across his mind's eye.

"We found it on a string around the baby's neck," Mother Marie said, breaking the silence. "And this we found also, wrapped in the child's blanket." She handed Pat a St. Thérèse of Lisieux prayer card, identical to the one the flower girl had given him in Paris. Pat took the card and turned it over, where he saw that a portion of the traditional prayer to the Little Flower had been highlighted in yellow: "... *in your unfailing intercession I place my confident trust ...*" Across the margin at the bottom was written, in Megan's hand, *M. François Duval, 33 Rue de Matisse, Paris.* He handed it to Catherine, who read it and then asked Mother Marie, "Did the police see this card?"

"Yes."

"Did they contact Monsieur Duval?"

"That I do not know."

"One last thing, Mother. We are looking for a girl, twelve or thirteen years old. We saw her selling flowers in the plaza this morning. She has dark hair and soft features, like a much younger child. Do you know her? Can you help us find her?"

"We are cloistered here, Madame. We rarely leave the convent and its grounds. It seems odd, though, to be selling flowers outdoors in the middle of the winter. I do not know the girl you describe, I am sorry."

Pat and Catherine spent an hour looking for the flower girl, in the plaza and up and down the dozen or so streets that fed into it, without success. None of the people they talked to, mostly shopkeepers, knew the girl. There seemed to be no doubt that Megan had confided in the child and then made a point of mentioning her in her false suicide note. If that was some kind of a clue or a lead, it wasn't much to go on, for how could she possibly expect that Pat would find the girl in Paris, a city of two million people? It seemed absurd that the child and Megan had joined forces, yet the girl seemed to know that Megan was not dead at a time when Pat thought she surely was. *And the child,* too, she said this morning, was in danger. She was wrong on that score, but nevertheless she seemed to know more about Megan's plight, whatever it was, than anyone in France, in or out of law enforcement. He would have liked to continue the search, but at Catherine's urging they pushed on. The DST, she said, could be a powerful foe when it was moved to act. It would have little trouble locating Catherine if it put its mind to it. They headed for the one place she would be known to surely go, yet for that very reason possibly the safest bet—Uncle Daniel's windswept, cliffside farmhouse only an hour away. They would arrive at night to his lonely place virtually at land's end. He would conceal them, lie if approached by the authorities, advise them on their search for Megan. From there, they could plan their next step, wait to hear from Doro, and, if necessary, flee the short fifty miles across the channel to England, an outing—also under the cover of night—that Catherine deemed not at all unlikely.

~ 14 ~

Paris, January 5, 2004

"Charles?"

"Yes, Mustafa, good morning."

"Good morning. You are at work early."

"Yes."

"Here it is midnight."

"You are working late."

"Yes, I have just spoken to Onyx. He is worried that we are losing valuable time, as am I. It has been a full day since the raid in Courbevoie. Where is Detective Laurence?"

"Yes, I understand. I am looking for her."

"We would like to help."

Charles Raimondi did not answer. Had Catherine Laurence deliberately fed him wrong information? He could hardly believe it to be so. Yet the house she identified in Courbevoie had obviously not been inhabited for months. And the neighbors knew nothing of a beautiful American blonde. And Laurence was missing, along with Patrick Nolan. Helping his Saudi friends snatch Megan Nolan was one thing, aiding in chasing down Laurence, a French citizen, a decorated policewoman who might be innocent, was another.

"Do you object, Charles?"

"No, but there are other considerations. Where is Onyx now?"

"In Paris, waiting to hear from me."

"I will call you back."

"Charles, the body in Volney park was one of Onyx's men."

"One of Onyx's?"

"Yes, we think Detective Laurence killed him. She also took his ID."

"I wasn't told this."

"I'm telling you now. Your Detective Laurence must be found immediately, and we would like to help."

"She could easily have left the country."

"Yes, but if she stayed in France, where would she go?"

"Her uncle lives on Cap de la Hague in Normandy. He is her only relative. I was about to send someone there."

"Let us do it, Charles. Chances are she is with Mr. Nolan. We just want to be the first to speak to them. We will then turn them over to you. The Moroccans have entrusted this to us. We would like to deliver. If Miss Nolan was involved in the Casa bombings, think of the repercussions. An *American*, Charles. A US citizen. The cowboy Bush would be brought down a peg or two, would he not? Humiliated, perhaps. You will get credit for a brilliant operation, and your government as well."

"What was Laurence doing in Volney park?"

"We think she was following Nolan, as she was ordered to do."

"What happened?"

"Onyx's men were following him as well. Their orders were to intervene if he threatened Laurence. As I have said, we think he is erratic, a dangerous person. He spotted one of the operatives and attacked him. Laurence intervened and one was shot. The other got away."

"You never told me that that body was connected to this case."

"I didn't see the need. We needed your help to clean something up, as you have needed ours from time to time. There was no need to know, Charles, but now there is."

It was true that Mustafa had more than once been helpful, not so much inside Saudi Arabia, where covert ops were virtually unheard of, but in other Arab states, where, as the second in line to the Saudi Interior Minister, his influence was great. There was a barely perceptible edge to Mustafa's voice, but nevertheless an edge. He needed this favor, and to grant it would not merely square the game. It would, Raimondi's instincts told him, put the old general in his debt. Such markers were the prized possessions of the intelligence world.

"Yes," Raimondi said, with what he felt was just the right note of hesitation in his voice, "so be it. But Mustafa, I want Laurence and Nolan in French hands. Speak to them and then call me. I will have people nearby who will take them from you. Your people must then disappear."

"You have my word, Charles. We have been friends a long time. What is the uncle's name and address?"

~ 15 ~

Normandy, January 5, 2004

Pat, Catherine, and Daniel Peletier sat in the living room of Daniel's hundred-year-old farmhouse on a bluff overlooking the English Channel. Daniel had lit a fire in the room's rough stone fireplace. Its crackling was a counterpoint to the muted but steady roar of waves crashing over the rocky shoreline some seventy-five feet below at the foot of the cliff on which the house stood, like a small fortress of weathered stone and timber. A local cheese, creamy and studded with roughly-ground black pepper, sat on a plate on the coffee table next to a bottle of Armagnac.

"You have been quiet, Uncle," said Catherine, placing her snifter on the table before her. Peletier—his mane of white hair swept carelessly back from a broad and handsome brow, his nose large and aquiline, his blue eyes piercing, looking more like an aging literary lion or a brilliant scientist than the retired officer that he was—had asked a question or two but otherwise refrained during dinner from discussing the subject on the forefront of all of their minds. They had dined on *pot-au-feu*—beef and vegetables stewed for hours over a low flame. That, a local bread, and a bottle of good Burgundy were devoured hungrily by all three, but especially by Pat and Catherine, who had eaten leftover rattatouille for breakfast and nothing since.

"Yes, *ma petite*. Now that we have eaten, we will talk. I am very sorry for the loss of your grandson, Monsieur Nolan." Pat and Catherine had related the events leading up to their arrival only an hour or so before, culminating in their fruitless search for the flower girl on the streets of Lisieux.

"Thank you," Pat replied, nodding in the old man's direction.

"Tomorrow I will send the sisters a small check and ask them to remember the child in their prayers."

Pat looked down at his hands, folded in his lap. He and Catherine had visited the baby's grave before leaving Lisieux and laid flowers on the small headstone. But the idea of a donation had not occurred to him and he felt ashamed. Inordinately so, he realized, as it was a small enough failure under the circumstances. It paled, for example, in comparison to his dragging Lorrie to die in the jungles of Paraguay and his breaking Megan's heart by ignoring her as a child.

"Thank you, Uncle," said Catherine. "We were planning on doing the same."

"*Bon*, a small sum will bring many prayers."

Pat, taken slightly aback by the swiftness and matter-of-factness of Catherine's lie, looked at her intently. "I don't know that there's much to talk about," he said, collecting himself. "Tomorrow we will return to Paris to speak with Monsieur Duval. You said yourself that French law enforcement is not looking for us."

"I said that French law enforcement—officially—does not appear to be looking for you," Daniel replied. "But someone is. Someone who has tried to kidnap you, Monsieur Nolan, and who has killed Madame Jeritza. Someone who uses people like Ahmed bin-Shalib in the field. Someone who appears to have the *support,* shall we say, of Charles Raimondi, ostensibly the Foreign Office's liaison with the DST, possibly DST himself."

"Who? Who is this someone?"

"Let us review. Geneviève LeGrand, whom I know personally and believe to be a person of integrity, calls Catherine in and puts her exclusively to work on finding Megan

Nolan, who is believed to have faked her suicide in further-ance of a terrorist plot inside France in conspiracy with her alleged lover, one Rahman al-Zahra. According to Raimon-di, they are believed to have worked together on the bomb-ings in Casablanca in May. A picture of Megan is produced, but not one of al-Zahra. Am I correct so far, *ma petite*?"

"Yes, Uncle, you are correct."

"You are further told, Catherine, that the Saudis have initiated this investigation, since it was they who had been tracking al-Zahra and Nolan. Further, however, that no Saudis were involved in the case in France, that it was you, and you alone, with DST as backup, who was working the case. Two men carrying Saudi Secret Police identifica-tion then accost Monsieur Nolan and you intervene, kill-ing one as the other escapes. You become suspicious and arrange, through Raimondi, for a raid on an empty house where Miss Nolan supposedly can be found. You watch as one of Monsieur Nolan's assailant's—identified as a known terrorist—along with three other armed Arab men, appear at the house and leave empty-handed. Can this be a deeply covert DST operation? I think not. I have spoken again to my source in Europol. Al-Zahra is completely unknown to them, as is Megan Nolan. And a terrorist plot involving them afoot in France? My source was shocked that some-thing of that enormity could be happening without Europol knowing. It is hard and fast European Union law that they be advised of all such investigations. Even the DST would not keep such information from The Hague. Raimondi, you are thinking, is up to no good, in league, it seems, with terrorists."

Pat watched as Daniel rose slowly after this speech and went to the fireplace, where he added logs and probed with a claw-handled iron poker until he was satisfied with the blaze. His thick cardigan sweater and corduroy pants did not hang loosely on a frame that Pat could see was at one time thickly muscled and still now at the age of seventy-two retained much of its strength and vitality. He replaced the poker in its stand and walked around the room until he was standing behind Catherine's chair. He rested a hand on his niece's shoulder. Without turning to look at him, Catherine placed one of hers on top of it.

"You look well, *ma petite*," he said.

"Thank you, Uncle."

"Quite beautiful and happy."

"Uncle ..."

"Yes, of course ... Tell me, what do you know of Charles Raimondi?"

"He is an arrogant fool."

"Do you know him personally?"

"The first time I met him he asked me to be his mistress."

"And you refused, of course."

"Of course."

"Good. We are done with arrogant fools, are we not?"

"Uncle ..."

"Yes, I know, I say whatever comes to mind. But I am old and do not have the time you have. The luxury of holding my tongue. Well, let us continue. Let us assume the incredible then, that Raimondi is acting on his own. Perhaps under threat of blackmail. Or perhaps for money. That for whatever reason he is aiding either the Saudis or an unidentified terror organization in the tracking and capture of Megan Nolan. Why? Why do these people want her so badly? Do you have any idea, Monsieur Nolan?"

"No," he answered, feeling exposed and again ashamed. It was his daughter, after all, that they were so coolly discussing in connection with all this death and destruction.

"But I can't say I'm surprised. Megan has a way of infuriating people, especially men. It looks like she made the ultimate enemy. She's not a terrorist, though. That's not possible."

"And you, Catherine. What do you think?" asked Daniel.

"I think Patrick underestimates his daughter. I think Megan has stumbled onto something. Something that has marked her for death. I think the fake suicide was brilliant, even though it failed. And then there is the trail she has left that only her father could follow. I don't know what she is thinking, what has led her to this, but I agree, she is not a terrorist. And she wants her father to find her."

Another lifeline, thought Pat, *another caress to ease my pain.* Watching Daniel circle back to the coffee table, he put these thoughts away to savor later. The old man lifted the bottle of Armagnac and, with a certain flourish, refilled all three glasses. *He's enjoying this,* Pat thought. *He's happy to be back in the game. And why not? How lonely must it be for a vigorous man to be stuck up here at the end of the world with nothing to do?*

"There is more," said Daniel, still standing and now facing Pat and Catherine. "I have been online and on the telephone since you called last night to say you were coming. Raimondi claimed that one of the Casa bombers survived and implicated Miss Nolan and al-Zahra. There was one surviving suicide bomber in Casablanca. He never talked, though of course the Moroccans tried. He was executed a few months later. There may indeed be an al-Zahra, however. No one has any details about him, but one or two very bright people think he may be the mastermind of the Casablanca bombings and of others as well. The United States embassy bombings in Tanzania and Kenya and possibly the USS Cole."

"Why?" Catherine asked.

"Bin-Shalib, the man who got away in the park, was thought to be involved, on the ground, in all three. But bin-Shalib is a follower, not a leader or a thinker. He would have to have had orders from someone. All three bombings seem to have had the same pattern: calls from airplanes, which are virtually untraceable, to operatives on the ground, recruitment of locals through a madrassa or hot mosque, the same type of explosives; and the use of suicide bombers as opposed to remote-controlled bombs. One agent in America heard *the Falcon* mentioned in celebratory phone conversations after the Casa bombings."

"The Falcon?"

"The Falcon of Andalus was an Islamic ruler of Spain in the eighth century. At the time, the Muslims ruled over the entire Iberian Peninsula, including Portugal and parts of southern France. It was the Golden Age of Islam. The Falcon is legendary among some Muslims today, especially the radicals, the killers. His name is a rallying cry."

"They want to return to the Golden Age," Pat said.

"Yes," Daniel replied, "to rule again in Spain and all over Europe. They believe it is their birthright."

"So how are they linking al-Zahra to the Falcon and the bombings?" Catherine asked.

"Abdur-Rahman al-Zahra was the full name of the Falcon of Andalus." Silence followed this statement. In it, Pat could hear the crackling of the fire, the rattling of a loose shutter in the wind, and, beyond that, the muted roar of the sea.

"That can't be his real name," Pat said abruptly. "Who is he?"

"No one knows," Daniel answered. "If he exists, he could be the most dangerous kind of terrorist. The kind with a respected above-ground identity, a wealthy business-man for example, whose affairs take him routinely to all the world's capitals. He could be a Saudi prince. There are some five thousand of them. He could be an Egyptian diplomat, or a scholar at a think tank. With such cover, a terrorist mastermind could do great harm and never be detected."

"So this is who is looking for Megan?"

"Who can say for sure? But it seems quite possible. I know you have been careful, but from now on you must make extreme caution the byword of your life. You are al-most certainly being hunted, Monsieur Nolan, by the worst kind of killers."

"Who think I will lead them to Megan."

"Yes."

"What do you suggest we do?"

"Stay here for now. It appears that no one has followed you."

"But Raimondi will soon turn in this direction," said Catherine. "It might seem too obvious a place to hide, but surely he will have a look."

"Yes, *exactement,* and we will be waiting for them."

"Uncle, no!"

"Yes, ma petite."

"You mean set a trap of some kind?" said Pat. "No, we'll leave in the morning. I'd rather be a running target." He looked again at uncle and niece and knew that all three of them were thinking of the beheading of the American re-porter in Karachi apparently orchestrated by al-Zahra and carried out by bin-Shalib. The salivating beasts in the room.

"We are not cowards in France, Monsieur Nolan," said Daniel, "despite what some Americans are saying. And we have not forgotten your sacrifices. We are only a few miles here from Omaha Beach and Utah Beach and the cemetery at Colleville-sur-Mer."

"Pat is right, Uncle," said Catherine. "We must leave early tomorrow. We will take some food and clothes and head for Paris."

"And if these terrorists arrive here after you leave? Do you think they will be kind to me?"

"You must leave, too," said Catherine.

"You mean run and hide?"

"Yes, precisely."

"Are you prepared to abandon Monsieur Nolan and come with me?"

"No, of course not."

"Such a simple matter."

"Yes."

Pat watched as Daniel and Catherine stared at each other for a long moment, a moment in which even a stranger could see their eyes doing all the communicating that had to be done.

"My heart is in play as well," said Daniel finally." You are the last of my blood. Perhaps I will stay and distract Raimondi's people, whoever they are. Perhaps I will come with you. I have contacts in Paris. We will decide tomorrow."

Pat and Catherine exchanged a swift glance. There was no way, their eyes said, they were letting Daniel stay here alone.

"I will retire," said Daniel, finishing his drink and then rising. "Tomorrow I will go into the village very early. There are people in the area who will give us an early warning of approaching strangers and I dare not use the phone."

"Good night," said Pat.

"*Bonne nuit*, Monsieur Nolan."

"One last thing," said Catherine.

"Yes, *ma petite*."

"I gave your private cell phone number to a young man who is helping us. His name is Doro. I do not know the last name."

"How is he helping?"

"He is trying to locate Megan Nolan. He is a gypsy and there is reason to believe that she is in hiding with a gypsy clan."

"*Bon*," said Daniel, nodding and flashing a short-lived but very charming smile. "An unlikely ally, but nevertheless an ally. *Bon. Bonne nuit, chérie.*"

"*Bonne nuit, oncle.*"

Pat and Catherine watched as Daniel left the room, then turned their attention to the fire. Pat sipped his Armagnac, then, setting his glass aside, watched Catherine's slender hands caressing her snifter as she brought it to her lips, her long lashes hooding her half closed eyes. He noticed, for the first time, the strength of her features, seeing in them the bones and the vigor of Daniel Peletier and, he imagined, her father. Twice during their long talk with Daniel she had somehow known he had been brought down, and twice she had, with her touch light, lifted his spirits.

"Let's go outside, out back," Catherine said, setting her glass down. "The sky has cleared and there's a wonderful view of the sea."

The sound of the still unseen sea crashing below them increased steadily as Pat followed Catherine along a flagstone path that led to a wide patio at the edge of the bluff. Crossing it they came to a waist-high stone wall, beyond which was a seemingly vertical drop to the rocks and surf below. To the right he could see a natural stone arch, high and gracefully curving like the door to a great cathedral. The water that made it over the rocks directly below sprayed through the arch and into what looked like a small cove just beyond it. The lowering sky had indeed begun to clear, permitting sight here and there of bright moonlight, or the promise of bright moonlight, behind high, swiftly moving clouds.

"That is Smuggler's Cove," said Catherine. "At least I called it that as a child. At low tide there is a small beach. My father taught me to shoot down there when I was twelve. Do you know guns, Patrick? Can you shoot?"

"No, but I can learn."

"Tomorrow morning the tide will be out. I will take you down there and show you the handling of one or two of Uncle Daniel's collection. You can choose one to bring with you to Paris."

"How do you get down there?"

"There is a path that winds down the cliff. It starts there, where the stone wall ends."

"Fine. Good. *Très bien.* I will learn to shoot... Catherine?"

"Yes."

"What about your job, your career? If you're wrong about Raimondi, you'll never get it back. You might go to jail."

"Yes, I've thought about that."

"And?"

"If I am wrong about Raimondi, then that means that the DST is indeed hunting both you and Megan and that they are in league with the likes of Ahmed bin-Shalib. I took an oath to defend the French constitution. It did not include working on the side of monsters, beheaders, or slaughterers of innocent people."

Catherine's voice rose as she finished her sentence, and Pat could see a hard look in her exotic eyes, the look of someone who had made a decision and accepted its likely consequences. Despite that look, he pressed his case.

"Even if you're right about him, the risk is enormous. There must be someone in authority you could go to."

"No. He is very powerful. He will be believed over me."

"You could walk away from me, Catherine. I would understand."

"If I did, what would you do?"

"I would try to find Megan."

Catherine remained silent. The clouds were scattering rapidly now. Like celestial curtains, they opened onto the amazing sight of a full moon bathing the sea and the jagged coast with its pure silver light. Below, the crashing waves and dark rocks were now lit as if by spotlights. Through the arch, the small strand of sea-washed beach could clearly be seen.

"*You* are worth the risk, Patrick," she said finally. Then she took his hand and put it on her chest. He could feel her heart beating rapidly and strongly. "I will not leave you. I could not."

Pat took Catherine in his arms before she could say anything else. Five inches taller, he bent his head down to her face and kissed her, feeling, just before he did, the cool, freshening wind on his face and the hot tears running down her cheeks.

~ ~ ~

Changing by candlelight in his second-story room at the rear of the house, Daniel Peletier thought slowly about all that he had learned in the last two days. He had intended to warn Nolan and Catherine off of their search for Nolan's daughter, to lie to them if necessary to get them to leave the country immediately. Rahman al-Zahra—whoever he might really be—was not a foe to be taken lightly. He had somehow corrupted Charles Raimondi, who, now that he suspected that Catherine could expose him, would be desperate: to stay in control, to save his job, his career, his life. Until he was stopped, he would have great resources at his command. An untrained American and a lone policewoman. What chance would they have against such enemies? Yet he could tell after an evening with Nolan that he would not be denied. He would risk his life to save his soul.

And Daniel's Catherine had returned. The spirited and determined young woman who had slowly disappeared after her wedding day had arrived in full glow at his door. He had no doubt that it was Patrick Nolan who had awoken her, who had stirred the ashes of her soul. He knew within a moment or two of their arrival that there would be no stopping them. No one could or should be stopped when they are on the path to their destiny. All futures ended in death, did they not? *Moi aussi* ...

Daniel blew out the candle and was about to get into bed when moonlight filled the room through the high window that faced the sea. He cinched his thick velour robe as he crossed to the window and, once there, had a clear view to the patio and the stone wall, and Catherine and Nolan in each others' arms.

No, you are not exaggerating, he thought, they will not be stopped. They are more afraid of stopping their quest than of dying. So be it. May God and the saints in heaven protect them.

~ 16 ~

Normandy, January 6, 2004

"Which do you prefer?" Catherine asked.

"The Beretta."

"It seems so small in your hand."

Pat smiled. The .25 caliber Beretta was a compact gun. It *was* small in his hand. But it had a better feel than the larger models he had shot, a 45 Luger and a 57 Magnum. With the Beretta he had begun to hit his targets at twenty-five feet and to appreciate the oddly gentle, steady squeeze of the trigger required to fire it accurately.

"Good, its yours. Uncle Daniel will be happy for you to have it. Let me show you how to load the clips."

They had been up before dawn, murmuring to each other in Daniel's rustic kitchen, unchanged in probably fifty years, while coffee brewed and they waited for thick slices of last night's bread to toast. After a night under a down quilt in Catherine's arms, this was the best breakfast Pat had had in years. On the beach, as predawn turned to dawn and dawn to sunrise, Catherine demonstrated the weapons for him, firing at pieces of driftwood she had arranged on a shelf of rock that jutted out from the arch into the water, which now lay as flat as a lake after the storms of the last few days.

They lay the clips on the same rock shelf, along with the box of copper-tipped, hollow-point cartridges Catherine had brought for the Beretta. Watching her, Pat followed suit and they methodically loaded about ten clips as the sun began finally to warm them. Despite the grimness of the activity, Pat's thoughts were on Catherine. The lushness of her body, the feel of her hands and lips on his.

She had put on one of Daniel's bulky sweaters, but she was not shapeless to Pat. Watching her hands at their task, the sunlight flashing off of a gold bracelet on her right wrist, he could not remember the last time he had felt this alive. Could it be thirty years? He felt sadness and exhilaration at this thought, a mix of emotions that had occurred regularly since the moment in the All Souls morgue when he realized what Megan had done.

"What are you thinking?" she asked.

"Of you."

Catherine smiled, and their eyes met for a second.

"What shall we do?"

"Daniel has to come with us."

"Yes, I agree, but he is stubborn. He may have other plans."

"Like lying in wait for these people?"

"Yes."

A dozen or so seagulls appeared, from nowhere it seemed, and began to circle the now tame breakers, crying their screechy cry as they fished for their breakfast. Pat and Catherine watched them, taken outside of themselves and their human worries for a moment or two by the carefree and seemingly effortless force of nature at work.

"It's a beautiful spot," Pat said.

"Yes. My father and uncle were raised here. Their parents farmed it. I spent all of my childhood summers here."

"Why did you become a policewoman?"

"Because of my father and Uncle Daniel."

"Was your father like Daniel?"

"Yes, strong and handsome and very proud."

"Did he really commit suicide?"

"No, he died in his sleep three years ago."

"You were doing your job."

"Yes."

"And now?"

"Now I am breaking many laws."

"How does that feel?"

"I am getting used to it."

Catherine's beautiful face remained deadpan for a second after she said this, then it broke out into a wide smile that charmed and confused Pat, reacquainting him as it did with the essential mystery of woman to man. *C'est la vie*, it seemed to say, *the die is cast, I will roll with it, fuck the world.* Or none of the above.

"And *your* parents?" Catherine said.

"My father was in the merchant marine," Pat replied. "He died when I was fifteen. An accident on his ship."

"I was told once that before we are born we choose our parents."

Pat did not respond, letting this statement sink in. Choose our parents? Choose our parents?—his thoughts turning not to himself but to Megan. Why choose me? And Lorrie, or the total absence of Lorrie? Or the total absence of both of us, for that matter?

"Do you believe that?" Catherine asked.

"I don't know. My father was never home. When he died, my mother started drinking. My brother and I were on our own pretty early on."

"You were left alone?"

"Yes."

"Perhaps that is why your daughter chose you."

Pat shrugged. His parents' old-world Catholicism, with its emphasis on suffering and guilt, had never held any charm for him. Lorrie had had an avid interest in the spiritual. She had spoken of *karma* and *chakras* and *sitting zazen* and had once tried to explain to him how each of us creates all the things we see and hear and touch. A tall order for a hard-nosed, genetically skeptical Irish kid, but her passion was authentic, as were all things about his young, beautiful, and headstrong wife of eight months. There was no guilt in her spiritual world, and maybe he would eventually have entered it. But she died, and his interest in higher, transformative powers died with her. Her death was enough of a transformation for the raw, twenty-year-old Pat Nolan.

"You mean so she could be left alone?" he asked finally.

"How cruel a thing is separation when all one wants is to be united to someone."

"That's not what Megan wanted all these years, Catherine. She left home. She hasn't put a foot across my threshold in over twelve years."

"But you are searching for her, no?"

"Yes, of course. She's my daughter, my blood."

"Your love must be very powerful."

"Catherine ..."

"We should go," Catherine said, placing two fingers against Pat's lips. "We dare not linger. We will talk more later."

Pat held Catherine's fingers to his lips and kissed them, then nodded his agreement. They stuffed the guns, the clips, and the box of loose rounds into their coat pockets and together turned toward the arch, at the foot of which began the path back up to the bluff. Just before the first step there was a hollow in the cliff wall, which Pat impulsively pulled Catherine into, taking her rapidly in his arms, and, swiftly finding her lips, kissing her, opening his mouth to drink headily from hers. Surprised at the urgency of his desire, he pulled away and smiled, realizing he was blushing, perhaps for the first time since high school.

"You have swept me off my feet," he said, "at the age of fifty."

"Such a young and handsome fifty."

He was about to kiss her again when he stopped and looked up. "Did you hear something?" he asked.

"A car door?"

"I think so."

"Uncle Daniel leaving for the village."

Pat nodded, his mind turning away from his burst of passion and back to the reality of their situation. "We can't wait here," he said. "We would be the ones to be trapped, with our backs to these cliffs."

"I agree. He loves me. He will come if I ask him."

"Good. He can help us in Paris." Then, looking up again, Pat asked, "where does he keep his car? I didn't see it last night."

"In the barn."

"That sound was much closer."

"You're right," Catherine replied, her hands gripping Pat's waist a bit tighter. He could see by the look in her eyes that she too had returned to reality.

"Is there another way up?" he asked, trying to keep his voice casual.

"About a quarter mile down the beach there's a path up and over the hills. The tide looks to be turning, but we could make it."

"It's probably nothing. Let's go back up here."

"Yes."

Pat in the lead, they mounted the first rocky step. About twenty feet up, Catherine grabbed his arm from behind and brought them both to a halt.

"What is it?" he asked.

"I hear voices," she whispered, putting her index finger to her lips.

One more step and Pat would be able to see over the crest of the arch to the remainder of the ascending path, all the way to the top of the cliff, to the area actually at the stone wall where he and Catherine had kissed last night. Stepping back and hugging the cliff wall, they strained to hear the sound of voices from above, but the wind had changed and they heard nothing but the screeching of the gulls. Their view to the top was blocked by the steeply rising leg of the arch that was also concealing them.

"I'll poke my head up," said Pat.

"No, someone may be coming down."

"Yes. I'm not cowering here. It's probably nothing."

Paranoid, Pat drew the Beretta from his pocket, unlatched the safety, and held it to the side of his face as he gingerly mounted the next step, bringing the full remainder of the path to eye level. The path was empty, but up at the stone wall a large man in a hooded sweatshirt and some kind of fatigue pants—a massive man, taller and bulkier by far than Pat—was holding Daniel Peletier by his long white hair, gripping it firmly from behind so as to pull Daniel's head sharply back. In his other hand he held a bunched up portion of the back of the old policeman's pale blue flannel nightshirt, its tail flapping incongruously in the stiffening morning breeze. Behind them was another man, his forehead bandaged, in a hooded jacket and jeans, holding the muzzle of what looked to Pat like an automatic rifle to Uncle Daniel's left temple. On the clearest, prettiest morning since he had arrived in France, Pat had no trouble seeing the white fields and dark orbs of the old man's eyes, opened wide with fear, yes, but also with defiance and an unmistakable contempt.

Before Pat could do anything, before he could *think* of doing anything, the man holding Daniel lifted him up and threw him headlong over the stone wall. For Pat, all of eternity elapsed and all doubt he had ever had about good and evil vanished in the heartbreaking two seconds before Daniel—who had fed him meat and bread and wine, who had allowed him to sleep with his beloved niece in his beloved home—crashed into the jagged rocks below. He chanced one last look up and saw the big man leaning over the wall to get a better view of his handiwork and the smaller, bandaged one—his right hand hooding his eyes—scanning the coast first to the left and then beginning to swing to the right toward Pat. Ducking quickly down, Pat turned to Catherine, who had seen nothing, and looked her directly in the eye.

"You're sure we could we get through?" he said, pointing to the far end of the small beach.

"Yes. The tide is not fully in. What is it, Patrick? Tell me."

"And we could get up the cliff?"

"Yes, I told you, I know a path across the hills. But I'm not going until you tell me why. What did you see?"

Pat's mind raced ahead, to escape, and back, to the last death he had caused, Lorrie's, and the sorry life he had led since then. He knew that all he could do was soften the blow, and so he did.

"Your uncle is dead. Two Arabs just threw his body off the cliff. One of them was our friend from the park. We have to go. There may be ten of them up there. And they've seen your car. They'll wait for us."

Catherine shook her head rapidly, back and forth, back and forth several times, and then rushed forward to climb the path. Patrick, moving quickly, placed his large body in her way. She bounced off and then tried again, this time clawing at his chest and then his face. She continued to struggle as he wrapped his arms around her and pinned her against the cliff wall.

"Catherine, Catherine," he said, whispering, his voice suddenly hoarse. "Catherine. We can't let them see us. There's nothing we can do." She continued to struggle for a moment or two, trying to free her arms, but Pat was too strong. Sobbing, the fight went out of her. He loosened his hold so that he could look at her. Her head was buried in his chest. When she raised it, he could see that her tears had stopped flowing, and that they had been replaced by a wild and fearsome look, a look that spoke of terrible pain, as if she were keening with her eyes, but also of something else, something that confused him at first, until looking deeper he saw what it was: revenge.

"We will circle back," she said. "I know the landscape, the farms along the coast, the back roads."

"Maybe," Pat replied, "but first we have to get off this beach."

~ ~ ~

They did get off the beach, and they did circle back, and thirty minutes later they were laying on their stomachs on a rocky knoll on the opposite side of the house. Some twenty feet directly below them, in a hollow next to a small stream that ran to the sea, was the smokehouse, now falling apart, built by the farm's first owner a hundred and fifty years before. In the distance they could see Catherine's Peugeot parked under and in between the two massive evergreens that stood to the right of the long gravel drive that led from the cliff road, as the locals called it, to the house. Another smaller evergreen stood on the near side of the drive, at the edge of the house's hardpan front yard. A black Citroën sedan was parked beneath it. Standing at the car's rear were two bearded and scruffy-looking men—not the ones from the cliff—with AK-47s slung casually over their shoulders. Two more Arabs, both in their mid-twenties.

"Do you see another car?" Catherine asked. "Between the trees? Anywhere?"

"No. I think we're dealing with four altogether."

Catherine did not reply, but continued to scan the scene before them. They had given the house a wide berth on their route back, climbing the bluff near a small bay, crossing the cliff road and then scrambling inside the tree line of the ridge above it until they deemed it safe to re-cross the road and make their way back; the knoll above the smokehouse, because of the view it afforded, had been their destination from the beginning. They could go no farther, however, because beyond the smokehouse and the stream was a rocky scrim, wide open and treeless, that led directly to the house. The only thing in between was the lone pine tree with the Citroën parked under it—and the two muja-hideen types standing at its rear.

"We can't get closer until tonight," Pat said, looking at his watch, which told him it was now all of seven AM. "That's a long wait."

"I will call them," said Catherine.

"Call them?"

"Yes, I have my cell phone."

"To say what?"

"I will leave a message for Uncle Daniel: meet us at the smokehouse: They will hear it and come for us. We will kill them as they approach."

"What if only two come?"

"The others will hear the shots. They will come to investigate."

"No, they'll assume we have been killed."

"They want you alive, Patrick. They want you to lead them to Megan. Do you know where she is, by the way?"

Pat took his eyes off the two Arabs to look at Catherine. "Are you saying you don't believe me? What was last night all about?"

"No, Patrick, my love, I am saying if you do know, they will force it out of you. Better to tell them and die a quick death than be tortured."

"I don't know, but they won't believe me, so they'll torture me, anyway."

"We shall kill them first."

"What if one of them picks up the phone?"

"I will blurt out my message, pretending that I assume whoever answers is Daniel."

"Okay, make the call."

Catherine dialed Daniel's landline and waited for his recorded greeting to end. "Uncle, we are at the smokehouse. Please come to meet us. Someone in the village said you had visitors this morning. What visitors? I am worried. We will wait here for you."

Catherine ended the call. "We will separate," she said. "You to the right and me to the left. Find a spot behind a rock. Lay out your extra clips. When you hear me fire, you fire. Remember, aim low. *Bonne chance*, Patrick."

"And to you, Catherine."

They took up their positions and watched as the two gunmen near the car continued their casual chat. A few minutes later—a long few minutes later—another man, the one with the bandaged head, emerged from the house and said something to the gunmen. Then all three looked in

the direction of the smokehouse and bandage-head pointed
at it. As he did, Pat involuntarily squeezed harder on the
handle of his Beretta, wondering if he had been spotted as
he lay prone, peering discreetly around a large boulder. The
gun now seemed too small and toylike to do any damage,
and he rued the fact that he had not chosen one of the bigger weapons. He glanced over at Catherine and saw that
she was intently watching the three men. She had taken
off her heavy wool coat to lay on, the morning sun warm
enough. She was probably oblivious to the weather, anyway.
Pat's heart ached suddenly at this sight and the simultane-
ous thought of losing her. She looked over at him then and
raised and slightly shook a clenched fist. *They are coming. Be
strong.*

Pat nodded in response, and then looked back toward
the house. The large man who had thrown Daniel Peletier
to his death now appeared and said something to the other
three. Then the two gunmen began walking slowly toward
the smokehouse, first unslinging their rifles and carrying
them at the ready. The other two moved to the other side of
the car to watch.

Fuck, Pat thought, looking over at Catherine, who
turned to look at him, then simply pointed to the two men
who were coming toward them. When, thirty seconds later, they got to a point about ten paces from the front of
the smokehouse, Pat, watching with his Beretta pointed at
them and his finger lightly on the trigger, heard two loud
blasts from Catherine's Magnum. He fired as well, emptying his clip in the direction of the two men. Both went down
and lay there on the open scrim, their weapons under them.
Then, to Pat's amazement, Catherine scrambled down off
the knoll toward the dead bodies. Reaching them in a flash,
she kicked them over, grabbed their AK-47s and ran back,

where she immediately dropped one rifle and began firing the other one in the direction of the men back at the car, who, rifleless, took cover behind it.

Pat hustled along the ground to Catherine and picked up the second rifle. He had never fired one but he would learn on the job.

"The safety's off," she said, "it reloads automatically. Aim at the car. I will circle around. Fire once every five seconds. The clip is full. Don't put it on automatic—here." She pointed to the lever on the side of the weapon. Then she took quick aim and fired off another burst at the Citroën. "We must keep them pinned down."

"No," Pat said. "I don't like it. You'll expose yourself. They'll separate and trap you."

"Yes. They"re confused. I must do this now. We need a car, Patrick. We can't walk out of here."

They were lying prone at the top of the knoll, side by side, their rifles pointed at the Citroën below. As they talked, they looked straight ahead. Catherine, her rifle on its four-round shooting mode, fired off a burst. Pat followed suit, getting a quick lesson in the oddly delicate yet rock-solid feel of the famous Kalashnikov as it pushed back against his shoulder.

"I'll go," he said. "You're a better shot. You can keep them pinned down. And if I can draw them out, you could actually hit one. That's the whole point, no?"

"No, I'm going."

Before Pat could answer, the large man, the body-tosser, emerged from the front of the Citroën in a mad low dash toward the house. Catherine and Pat fired simultaneously, and to Pat's astonishment, the man went down, falling hard, face forward, onto the stone steps that led to the house's wide front porch. Then their attention was diverted by the sound of the Citroën's engine starting and the car's tires screeching as it backed sharply away from them and headed down the driveway. They fired at it, but in an instant it was gone, out of sight behind the tree line, where the driver switched back toward the cliff road.

"I don't think there are others," said Catherine. "They would have come out to help. Let's get to my car."

They went cautiously, keeping low, but soon it was clear that there were no more terrorists about. Before getting into the Peugeot, Catherine and Pat stepped over to the large man whose body, shot in the chest and head, lay on its side half on the ground and half on the house's stone steps.

"He threw the body," Pat said.

"Are you sure Uncle was dead?"

"Yes, I could tell. He was dead already."

Catherine did not respond. Toeing the body onto its back, she dug out the man's ID from around his neck, then pulled his billfold out of his back pocket. It contained a thick wad of hundred euro notes and nothing else. On the belt of his fatigue pants was clipped a cell phone, which she took also. Her own cell phone she removed from the front pocket of her slacks and put into the glove box of the car. Then, returning to the body, she placed the muzzle of her AK-47 against the dead man's crotch and calmly squeezed off a burst of four rounds. Where the crotch of the man's fatigue pants had been, Pat could now see a ragged gaping hole. "He won't be able to enjoy his virgins now," she said, and then, leaning over, she spit on his face.

In the quiet that ensued, Pat remained still, motionless, as if to hold off making what Catherine had just done a historical fact. "I'll search the others," he said finally, still not moving.

"Yes, good," Catherine replied, still outwardly calm, as if she had been interrupted while folding laundry or putting away groceries. "Take their extra magazines and ammunition, and their cell phones if they have them. I will hunt down Uncle's cell phone. Doro will be calling."

When Pat returned from searching the bodies on the scrim, Catherine was in her car, in the passenger's seat, her head down, sobbing. He slipped behind the wheel, saw that the keys were in the ignition, and started the engine. When he looked at Catherine, she was drying her eyes with the sleeve of Daniel's bulky old navy blue sweater.

"Paris," he said. "Monsieur Duval."

"Yes," Catherine answered. "Thirty-three Rue de Matisse."

~ 17 ~

Morocco, April-May, 2003

Throughout April and into early May, Megan visited Abdullah al-Azim's shop weekly and sometimes more often. Abdullah made a living as a pharmacist, but his passions were history and politics. Once he got going on these subjects, it was hard to stop him. Their slow-moving chess games were pretexts. When customers came into the shop, as they often did, Megan stayed seated at the table in the corner, returning their stares until they looked away. Shamelessly, she taped all of her conversations with the pharmacist, as well as all of the conversations Abdullah had with his customers, even those in Arabic and Berber. She turned on the small, expensive, extremely high-performing recorder hidden in her bag before entering the shop and did not turn it off until she was back out on the street, usually an hour, sometimes as much as two hours later. She wore Western clothes, usually jeans or cotton slacks with a light sweater or a layer or two of loose tops. She wore the djellabas she had bought in her small suite at the Farah Hotel, or occasionally when she was with Lahani at his place. Hakim walked her to and from Abdullah's shop and a cab driver she had hired on a permanent basis took her back and forth from the hotel to the Carrières Thomas market square.

She heard a lot of Muslim history in the shop: the life and times of the Prophet, the spread of Islam to the east and west and south after his death, the forceful expulsion of Muslims from Spain in 1492—and from all of Europe in 1683—Napoleon's conquest of Egypt in 1798, the abolishment by the Turks of the caliphate in Istanbul in 1922. This last was, according to Abdullah, "the final blow to the pride of a shame-based culture." As to the modern faith, it had been corrupted from within, by oil, hatred, and fanaticism: the Wahabis in Saudi Arabia who preached annihilation of everyone except themselves, the Shiites in Iran who stoned children to death, the tribal councils in Pakistan who ordered the gang rape of women who committed adultery, the "leaders" of Hamas and Hezbollah who sent teenage boys and girls to blow themselves up in crowds of innocent Israelis. Much of this Megan knew. She had been reading and writing extensively about Islam for more than two years. Nevertheless, she listened attentively. She could afford to be patient. Lahani had obtained a special visa for her that allowed her to stay in the country indefinitely. After each visit, she dated and labeled her tape according to the participants in the conversation—usually just her and Abdullah, though occasionally others, *two Berber women, neighboring shopkeeper,* etc. were included.

On the issue of terrorism, the pharmacist was of the strong opinion that al-Qaeda, having aroused the sleeping American giant, was now more interested in retaking Europe than in lashing out in anger at the United States. Only a fool would believe that America could be defeated, and Osama bin Laden, whatever else he was, was no fool. It would be far from preposterous, however, for him to believe that Europe could be reclaimed by exerting pressure from within and without. "It lacks the will," Abdullah said. "It is like the lamb who trusts its butcher." He cited excerpts from bin Laden"s taped messages and myriad postings on jihadist Web sites to support this theory. He knew of the Falcon of Andalus as an important figure in the history of Islam, but, like Professor Madani, the scholar Lahani had sent Megan to, he was unaware of a myth involving his return. "But it is a brilliant idea," he said to Megan, "to rally the angry, humiliated masses behind the Falcon, risen from the dead to return Islam to its full glory, its rightful place as the dominant force on the planet."

Only once was Megan exposed to the young male Muslim anger that she had seen so much of in Europe. On her third or fourth visit, sometime in mid-April, a man of perhaps twenty-five, in need of a shave, in jeans, running shoes, and a Western-style leather jacket, came into the shop asking for a toothache remedy. Megan and Abdullah were sitting at the chess table in the corner, a sight the man reacted to with a contempt that he made no effort to conceal. Abdullah rose and, after a series of questions in Arabic, he took the man through the curtain behind his counter. When they came out a few minutes later, the man hurried out without looking at Megan.

"I am going to purchase an ingredient I need," Abdullah said. "He has a cracked tooth that is very painful. It should come out, but he is deathly afraid of the dentist. I will only be ten minutes or so. You will no doubt need at least that much time to contemplate your next move."

Megan knew what her next move was going to be. She didn't care about the game, anyway. She had been left alone in the shop before and had spent the time sticking her nose and her finger into some of the more exotic sounding powders that lined the room. She was about to get up to wander around when a movement through the slats of the shuttered window to her right caught her attention. Two of the three young men she had seen praying on her first visit were in the dirt courtyard, smoking. The movement she saw was the man with the toothache joining them. Having seen him up close, having felt his hostility fill the shop, she remained seated and studied his companions, comfortably concealed behind the wooden shutter but able to see through the thin, sun-filled spaces between its slats. Also in their mid-twenties, the other two were dressed in Western-style clothes as well. Both needed shaves. All stood under a corrugated steel awning that rested on poles in the ground on one end and the tin roof of a small shed on the other. Morocco's brief and mild winter had passed and the days were getting hotter and dryer.

As Megan was studying them, a fourth man joined the three. Megan immediately recognized this man as Mohammed, Abdel al-Lahani's bulky, taciturn driver. He greeted them, his Arabic husky and guttural, and then proceeded to talk, commanding their attention with a presence and a confident, insistent voice that took Megan back, it was so out of character. They were only a few yards away. As their conversation drifted toward her, Megan took the recorder out of her purse and put it on the windowsill facing the courtyard. Abdullah had opened the unscreened window earlier to admit whatever breeze was out there but closed the shutters to keep out the African heat. On an impulse, she took her small digital camera out of her bag and snapped off a few pictures of the men, the viewfinder pressed against a slice of sunlight in between the shutter's slats.

In a few minutes, they were done. Mohammed left. The three young men continued to smoke in the shade of the steel awning. Then a female voice called to them from one of the houses or shops that lined the street and they left, too.

When Abdullah returned, Megan mentioned the men.

"I saw the toothache man with three others in the courtyard," she said. "When is he coming back for his remedy?"

"He doesn't work, our young friend, but he is very busy. His mother will stop by later. Why?"

"I would like to talk to him."

"You'd be wasting your time. I assume he was with his unemployed friends, the ones that hang out at the café next to the spice shop."

"Yes, but one was older, more your age."

Abdullah raised his thick eyebrows at this information, but said nothing.

"Who are they?" Megan asked.

"They are angry children," the pharmacist answered. "They live off of their parents. They drink coffee and smoke cigarettes. They play the victim game, as there is nothing else for them to do."

"Do you know the families?"

"Yes. I offered our young man an apprenticeship here last year. He sneered at me."

"Where do they get their information?"

"Haven't you noticed all the dishes? Everyone in this neighborhood is dirt poor, yet they all have satellite television. Al Jazeera is on all the time, twenty-four hours a day of jihadist propaganda. For their local poison they go to the mosque near the square."

"Why won't he talk to me?"

"You are a whore, and a Western one at that."

"Are there many others like this?"

"I only know his group, but I sometimes pass the mosque on a Friday afternoon. The crowd spills into the courtyard to hear the new imam."

"What is the young man's name?"

"Sirhan al-Majid."

"Can you help me talk to him, Abdullah? I am interested in this anger in the street. I have written about it, as you know."

"I will try, but do not expect much. He is a restless fool, nothing more."

"Thank you." Megan recalled the burning look in al-Majid's eyes as he listened to Mohammed in the courtyard. Restless fools, she knew from experience, tend to spill their guts. If she could get him to talk, from such dross she might find gold.

~ 18 ~

Paris / Riyahd, January 6, 2004

"What exactly did they tell you, Charles?"

"That a witness saw two Arab men throw the old man off the cliff. They were carrying automatic rifles."

"Who is the witness?"

"It was an anonymous call. A woman."

"You don't believe that my people did this, do you?"

"I don't know what to believe."

"As I said, our men went to Cap de la Hague. Monsieur Peletier would not cooperate. They left. Someone else is looking for our Monsieur Nolan. That is what I think."

"Who? Why?"

"To find his daughter, of course."

"Well, the DST is looking for her as well, now."

There was a pause as Mustafa al-Siddiq took this in. "How is that?" he asked, keeping his voice casual.

"The Cherbourg police called them. They hear 'Arab men with automatic rifles' naturally they think terrorists."

"Yes, but how do they know about Nolan *père et fille*?"

"They took apart Peletier's computer. Apparently he made inquiries to Europol concerning Megan Nolan and a suspected terrorist named al-Zahra. He was asked by his niece to run some fingerprints. One set belongs to a known terrorist, Ahmed bin-Shalib. They discovered that Monsieur Nolan was in the country. They called Paris and were told about the suicide."

"But they believe the suicide was real, no? The body identified by the father?"

"They are confused, Mustafa, but they have enormous resources and they are very curious."

"And what is your role?"

"I have no role. DST advised us of the situation because it appears an American citizen is involved."

"You told them nothing about me?"

"No."

"Well then, I will contact Onyx. I will tell him the chase is off. He and his people must leave the country."

"Why not coordinate with the DST? Your people developed this case. The background you can provide would be invaluable. We don't have to tell them of our initiative."

"No, Charles, we must withdraw. I am sure your DST will hunt down the Nolans and their friends and that justice will be done."

Now Charles Raimondi was silent. He had covered up the dead body—one of al-Siddiq's agents—in Volney Park. Now a respected former French policeman was dead. Thrown off of a cliff at around the same time other Saudi agents were in the vicinity. And neither Patrick nor Megan Nolan were any closer to being found. Had his decision to help al-Siddiq been wrong? Who actually was this Megan Nolan, and why exactly did al-Siddiq want her so badly?

"And you would like to be kept out of it?" he asked finally.

"I would prefer that, yes. We broke several rules, as you know. Why cause a fuss among the diplomats? They're sensitive to these things. Good-bye, Charles. I look forward to seeing you at our next conference in Brussels."

Charles Raimondi was a diplomat himself. His only connection to the world of intelligence was his role as liaison between the Foreign Office, where he worked as an assistant to the French Foreign Secretary, and the DST, France's very powerful and very secretive intelligence agency. He had often used this connection to impress certain people, usually women, but the aura of danger that he liked to surround himself with did not exist. Until now. After hanging up the phone he considered his situation. How exactly had the shooting in Volney Park occurred? Was it possible that al-Siddiq's men had attacked Laurence and Nolan first, rather than the other way around, as al-Siddiq had informed him when he asked for help in covering up the incident and getting the body returned to Saudi Arabia? Could a known terrorist—Ahmed bin-Shalib—be on the payroll of the Saudi Interior Ministry? Was it possible that al-Siddiq's people killed Peletier? Looking around his lavishly appointed office and down at his manicured hands, it occurred to him how much he had to lose if these questions were to be answered in the affirmative and his role—perhaps rashly undertaken—discovered. He had known al-Siddiq for many years and trusted him, but perhaps it *was* better that he and his people, including the secret agent oddly code-named *Onyx,* disengage, and quickly.

Only two people besides al-Siddiq knew of Charles's involvement in *l'affaire de Megan Nolan.* Catherine Laurence and Inspector Geneviève LeGrand. LeGrand was due to land in Nuremburg for a law enforcement conference in thirty minutes. He had left a message on her cell phone for her to call him as soon as she landed. Laurence had gone missing. Perhaps she had visited her uncle in Cap de la Hague, perhaps not. It would not do now to alert the local police to pick her up if she appeared in the vicinity. It would look too suspicious. He had asked the police in Rambouillet to look in on her husband's house on the chance that she was there. She was not, but it appeared, they said, that the house had recently been used by more than one person. There were several brands of fresh cigarette butts in the trash, two sofas had been used as beds, and the wood-burning stove was still warm.

What had at first seemed impossible, that Laurence was continuing the search for Megan Nolan on her own, or worse, in league with Nolan *père*, who was also missing, had now to be seriously considered. The thought of the two of them together—the sad and beautiful Catherine and the obtusely handsome and "rugged" Nolan, was very distasteful. Catherine was to be Charles's prize in this affair, one of the reasons why he had agreed to help al-Siddiq in the first place. The reward seemed worth the risk at the time. Now Catherine was officially on a leave of absence. He could not ask the police or the DST to track her down without risking exposing his own involvement. But Nolan was a different matter. Geneviève LeGrand would have no reason to question his instructions to her to aggressively hunt him down. She had been more than happy to help Charles in his *sub rosa* terrorism investigation. Perhaps he would have to bed her to keep her happy, which was why, always thinking, he had wired flowers to her hotel room in Nuremburg. His hunch was that if he found Nolan, Catherine would be with him. If he could get his hands on them, they might lead him to the mysterious Megan Nolan, a wanted terrorist. He might still do himself a world of good. Indeed, with al-Siddiq out of the picture, he would get *all* of the credit if he could pull it off.

Charles's phone rang and he saw on his caller ID screen that it was Inspector LeGrand calling. *You might get some small portion of the credit, my dear Geneviève,* he thought, reaching for the receiver and smiling to himself, *but your real reward will be a night or two with me. What more could you ask for at this stage of your lonely and empty life?*

~ ~ ~

Mustafa al-Siddiq wasted no time after his telephone conversation with Charles Raimondi. He immediately placed a call to a cell phone in Germany. While waiting for a return call, he reviewed the situation. Megan Nolan was still at large. Her father, who had identified a stranger's body as his daughter's and was therefore highly suspect, had escaped the net. Detective Catherine Laurence, assigned to follow Patrick Nolan, had, probably with the help of Mr. Nolan, killed four Saudi nationals, one in Volney Park and three at her uncle's house in Cap de la Hague. She had lifted the fingerprints of the two downed men in Volney Park and asked her uncle to run them through Europol's database. She had also asked her uncle to inquire with Europol about Megan Nolan. And, most intriguing, she had initiated the wild goose chase—as the Americans called it—to the house in Courbevoie, where it turned out no one remotely fitting Megan Nolan's description had ever lived. It was safe to assume that Detective Laurence and Patrick Nolan were searching—desperately searching—for Megan. And now the DST was in on the hunt. Megan Nolan would be a new name to them, but Ahmed bin-Shalib would not. The French were suspected by the Americans, rightly so in al-Siddiq's opinion, of being corrupted by huge Middle Eastern oil money. They would therefore be highly motivated to hunt down Megan Nolan if they had even a slight hope that she would lead them to the leader of the cell that beheaded the journalist Michael Cohen. The Chirac government could stay corrupted but take some heat off itself in America. In fact, the stakes were much higher than the French could even imagine them to be.

Onyx, a royal prince in a bloodline much favored by King Faud, was al-Siddiq's nephew, the only son of his beloved dead sister. Childless himself, al-Siddiq loved Onyx like a son. When last they spoke, Onyx had mentioned a prayer card found by his men in the house in Cap de la Hague, a prayer card from the Convent of St. Thérèse of Lisieux, with the name and address of a François Duval written on it. He would have to follow that lead on his own. The jihad was more important by far than one man, one life. It remained only for Charles Raimondi, the one person besides Onyx with knowledge of al-Siddiq's involvement in the case, to be dealt with. He had been feeding Raimondi caviar, handing him expensive gifts and stroking his bloated ego for years, all against the day when the ridiculous would-be Casanova might prove useful to him. That day had come and gone. While talking to Raimondi, al-Siddiq had flipped through his old-fashioned Rolodex and stopped at the diplomat's card. He was ready, therefore, when the return call came, probably from a cell phone in Greece or Turkey, though it could have been anywhere. He pushed the speakerphone button, then, reading from the card, said, "One Boulevard Capucine, Apartment 22." The phone on the other end went dead and al-Siddiq clicked off as well.

"Good-bye Charles," he said softly to himself. "You were an even bigger fool than I thought. And about as useful."

~ 19 ~

Paris, January 6, 2004

Catherine used one of the cell phones taken from the dead Arabs to call the Cherbourg police to report that she had witnessed two men, two Arab men with automatic rifles, throw an elderly man off a cliff in Cap de la Hague. Then she put her head on Pat's shoulder and slept. Two hours later, the Peugeot stopping and starting in city traffic woke her.

"We are in Paris?" she said.

"Yes. I"m glad you're awake. Where is Rue de Matisse?"

"There is a Rue de Matisse in Montmartre. We will head there. But first I have to use a restroom. Pull in at that gas station on the corner. When I come out I will drive."

Pat did as he was told, but before Catherine could exit the car, he took hold of her hand and held it firmly in his.

"How was your sleep?"

"Good. *Bon.*"

"I'm sorry about your uncle."

Silence. The silence that death brings when it hovers close to life.

"He was a good man, Patrick," Catherine said, speaking quietly but clearly. She was hurting, but relieved to be. As opposed to those moments in Cap de la Hague after learning of Daniel's death, when the pain was so great that her mind had banished it, leaving her free to take her revenge the way it should be taken: cold and quick. Looking at Pat, she could see the relief in his eyes as well. He had seen what he had seen and would have to live with it, but she was glad, for his sake and for hers, that she had returned to herself.

"And he liked you," she continued. "He approved of you. He hated my husband."

"He died because of me, and Megan."

"No, he died because evil has reappeared in the world."

"We will go back and bury him properly."

If we live, Catherine thought, and then realized that *if we live* would be built into every statement, every thought, every hope they had for the future from now on. Until there was no more future or until the people who were pursuing them—whoever they were and in whatever number—were killed. Looking down, she saw Pat's hand, his lion's paw of a hand, still gently clutching hers. Pulling it to her lips, she kissed it and said, "*Mais oui, chérie.* Of course."

"Catherine, one more thing."

"Yes."

"I left the prayer card with Duval's address on it in our bedroom in Cap de la Hague. I took it out to read the prayer to St. Thérèse while you were sleeping. I left it on the night table. I remembered it while driving."

"I see," Catherine replied. "They may not have found it. If they did, they could not know its importance. And only one survived, don't forget. And he fled abruptly, you recall."

"The police will have found it by now."

"Possibly. But we have no choice but to visit Duval. We will be careful. There is nothing else we can do. We have no other leads."

Thirty-three Rue de Matisse was a storefront on a corner across from the Cimetière de Montmartre, the famous burial place of many of France's favorite sons. Through the cemetery's wrought iron fence could be seen asymmetrical rows of stone markers and, in the distance, crypts, all weathered to a dirty gray that perfectly matched the watery grayness of the early winter day. The storefront's plate glass windows, on either side of an opaque glass door, were painted black. On each could be seen the faded yellow lettering, *Achat de Chevaux,* and beneath the letters a rearing white horse.

"Duval sells horses?" Pat asked.

"No, it must have been a butcher shop at one time, specializing in horse meat."

"I never saw *that* on Julia Child."

"Julia Child?"

"Never mind. What do you think?"

Catherine had driven past Duval's storefront twice and then found a place to park on a side street with a head-on view of it. She had been a cautious policewoman, a trait drilled into her head by her father and uncle from an early age. *Act swiftly and decisively when it is time to act, but until then take no unnecessary risks. Do not make assumptions.*

No suspicious cars or people were hanging about and no one had gone in or out of the old butcher shop in the last half hour.

"You must go alone, Patrick."

"Fine. But why?"

"He is expecting Megan's father, not Megan's father and a woman.

He likely will not talk with me present, or let us in for that matter. Besides, if someone follows you in, I will come. To lend my support. Do you have your gun?"

~ ~ ~

After two knocks, the frosted glass door swung open and Pat stood facing a dark-haired, dark-eyed gypsy boy of ten or eleven. He stood mutely, staring up at the giant *gadgo*—nongypsy—while a second boy, who had been sitting on an overstuffed sofa watching two televisions, jumped up and ran through a curtained doorway off to Pat's left. Pat stepped in and closed the door behind him. Across from the sofa and the TVs was a large dresser covered with statuary of what looked to be Catholic saints surrounding a gold-plated samovar. The floor and walls were covered by thick oriental carpets, and there were maroon brocade drapes covering the already blackened plate glass windows. Light came from several ornate lamps placed with no seeming plan in mind. Heavily shaded, these lamps did not do much to brighten the cavelike enclosure in which Pat found himself.

"*Je m'appelle* ...," he said to the boy.

"We saw you in your car," the boy said, interrupting and startling Pat with his strangely accented English and his directness. "Will you give me money for food?"

Before Pat could answer, a paunchy, thick-set middle-aged man, perhaps forty, perhaps fifty, came through the curtain and said something swiftly to the boy in a language Pat didn't know. The boy turned and ran into the back room. The man then went to the far end of the thick draperies to his right and, pulling them aside a few inches, peered out to the street for a long moment.

"What is your business?" the man said finally, turning to face Pat.

"Are you François Duval?"

"Yes, but there was another François Duval. My father. He died a month ago." The man was pale to the point of whiteness, and balding, his wisps of black hair sticking like painted stripes to his naked head in a bizarre gypsy version of a comb-over. His baggy gabardine trousers were held up by suspenders worn over a plaid wool shirt. He wore slippers on his feet.

"I am searching for my daughter. Her name is Megan Nolan. Do you know her?"

"What makes you think I would know her?"

"Your name and address—or your father's—were written by Megan on a prayer card and left at the Convent of St. Thérèse in Lisieux."

"Can I see this prayer card?"

"I seem to have lost it."

"Lost it? I see. Do you have money in your wallet, Monsieur Nolan?"

"Yes. How much do you want?"

"Do you have half of a hundred?"

"Fifty dollars? Of course."

"No, not fifty dollars." As he spoke, Duval drew a once white but now crumpled and dirty envelope from his shirt pocket. "Half of this," he said, presenting Pat with its contents: one half of a hundred-dollar bill.

Pat stood dumb for a second and then realized he was looking at Megan's half of the hundred-dollar bill he had torn in two at an outdoor café in Prague in 1992. He quickly extracted his half, forgotten these twelve years until now, and held it out toward Duval.

"Yes," said Duval, taking the torn bill from Pat's outstretched hand and placing it next to the one he was holding. "A perfect match. You are the father of Megan Nolan."

"Where is she?"

"I don't know, Monsieur, but I will find out."

"You don't know?"

"No, but as I said, I will find out where she is."

"Do it now. I'll wait."

"No, Monsieur, it is not so simple. Come back tonight, *a dix heures,* ten o' clock. I should know by then. Do not use the front door. There is an alley on Rue de Caulaincourt, across from the grave of M. Zola, a dirt path. It leads to the back door here."

"Fine," Pat said, turning to leave, "I'll be here at ten." Then he turned back and said, "Let me ask you, François, Why are you doing this?"

There was rustling and giggling at the curtain, and then the boys' heads appeared. Duval glowered in their direction and they were gone. The televisions were still on, one blaring a Popeye cartoon in French, the other a game show with half-naked contestants.

"My father died of cancer of the stomach, Monsieur Nolan. He refused to see a *gadgo* doctor or go to a *gadgo* hospital. Your daughter took care of him. For seven months, until he died, she took care of him. He had a gift, my father, the second sight. He could see your future and he could curse you if he wished. On his deathbed he gave me Megan's half of the hundred-dollar bill. He told me how to find Megan if you appeared with the other half. He said he would curse me from the grave if I refused or failed. I do not wish to be cursed. I am a gypsy. A curse from the grave would be worse for me than the danger that is following you. My father saw that danger, and I am afraid of it. After you leave tonight I will pack up my family and go away. Do not be late."

~ ~ ~

"You have been very tender," said Catherine.

Pat remained silent. They were sitting over coffee, after eating dinner, in a quiet corner of a nearly empty bistro a few steps from their nondescript hotel on Rue Gabrielle. Catherine had lit one of her Galloises before making this statement, and Patrick was caught up in watching her movements as she lit up, inhaled, and then exhaled as she spoke. She had said earlier while they were doing some quick shopping that she would smoke three cigarettes in the ten hours they had to kill before their meeting with Duval. This was her second. The first had been after they had made love in their tiny room at the Three Ducks Hotel. Her face then, half in shadow, had been aglow, her eyes glittering, her sadness exiled for the moment by the stronger demands of pleasure. Watching Catherine smoke brought the memory of that pleasure swiftly back to Pat.

"I am not the only one grieving," Catherine said. "You have lost a grandson."

"You have been tender as well."

"Thank you. It has been a pleasure."

They smiled across the table at each other, then Catherine said, "Tell me about your life, Patrick."

"My life?"

"Yes, your emotional life. The life of your heart. You know about Jacques. My failure."

"My emotional life. I see. Well, I can top you. I didn't have one."

"Why not?"

"All Lorrie wanted was a house in the suburbs, a couple of kids, to love me. I dragged her to the jungle to die. Then I abandoned Megan. I didn't deserve anything good after that."

"You punished yourself."

"Yes. And was proud of it."

"There must have been women."

Pat took a moment to consider this.

"There were women," he said, finally. "One or two loved me, I'm sure. But no one I would let myself love. Like I said, I was either too proud or too humiliated, or lost somewhere in between."

"And now?"

"Now?"

"Have you found yourself?"

"I don't know," Pat said, smiling. "But I've found *you*, and now that I have, I'm not letting you go."

~ ~ ~

When they drove past 33 Rue de Matisse at ten that night, Pat and Catherine saw two Arab men in ski jackets and jeans, their hands in their jacket pockets, standing on the entrance steps.

"The prayer card," Catherine said, turning left on Rue Caulaincourt. "The prayer card," Pat replied, turning his head to keep his eyes on the two men until they were out of sight.

"We have to go in," Catherine said. "They may be simply waiting for us outside."

"I agree."

They had not heard from Doro. Who knew if they ever would? François Duval was their best, possibly their only hope of finding Megan. They parked on Rue Caulaincourt and stepped quietly into the pitch-black alley, their guns drawn. They did not so much find the back steps as stumble upon them. The small porch was nearly completely covered by a wild vine of some kind. The door was locked. On the brick wall to the right, also covered with the vine, they could make out the faint outline of a window in the dark. Pat jimmied the lock with a pocketknife and they climbed into François Duval's bedroom, another carpet-covered cavelike room that was completely dark and reeked of incense and tobacco. They stood still for a long second or two, getting their bearings. A very faint light outlined the room's closed door. They opened it slowly and stepped into a small, dark, pantry-sized room with a mattress on the floor. Here Pat saw the curtain that the two boys had peeked their heads out of, a faint glow behind it. He moved it aside about six inches, his gun unlocked and gripped tightly in his free hand. Catherine joined him and they peered into the front room together. One lonely lamp glowed in a corner. Within its cone of dim light lay the headless body of François Duval. A few feet away the head was propped up against the leg of an overstuffed chair. Blood was everywhere. They took this scene in for a long moment, the silence surrounding them stony and deep and heavy with death.

"I have to search him," Pat said, thinking of Megan, the idea that this is what could happen to her finally penetrating all of his defenses, encircling his heart like a band of ice. He had heard Catherine gasp, but was only vaguely aware that she was gripping his arm until he made a move to enter the room.

"No," she said in an insistent whisper, trying to pull him back, her grip like a vice on his bicep, "there is nothing we can do. We must go." As she was saying this, the cell phone in her shoulder bag rang. She continued to pull maniacally on Pat's arm, urging him toward the bedroom while reaching into her bag with her free hand to find the phone. But Pat was having none of it. He jerked his arm free, causing the shoulder bag to fall to the floor and its contents to spill out. Catherine fell to her knees to search in the dark for the phone, desperate to silence its irritating chirpy ring.

Pat watched her for a second, then, hearing the front door click and swing open, slid the curtain aside and saw both Arabs from the street coming right at him. Both were carrying drawn pistols, but they did not see him in the dark. He shot the first one in the chest, causing him to crumple to the floor and giving his partner a chance to duck and at the same time point his gun in Pat's direction. But before he could fire, Pat shot him twice, once in the shoulder and once in the forehead, a lucky shot.

Stepping quickly into the room, Pat kicked their guns away and placed his index and middle fingers against their carotid arteries, making sure both were dead. Then he heard Catherine's voice and, turning, saw her kneeling and talking on the cell phone. "*Oui, Doro, c'est moi, Catherine. Oui, Daniel est mort. Oui, oui, demain, Champ de Mars, a huit heures.*"

~ ~ ~

They drove in silence back to the Three Ducks. In their room, the things they had bought that afternoon sat forlornly on the dresser: face cream, gloves, and a thick scarf for Catherine, socks and a new shirt and sweater for Pat. Near them was the wine they had bought, thinking of a nightcap. This Pat uncorked, pouring out two glasses. He drank in silence while Catherine undressed and got into bed, leaving her wine untouched. There had been no sign of the children or of Duval's wife. Whether that was good or bad was a question that hung between them, unasked.

Tomorrow morning they would meet Doro. He would tell them where Megan was. If he really could be trusted. That question also remained locked in Pat's head, along with the day's images: Daniel Peletier, legs and arms akimbo, falling to his death; Catherine shooting one of his killer's in the groin; François Duval's leering head. Catherine had made sure that they were not being followed on the short ride to the hotel, meandering through adjacent neighborhoods and checking her rearview mirrors constantly. Nevertheless, Pat pushed the dresser against the door before settling into a shabby plush chair near the room's one window, with its view of the now-quiet Rue Gabrielle.

As he drank and listened to Catherine's regular breathing, more questions without answers came to his mind. What had Megan done to lay down such a trail of blood to her door? And how could they possibly prevail against the host of vipers that were arrayed against them?

~ 20 ~

Paris, January 7, 2004

Catherine and Pat, wary of traps, arrived an hour early at Paris's Champ de Mars. The weather had turned colder, but the morning sun was bright and the sky above the city was, for a change, a pale and pretty blue. Starkly leafless trees and an occasional ornate lamppost dotted an otherwise wide open and windless landscape. They quickly spotted the meeting place Doro had designated, a bench facing a triangular flower bed in the middle of the park, and watched it from another bench fifty or so yards away. Nearby, a young mother walked a child in a sturdy, hi-tech stroller, and in the distance, near one of the park's entrances, a kiosk selling newspapers and hot chocolate was doing a brisk business. One or two of its patrons, bundled against the cold in overcoats and scarves, had tucked their papers under their arms and were slowly negotiating the paved paths that dissected the park's wide winter-blond central field. Promptly at eight, Doro approached the bench alone and sat. Pat and Catherine, their hands on their guns in their coat pockets, walked over and joined him, one sitting on either side of the young gypsy. They nodded in greeting and waited while the boy lit a Gallois, declining his offer of one.

"Doro," Catherine said, "do you know a man named François Duval? A gypsy?"

"Yes, he is of my *vitsas*, my tribe. Megan stayed with his father in Paris for several months. What of him?"

"He is dead. We found his body last night, just as you were calling. It was the Arabs again."

"Dead?"

"Yes, beheaded."

"Beheaded ... And his wife and children?"

"We don't know."

"How did you find François?"

"We were given his name in Lisieux, at the convent. Megan had written his name and address on a prayer card and left it with the child."

"Did you find the child?"

"The child is dead."

Doro looked at Pat. "Ah ... I am sorry, Monsieur."

"Thank you."

"Did François tell you where your daughter is?"

"No, we were too late."

Pat had been listening to Catherine and Doro, but also scanning the park, his right hand gripping his Beretta in the pocket of his leather jacket, the same weatherbeaten bomber jacket he had worn since his arrival in Paris. He gripped the gun as much as a defense against Doro as against Islamic fanatics charging at them across the park. The population of people in the world he trusted had dwindled to one: Catherine.

"His father agreed to help Megan," Pat continued, "to lead me to her. He must have left information with his son."

"So now the barbarians know where Megan is."

"Probably."

"That is good."

"Good? Why?"

"Because I also know where she is. We will go there and we will kill them."

"Where is she?" Pat and Catherine said simultaneously.

Doro did not answer. He too had his right hand in his jacket pocket, and he too now scanned the park.

"The Nazis killed a million gypsies, Monsieur Nolan," Doro said, completing his scan and returning his gaze to Pat. "Did you know that?"

Pat took a breath and looked from Doro's darkly handsome eyes to the trail of smoke he was exhaling through his flared nostrils. *The Nazis?* he thought. *Where's Megan?* But he bit his tongue. The boy, probably not yet twenty, was his last chance of finding his daughter.

"Yes," he replied. "I knew that."

"You may think one or two more are of little significance."

"I don't think that."

"There is no holocaust museum for us, no homeland."

"No."

"But that is as we want it. We are gypsies. Do you understand, Monsieur Nolan? We do not want a museum, we do not want a homeland. We want no records kept of who we are and where we go and what we do. We do not assimilate. We have our ways and we have each other, and that is all."

"I understand."

"I don't think you do."

Pat did not reply. He glanced at Catherine, but she was quietly scrutinizing the young man sitting between them and he could not read her eyes.

"Where is Megan?" Pat said finally.

"She is with my uncle Corozzo in the Czech Republic."

"Will you take us to her?"

"Yes, but we must use her to draw the barbarians to us. If you cannot agree to this, then I cannot help you."

"I understand, but Megan may have something to say about that."

"You will talk to her. Tell her of Annabella and the others."

"I will try. That's all I can do. You have my word I will try."

"Good. That is enough. We are agreed."

"We must hurry," said Catherine. "The Arabs have a ten-hour head start."

"No *gadgo* can approach Corozzo's camp without him knowing it," Doro said. "If they arrive in force, he will run and we will catch up with him. We will meet in Waldsassen, in Germany, and from there cross into the Czech Republic. Corozzo and his people, and your daughter, are in an abandoned mining camp in the forest near Kolin, a small city of no importance."

"Where in Waldsassen?" Catherine asked.

"Do you know Waldsassen?"

"No."

"It is near the Czech border. Outside the town there is a small amusement park, on the banks of the river Ohře. It will be closed for the winter. Go to the carousel at six tonight. If I am not there, come back at midnight. I will call you if there is a problem."

"What kind of problem?"

"I have to find a place to cross the border. It should be easy, but sometimes there are patrols. We may have to wait one, maybe two nights."

Doro began to rise from the bench, but Pat took hold of his arm and stopped him. As he did this, the two men in overcoats carrying newspapers that Pat had seen earlier veered sharply toward the bench. Both Pat and Catherine drew their guns. Doro, using his free arm, held his hand up, palm forward, to the two men, who stopped about twenty yards away. Both had their hands in their pockets, ready to draw weapons. They were not, Pat realized, Parisian businessmen, not men at all, but the two teenage boys who had been with Doro at the house in Rambouillet three days ago.

"Yes, Monsieur Nolan?" said Doro.

"What about *your* word, Doro? Is it any good?"

"Monsieur Nolan, I could have killed you in Rambouillet three days ago. I could have had the police here when you arrived. I am going to kill the men who killed my grandmother, with or without you. I am bringing you to your daughter because Annabella would have wished me to. Not all gypsies are liars and cheats. Most, but not all. I will see you tonight in Waldsassen."

~ ~ ~

On the way out of the park, Catherine and Pat were passing the kiosk when Catherine stopped suddenly to stare at the neat stacks of newspapers lining the top of its tiered counter. Reaching down, she picked up a copy of *Figaro* and began rapidly reading a front-page story. Over her shoulder Pat could see the headline, *Diplomat Slain on Paris Street*. Below it were two black-and-white pictures side by side. On the left was an effetely handsome, well-dressed man in his late thirties behind a desk, smiling as he talked on the phone. On the right was the same man lying face up on a sidewalk, his legs twisted under him, blood staining the front of his stylish camel hair overcoat. The caption read: *Charles Raimondi in bis office in 2002 and as found yesterday near his apartment on Boulevard Capucine.*

~ 21 ~

Morocco, May 14-15, 2003

"When do you think ensoulment takes place, Megan?"

"Ensoulment?"

"Yes. You have heard the word before, have you not?"

"I haven't, actually."

"But you know what it means."

"Of course."

By late April Megan knew she was pregnant. Not only had she missed her second period, due April 20th, but the telltale signs were there. The slight heaviness in her breasts, the backache, the morning sickness of a month ago, which she had refused to acknowledge at the time. She had experienced these symptoms before. Selfish of her pleasure, her good health, her freedom from the hassles of prophylactic measures, she had used abortion as her surefire method of birth control. With Lahani, she had insisted on condoms, a first for her. In Morocco, abortion was illegal unless the mother's life was in danger. But obviously something had gone wrong. And now this question from Abdullah, who was sitting silently across from her at the chess table, waiting for her answer.

"I don't know," she said.

"As a Christian, I believe it takes place at conception," said Abdullah. "Any other moment would be arbitrary, established by man for his convenience."

"I didn't say I was having an abortion."

"You asked for a remedy."

"I asked if there *was* a remedy."

Megan rose and went to the front door; she could see through its bead curtain to the street. A portion of pavement had buckled in front of the shop, opening a fissure several feet wide and a foot or two deep. It had filled with water from a morning downpour. Three children, two gangly girls and a small boy, were jumping back and forth over the water, laughing and pushing each other whenever there was hesitation. Steam was lifting around them as the noon sun did its work.

"I can return to France," Megan said, her back to the pharmacist. This, of course, was what she was trying to avoid, at first telling herself that she did not want to lose the foothold, however tenuous, she had established in the Carrières Thomas neighborhood, then admitting that the idea of another *procedure,* another stainless steel *scraping* of her uterine wall, had become, suddenly, quite repulsive. Hence the request, illusory she knew, of Abdullah for a *remedy,* the dream of every woman with an unwanted pregnancy on her hands, a vial of liquid or a powder that would make it, magically, go away.

"If you have this child, Megan, I will raise it."

Megan turned abruptly and looked hard at Abdullah, as if seeing him for the first time. His dark eyes shone brightly above his hawkish nose, his thick brows knitted together. *For this man, a stranger, to fight for a child's life like this. Amazing.*

"Are you married, Abdullah?" she said. "I've never asked."

"And I've never volunteered," Abdullah replied. "I'm not, but I was. My wife was killed. In Cairo, where I was teaching. And my three daughters. Their throats slit by Islamic fanatics. I was at a conference in Beirut, otherwise I would have been killed as well."

"What did you do? I mean, why did this happen?"

"I spoke my mind. I named evil for evil. I said that the Islamic fundamentalists had turned their backs on God. That the fanatics among them used the Kuran, used Muhammad's life, to justify beheadings and the slaughter of innocents. That the average Muslim, the nonfanatic, did not seem to mind all this bloodshed in the name of his God. In my classroom I said these things. The word must have spread. It is not far from the university, from anywhere in Egypt, or the Middle East for that matter, to the places where Satan dwells. Not far at all."

Megan took a deep breath and remained silent. She could hear the children playing outside and the voice of the shopkeeper next door trying to shoo them away. The women's clinic she went to to confirm her pregnancy had been on the same street as her hotel, the wide and tree-lined Avenue des Forces Armées Royales. She had walked the two miles back to the Farah, breathing air refreshed by the unexpected shower, and thinking of the unreal possibility of keeping the child. Of finishing her work here in the next month or two and then flying home to Connecticut. Of the look on her father's face when she told him he would soon be a grandfather. Then she remembered her first pregnancy at age seventeen: the abortion that quickly followed; the surprising joy of keeping it secret from her father; the long, windswept, melodramatic walks she took, the hood of her sweatshirt blocking out the world, planning to the last detail the scene where she would drop the abortion bomb on Paddy, as she often in those days condescendingly referred to her father in her thoughts, just before she left for Europe. The scene never played out. How would it go now? Dad, I'm giving you *a grandson; the others I killed.*

By the time she walked through the hotel's glass-and-steel front doors, she had cast these thoughts away—good and bad, bitter and sweet—had managed to harden her heart once again, in the old Megan style, against the idea—with all of its insistent, primeval pull—of home and family. But now the look on old Abdullah's face, more defiant than sad, devoid of self-pity, brought them back in force.

"Abdullah ... ," she said.

"There is nothing you can say, child. What is done is done. But I would be putting my own soul in jeopardy if I did not try to prevent the killing of this innocent babe. It is a terrible and tragic destiny to be killed by your own mother before you are born. To be so unloved."

Megan did not speak. When RU-47, the so-called "morning-after pill," had become available over the counter in France in 2001 while she was seeing Alain Tillinac, she had taken it without hesitation. Which meant she might have aborted a few dozen or so more "innocent babes." Unloved innocent babes. Suddenly she was crying, thinking of what she had done and why, images of herself as a child—lonely, abandoned—and the hardened, cynical adult that child had grown up to be side by side in her mind. *Child,* Abdullah had called her, without a trace of irony or bitterness, indeed with a tenderness that had pierced her heart.

"And you?" Abdullah asked. "Do you have a family?"

"I have a father," Megan replied, wiping away with her hands the first tears she had shed in more than fifteen years. For the first time since she could remember, she had referred to the fact of her having a father without irony. Yes, she had a father.

"A father."

As he said these two words, Megan could see sadness stealing the light from the pharmacist's eyes, like a curtain being slowly drawn across them. She knew what he was thinking: *I was a father once.*

"Yes," she said.

"Perhaps you should go to him."

"Maybe. I don't know what to do."

"My dear Megan, my offer stands."

~ ~ ~

When Megan returned to her room at the Farah, she found two notes on her bed. The first was from the hotel manager:

> *With deep regret I am compelled to inform you that you must vacate your room by Friday, May 16. We have a long-standing booking for a United Nations conference which will require most of our rooms. I apologize for not inform-ing you when you arrived, but we did not ex-pect your stay with us to be as extended as it has been. The Hyatt, only two doors down, has a reputation for excellent service. If you would like, I will be happy to reserve a room for you there. With deepest appreciation.*

The second was from Abdel al-Lahani:

> *I have unexpectedly returned for a few days. Shall we have dinner tomorrow night? I will meet you at the Farah bar at nine unless I hear from you to the contrary.*

Over the last two weeks, Lahani had been urging her to stay at his place. She could have her own bedroom if she liked, he had said, and a room could be easily converted into a study for her. She had smiled and declined. Lahani was too rich and too powerful a man to be overseeing her life in that way. She had already taken and would in the fu-ture take other things from him, but not the roof over her head. She would not let him view himself as her keeper. The sixteenth was only two days away. Before settling into a long hot bath, she dialed the manager's office and asked his assistant to book her a small suite at the Hyatt.

The next evening, her last at the Farah, she went down early to the bar, called the Oasis, located off the lobby at the rear of the hotel. She liked to sit by herself under the trellis of the bar's patio at this time of day when the sun was about to set and it was bearable, sometimes pleasant, to be out of doors. The patio was bordered by a long reflecting pool on which floated paper lanterns lit by candles. Beyond the pool were the hotel's formal gardens, and beyond them its tennis courts and swimming pool. As she sat waiting for her gin and tonic, she could hear above her head birds chirping in the branches of the leafy vine that twined itself over and around the trellis, and in the distance the muffled rhythmic thuds of a tennis match. She had placed her order at the bar on the way in and it was brought to her now by Elnardo, the handsome mulatto waiter who had, after a month of trying, finally stopped hitting on her and settled in to a half formal, half friendly relationship in which they bantered back and forth in French about the doings of Megan's fellow guests. A four-month stay had earned her this extra amenity, one she enjoyed wherever she went and happened to stay long enough. Elnardo wore a pencil-thin mustache that went well with his broad smile and sly eyes. Perhaps forty or forty-five, in his white waist jacket and black bow tie, with his hip, Parisian French, he was the perfect player on a stage set to take full advantage of Casablanca's colonial heritage.

"*Bonsoir, mademoiselle,*" he said, tray in hand, placing her drink and a crisp cloth napkin on the table.

"*Bonsoir,* Elnardo."

"Are you waiting for someone?"

"Yes."

"Shall I take an order?"

"No, he'll order when he gets here."

"Very well."

"Are you prepared for the flood?"

"The flood?"

"Yes, of *les politiquement corrects.*"

"*Je ne sais ...*"

"The UN conference coming in."

"Not here, Madame."

Megan smiled at Elnardo's use of the more formal *Madame.* Perhaps he was concerned that Lahani, whose appearance on this very scene some three months ago had markedly dampened the suave waiter's ardor, would appear now and be mistaken as to the nature of his attentions to the beautiful American.

"Yes, on Friday. For once I am ahead of you, Elnardo."

"I'm surprised I have not been told."

"I've been asked to leave to accommodate them."

"Asked to leave?"

"Yes, but I'll be back for drinks. I would miss our tête-à-têtes."

"As would I, mademoiselle."

A short time later, Megan watched as Lahani arrived, stopping at the captain's podium to shake hands with the majordomo type there who was in charge of the prized patio seating. Probably handing him a hundred dollars. Banking it, as he would say, for the next time, when he actually needed a table. She was familiar by now with the way in which her new lover kept Casablanca—both its servant class and its society types—in his thrall. Wherever he went he was known and deferred to. It wasn't just money, Megan reflected as she watched Lahani chat with the tuxedoed captain. Or merely movie-star looks, though he had both in spades. It was power; power made more, not less, palpable because it was forever in reserve, wielded when necessary with the lightest, the most unnerving, of touches. Dressed in a stylishly cut navy blue blazer and white lightweight flannel slacks, all eyes, certainly the women's, were on Abdel al-Lahani as he took his leave of the waiter and headed toward Megan. He kissed Megan's hand and told her in a whisper that she looked beautiful before sitting down. Elnardo, hovering nearby, appeared immediately and took Lahani's order of Gray Goose on the rocks with a twist of lime.

"So," Megan said, "what happened in Angola? Why have you returned so quickly?"

"The Americans changed their minds, or rather their bankers did."

"Why?"

"The risk was high and the government wanted ninety-five percent of the profits."

"Only ninety-five percent?"

"Yes. They knew they weren't dealing with one of the big boys and thought they could hold a gun to their heads. The bank said no."

"What was Luanda like?"

"A backwater."

"Did they pay your fee?"

"Yes, of course."

"Good, you can afford dinner. I'm starving."

Lahani smiled and then nodded to Elnardo as the waiter placed his drink on the table and left.

"Where would you like to eat?"

"You decide."

"I have something to tell you first. I hope you won't be offended."

Megan, instantly alert, did not reply. In the three months she had known Lahani, he had not once by word or gesture made himself even the slightest bit vulnerable. He was possessive of her in the way that all powerful men are possessive of their women, but he was never jealous, never weak. It was weakness that was exploitable, that turned men into fools. She had no diabolical plan to exploit Lahani, nor had she any of her other lovers. But by their need they seemed to beg for it and she accommodated them whenever she could, which was most of the time. Thus she was able to travel first class and stay in suites in the best hotels in the world. She remained silent, but so did Lahani.

"I'm listening," she said finally.

"I know that you are pregnant."

This was a shock to Megan, a complete shock. But she knew better than to lose her composure. If Lahani was to be beholden to her in some way, then she did not want to squander the newly acquired chips she held with an emotional outburst, the kind of reaction that in the games that men and women played would enable him to too quickly start regaining lost ground.

"What are you talking about?" she said.

"I have been worried lately for your safety. Carrières Thomas is a very dangerous place. I had you watched while I was away this time. You were seen going into the women's clinic. When I was told I became worried. I thought you might be ill. I never dreamed you were pregnant. I know the owners of the clinic. I prevailed upon them to give me a copy of your chart. I am to be a father, but I am sorry I learned of it this way, sorry to have to tell you of this ... this invasion."

Megan took a breath and then a sip from her drink, assessing this information at a rapid rate, as if it were necessary to do so for a reason that was specific and important but that she could not put her finger on.

I bad you watched. I know the owners. Your chart.

"I'm surprised, Del," she said, "but I'm not upset."

"You're positive?"

"Yes. You were worried about me."

"I was. It all seems so cloak-and-dagger, but I was hoping you'd see it that way."

Megan finished her drink, baby's first gin, remaining silent. Silence, she knew, was a reaction, but much less open to interpretation than anything she might say at this moment. In her heart there was a strange mix of fear and anger, but her instincts, honed over twelve years of dealing with men in every stage of their development, in every European capital, told her that it was imperative not to give voice to either.

"Of course I will pay for everything," said Lahani, "and acknowledge the child."

Acknowledge the child? Megan thought. But all she said was, "Let's talk about that later, Del. Right now I'm starving."

~ 22 ~

Morocco, May 15, 2003

Megan awoke alone just before dawn in Lahani's custom-made king-size bed. Moonlight flooded into the room through the French doors that dominated the far wall, moonlight so bright that the shadows of the doors' diamond-patterned mullions were cast in sharp contrast on the room's large expanse of white-carpeted floor. The gossamer curtains that covered the floor-to-ceiling windows on either side of the doors were billowing gently into the room in the night breeze. Megan had placed her shoulder bag on the sill of one of these windows before putting on one of Lahani's silk shirts and getting into bed with him when they arrived after their late dinner. She lay for a few seconds and watched the ceiling fan above the bed spin slowly. The sex was so good, she was certain, that he would never guess that it was to be their last. She rose and went to her bag for a cigarette. Lahani had been absent in the middle of the night before, sometimes working in his study, sometimes leaving her a note to say he had left on a business trip and would call on his return. As she lit her cigarette, she was hoping it was the latter this time. She would never have to see him again. The acting she had been doing for the past hours would be over. And she would have control of the child. Complete control.

As she smoked, voices drifted into the bedroom from somewhere in the apartment. Naked and feeling suddenly vulnerable, she found Lahani's shirt on the floor next to the bed and put it on. One of the voices was Lahani's. The other she could not make out until she remembered the forceful, oddly sing-song Arabic of Mohammed as he spoke to the three young men in the Carrières Thomas souk court-yard a few weeks ago. She took the tape recorder from her bag, turned it on, and slipped it into the monogrammed front pocket of Lahani's pure white, beautifully tailored shirt, stepping silently into the long hall that led from the rear of the apartment, where the bedrooms were located, to the living room and kitchen area. Before the corridor ended she stopped to listen. The voices, definitely those of Lahani and Mohammed, were much clearer now. Breathing slowly, calmly, remaining in the shadows of the hall, she peered into the living room where she saw Lahani and his stocky driver sitting across from each other in brocaded wing chairs, a small inlaid table with glasses of water on it between them. Their faces were illuminated by a shaft of moonlight from the slightly ajar door to the balcony behind them. They talked quietly for some five minutes, Mohammed leaning forward at one point and seeming to repeat several times the same questioning phrase. From outside, the call to morning prayer could now be heard, piped here as almost everywhere in Casablanca through loudspeakers, but nevertheless strangely beautiful and compelling. Megan watched as the two men stood and faced east then went through the ritual of bowing, standing again, prostration, sitting, and finally prostration again, reciting the prayers of *salat* as they did. When they were done, they exchanged *inshallahs* and kisses on each cheek and then Mohammed left and Abdel went out to the balcony.

Megan had been with Lahani on many occasions coincidental with the prescribed times—before dawn, midday, four PM, sunset, and before midnight—for the *salat* ritual, and had never seen him pray before. Pondering this, she reached into her shirt pocket and turned off the recorder. The clicking sound this action made was not loud—it was all but silent—but it made Megan paranoid. Before turning back toward the bedroom, she chanced one more look into the living room. There, standing in the entrance foyer, was Lalla, staring at Megan as she placed her key into a deep pocket in her djellaba. Lalla's eyes were as clear and as piercing as the ones on the Afgahni mountain women she had seen in *National Geographic* pictorials. Megan nodded and said, *sabaah al-khayr, Lalla*—"good morning, Mrs."—having picked this up along with a few other stock Arabic phrases during her time in the country. Then she turned and walked slowly back to the bedroom, where she quickly put the recorder back in her bag.

This taping was not impulsive, as the previous one of Mohammed and his young friends had been. She was angry at Lahani, but frightened as well, and knowing someone's secrets was always a useful means of protection. In the bathroom, she brushed her teeth and dabbed perfume in strategic spots on her exquisite body, then she slipped off the silk shirt and got into bed. She would have to act for a few more hours, something she had been doing well for many years, given all the men she had seduced who she basically despised. It was different now, though. There was vastly more at stake. Lahani had spoken of dual Saudi and American citizenship for their child, whom he expected confidently would be a boy. Of private tutors, of his son's role in the family business—this the first mention of a family by the charming but highly discreet Lahani. It wasn't simply these remarks that triggered Megan's reaction, though they were bad enough. It was Lahani's attitude. He seemed to *know*, as *a fact*, that Megan would bear the child and that he would control its destiny. This chilled her, because it struck her that she was in a Muslim country, where fathers reigned supreme and where Abdel, the Muslim father of her child, had untold wealth, power, and connections. Her response had been to demurely agree while secretly planning to get on the earliest flight to anywhere in Europe.

Lahani was the lover that women dreamed of, strong, masterful, and ready at short intervals to give and receive great pleasure. She was sure he would want to have her when he returned to bed. He did, and she acted her part flawlessly, receiving him with award-winning delight. But while he was inside her, pressing his body insistently against hers, slowly getting ready to climax, she remembered him in a different prostrate position as he prayed just a few minutes earlier. The devout Muslim acknowledging his God was now thrusting at her and moaning. Something dark and cold took hold in Megan's heart, something beyond mere fear, as Lahani's moaning increased and he had his orgasm and she managed to fake hers. Afterward Lahani fell soundly asleep, as he usually did after they made love, and Megan slowly rose and went into his lavishly appointed bathroom where she washed his semen from her and then, not satisfied, decided to take a shower, to wash again.

In the tile-and-glass enclosure, the hot water loosed the cold fingers gripping her heart. She stood for a long time, her head bowed, as the water from the shower mingled with her tears. But there was no self-pity in Megan Nolan. None. Composed again, her eyes red but dry, rubbing herself down with one of Lahani's thick Egyptian cotton towels, she acknowledged that she had played her game of seduction and plunder one time too many. And that she had played that game with the wrong man. She could not have picked one more wrong than Abdel al-Lahani, who, powerful and single-minded, neither desperately needed her nor supinely loved her like other men had. And there was something else about him, something having to do with his praising Allah so humbly and then fucking her so proudly. Something that made her skin crawl. Now, for the sake of the child in her womb, she would have to outwit him.

She had no doubt that she would.

~ ~ ~

Two hours later, Mohammed drove her to the Farah and waited while she packed her things and checked out. He dropped her off at the front of the Hyatt and again waited in the circular drive while she went in. Instead of checking in, though, she went up to the second-floor coffee shop where she could look down and see Mohammed standing, still and observant, at the passenger side of the limo, watching the hotel's front doors. She gave her two large suitcases to the concierge along with a large tip and asked him to have them put into the room she had reserved the day before, knowing that if she checked in herself, the hotel would hold on to her passport for a day or two while they registered her with the Foreign Office. Then she walked out the back of the lobby and along the winding garden paths that connected most of the swanky downtown hotels until she reached the terrace of the Oasis, the Farah's bar. There, she eventually found Elnardo carrying Bloody Marys to a group of early tennis players. When he was free, she asked him to get a cab to meet her at the Farah's service entrance, which he did, un-questioning and with a friendly, conspiratorial smile.

In the cab, Megan asked the driver to recommend a quiet pension in the city's old colonial neighborhood. He took her to a place called La Parisienne that looked charm-ing, but she didn't go in there either. She sat on a small strip of grass across the street and watched a group of boys play-ing soccer on a dirt field next to a cemetery. When she was sure she was not being watched herself, she picked up her two small bags and walked around the corner to La Porte Rouge, whose red door and small sign she had spotted from the cab. In her room she called Air Maroc and booked a fight to New York for the next day at one PM. Then she called down to her host, a fat Frenchman whose bald head was sweating despite the fact that the place had more than adequate air-conditioning, and asked for ice. He reminded her that he needed her passport and she assured him that she would drop it off on her way out later in the evening. When the ice came, she wrapped a large handful of it in a towel, which she held to her forehead as she lay down on the bed. To wait.

She would not get her story, but she had other things on her mind now. Her father, for example, and making amends. Thinking of him and his reaction to her news, she let her memories come. Of her aching love for him as a girl. Of her bitter tears when he left on his long trips. Of how unimaginably happy she had been when he bought the house in New Canaan and then eventually stopped going away. Of how content she had been—more than content, ecstatic in the way only a lonely little girl can be—to have the small pieces of himself he was willing—or able—to give in the years that followed. Of the nights she cried, fearing that he would leave her again. Of how her preteen friends had envied her her movie-star-looking father. Of their rare but wonderful outings to the mall, to the movies, to the park. Pat would help her raise the child, and in this way she would make amends. At this thought, unthinkable only a few weeks ago, Megan smiled her first genuine smile in a long time.

While placing her call to Air Maroc, Megan had thumbed through the Porte Rouge's information portfolio, where she had come across a small color brochure that urged her to visit its sister hotel in Paris, the Hotel Lorraine on Rue des Fleurs. While idly looking through this badly done three-page leaflet, a postcard with a picture of a saint on it—St. Thérèse of Lisieux—had fallen out. She had picked it up and brought it to the bed with her, and now, still holding the ice to her head, she lifted it and read the prayer on the back:

MIRACULOUS PRAYER TO THE LITTLE FLOWER

O Little Flower of Jesus, ever consoling troubled souls with heavenly graces, in your unfailing intercession I place my confident trust. From the heart of our divine Savior, petition those blessings of which I stand in greatest need, especially ... (Here mention your intention). Shower upon me your promised roses of virtue and grace, Dear St. Thérèse, so that, swiftly advancing in sanctity and perfect love of neighbor, I may someday receive the crown of life eternal. Amen.

Megan turned the card over and looked at the picture of the simple and vastly humble Carmelite nun who had died at the age of twenty-four and was canonized twenty-eight years later by Pope Pius XI. *Here mention your intention,* Megan smiled again, though this one was quite rueful.

"Take care of my baby, St. Thérèse," she said out loud, her first prayer since she left the church at age six, right after her first communion. She had wondered at the time if her father would notice, sure that he would not, and of course she had been right. He would notice the change in her now, though. Of that she had no doubt.

~ 23 ~

Paris, January 7, 2004

As Pat and Catherine were reading of the murder of Charles Raimondi, a tall, handsome Arab, carrying a Vuitton briefcase, and his squat, balding, not-so-handsome older companion, also Arab, were checking out of Paris's Ritz Carlton hotel. Both were well-dressed, the tall man elegantly so, the smaller one, though his clothes were perfectly cut, not quite able to pull it off, like the proverbial farmer visiting the big city. Outside, they stowed their Gucci bags in the trunk of a waiting Mercedes sedan and then got in the backseat. In front were two men of similar age, size, and bearing, but wearing jeans, Nike sneakers, thick sweaters, and leather jackets. They drove west through the city on Avenue Victor Hugo into the Bois de Boulogne, the famous woods that at night were awash with characters out of a Fellini movie, all looking for sexual and/or commercial success, but that in daytime were just a large, pleasant, heavily wooded park. Making their way deliberately—and watchfully—around a placid lake, they came finally to a car park behind a boathouse that was closed for the winter. Here, all four men quickly stripped and the two in the back exchanged attire with the two in the front. The tall Arab handed two passports and an envelope containing two airline tickets to his counterpart in front, and then he and his companion exited the car and watched as it slowly drove off. They walked across the car park—looking like any two of the more than six million North African Muslims who had immigrated to France in the last ten years—and got into an older-model gray Peugeot. In the backseat were two young Arab men, Saudis, in their mid-twenties, dressed in jeans and ski jackets and woolen caps and gloves. Nods and one-word greetings were exchanged, and then they left the park, the small, squat man driving.

The tall one still had his briefcase. He opened it as his companion headed out of the city, extracted one of a dozen or so slender compact cell phones, and pushed one of his speed dial buttons. When it began to ring, he put it on speakerphone and placed it on the console of the small car, between him and his companion.

"Yes, Onyx," a man answered.

"You have heard?"

"Yes, I saw it on CNN an hour ago. Where are you?"

"I am about to get on a plane."

"And Mohammed?"

"He is with me."

"Good. It is best."

"Yes."

"Did you go to the convent?"

"Yes."

"Anything?"

"No, no luck."

"And the father and the French detective?"

"I have lost them."

"As I said, I can no longer help you."

The tall man was silent, as if to express his reluctant acceptance of this fact.

"Are you coming to Riyadh next week?"

"Yes," the tall man answered.

"Good. I will stop by to see you. God be with you."

"And with you, Uncle."

The tall man clicked the phone off and, cranking the window down a few inches, slipped it into the stream of traffic.

"You did not tell him about the two men lost last night," said the driver.

"No, I did not."

"You should have sent me."

"It is just as well. If the father and the woman arrive in Kolin, we will kill them, too."

"We are better off, just the two of us."

The tall man did not answer. He was thinking of Megan Nolan. She was smarter and braver and much more vicious than he had thought. "It was bitter cold that night," the old nun had said. "To leave the child out like that, Monsieur ... Yes, it was quite unfortunate." She had killed the child. Soon, she would pay with her own life, worthless as it was. In the trunk of the Peugeot was a small arsenal: grenade launchers, dozens of grenades, AK-47s, handguns, and enough hexogen to blow up all of Kolin if necessary. The two in the back, Jamal and Kumar, raised in the best madrassahs the kingdom had to offer, were explosives experts as well as religious fanatics. They were living only for the day when they could sacrifice themselves on his orders.

They were heading east on the Periphique, the ring road that circled Paris, in moderate traffic. The drive to Prague would take about seven hours. From there to Kolin was no more than another hour. By this time tomorrow, it would be done.

"There are four of us, my friend," the tall man said, remembering finally that his companion had spoken and should be answered.

"You mean our martyrs in the back? Soon we will be two again." They were speaking in French, a language they knew to be completely foreign to Jamal and Kumar.

"Yes, of course," said the tall man. "They will be in heaven with their virgins."

"And soon the Falcon will fly back to Andalus, *inshallah*."

"Yes, Mohammed, *inshallah*."

~ 24 ~

Nuremburg, January 7, 2004

Geneviève LeGrand, having interrogated many sus-pected criminals in her day, felt uncomfortably like the tables had been turned. She mused for a moment about the cause of this role reversal, Charles Raimondi, whose duplic-itous life and sudden, brutal death had brought her interro-gators so swiftly to her hotel room door in Nuremburg. She had allowed herself to believe that she was still desirable, that her beauty was not marred, but rather enriched by age. How foolish. How utterly banal. Personal humiliation, however, she could accept. She understood that suffering was the price of vanity. But now it seemed that in addition to personal humiliation, her fantasy of a romantic liaison with the handsome and much younger Raimondi might have caused the demise of her career and her professional reputation as well. That would be a bitter pill.

"Did you call him when you saw the flowers in your room, Geneviève?" Marcel Dionne asked. He was the good cop, handsome, baby-faced, using her first name, speaking softly. Only he wasn't a cop. He was DST, and not simply DST but a member of a special homeland security antiter-rorism unit so secret that only those at the highest level of law enforcement in France even knew it existed. LeGrand did not miss the irony in the fact that, as an assistant chief inspector of police, she had been one of the recipients, two months after 9/11, of a memo from the interior minister himself advising of the formation of this task force and urg-ing the fullest cooperation with its members.

"Yes."

She had placed the flowers—hothouse roses and carnations—in a tall glass vase on the room's spacious desk, where she could see them from bed. Looking at them now, it was hard to believe that Raimondi was dead and, more incredible, that he was the subject of an antiterror investigation. But there it was.

"And? What did he say?" Dionne pressed her.

"He said a complication had arisen regarding the Megan Nolan case. He told me not to discuss the case with anyone until he and I could meet and talk in person. We arranged to have dinner when I returned to Paris."

"Did he mention anything specific about Megan Nolan or her father?" This question came from the bad cop, André Orlofsky, Dionne's superior. Small, wiry, his eyes unreadable, his voice carrying a hint of menace, Orlofsky's intensity permeated the room, touching a chord of fear in LeGrand that she did not know was there.

"No," she replied.

"Did Catherine Laurence come up?"

"No."

"Rahman al-Zahra?"

"No."

"Anything besides what you've told us?"

"No."

"Do you know a man named Mustafa al-Siddiq?" asked the third interrogator, the young American in jeans and a rumpled corduroy jacket. Aside from *Bonjour, enchanté*, spoken in perfect, nearly unaccented French when he was introduced by Orlofsky, this was the first time the FBI agent with the improbable name of Max French had spoken.

"No."

"How did you know Raimondi?" French asked.

"We met at a conference some years ago and our paths crossed occasionally since. We were acquaintances," Le-Grand replied and then paused, waiting for the next question. When none came, she added, "That is all."

"Why the flowers?" French asked.

"He was wooing me."

"Why?"

"I thought it was because of my great beauty, but I believe now I was wrong."

French, Geneviève noticed, did not smile at this answer, but a certain light flashed in his eyes which she read as an acknowledgment that he had been forced to insult her and that she had been forced to accept it gracefully, given her behavior. *Perhaps they will believe me, and perhaps—just perhaps—I will not only keep my job but be able to be of some assistance.*

"We are going to tell you what we know, Inspector LeGrand," said Orlofsky, "because we are hoping that you will then be able to give us some insight, once your blinders, shall we say, have been removed. But first tell us again about your unauthorized investigation into the false suicide of Megan Nolan."

LeGrand had just finished showering when the knock had come on her door. In a thick terrycloth hotel robe, with a towel folded on her head, she had scrutinized three somber faces and three sets of impeccable credentials and known immediately that something was wrong. She had asked the men to wait outside the room while she dressed, but they would have none of it, entering swiftly and going so far as to check her person and the entire room for cell phones and weapons before allowing her to pick out her clothes and change in the lavatory. They had gotten right to the point, or rather Orlofsky had. *Daniel Peletier was dead. Thrown off a cliff by two Arab men. His computer had led them to Cath-erine Laurence. Laurence had asked Peletier to run the prints of a known terrorist and had inquired about one Megan Nolan. Laurence had called Charles Raimondi and had lunch with him three days ago. Raimondi was killed execution-style last night. Earlier he had called LeGrand on her cellphone. Laurence works for LeGrand. Talk to us.* These sentences, delivered staccato-like by Orlofsky, were blows. *Peletier dead. Raimondi dead. Deceived by Catherine Laurence—the young and beautiful and desirable Catherine Laurence.*

But LeGrand was a professional. She was on their side. She gathered herself and quickly recounted the history of the Megan Nolan affair, starting with Charles Raimondi's visit to her office on January 2 and ending with his request two days later for Laurence's cell phone number and address, which he was given. *Did she think it odd that Laurence would go on leave in the middle of the case?* We both thought the case was solved. *Did she know Daniel Peletier? Yes. Did she know he was Catherine's uncle? Yes. Did she have any reason to believe there was a link between his death and Catherine Laurence or Patrick Nolan?* No, of course not.

Geneviève composed herself once more before repeating her story, amazed in retrospect at its brevity and sparsity of detail. And disgusted with herself for having permitted Charles Raimondi to dictate procedure to her, and worse, to keep the case secret from her superiors. She was sitting on the edge of the room's large bed. When she was done, she stared at the three men, who stared back at her. French had remained standing, but Dionne and Orlofsky had taken chairs and sat in them facing her. She had put on the chic business suit and silk blouse she had worn to her seminar that day, but no makeup, and her hair was simply drying as they spoke. Vanity had vanished from her thoughts.

"What's going on?" she asked.

"Until yesterday," Orlofsky replied, "no one at DST had ever heard of Megan Nolan or her faux suicide."

"But Raimondi was the liaison to the DST from the Foreign Ministry, was he not?" said LeGrand.

"He was," said Dionne, "but he had no authority to initiate an operation. He was a professional diplomat who was part of our intelligence interface with foreign governments, that is all. He did this completely on his own."

"Mustafa al-Siddiq is the number two man at Saudi Arabia's interior ministry," said Orlofsky. "Among other things, he is in charge of their secret police, the *Mabahith*. He and Raimondi spoke several times over the last week. There was also a fax from Raimondi to al-Siddiq, five pages, contents unknown. Three dead bodies were found at Daniel Peletier's farm. All were carrying *Mabahith* credentials."

"So Raimondi was cooperating with the Saudis in an unauthorized Saudi operation on French soil," said LeGrand.

"Yes," said Dionne, "to find Megan Nolan, who he claimed—or believed—was a terrorist. We don't know which."

"Do you have leads on his murder?"

"None."

"There was a photograph of Megan Nolan in my file," said LeGrand. "I never thought to ask her father for a current picture."

"We have your file," said Orlofsky. "We have seen the picture. It is her, and it looks to have been taken in a souk—a small market—in a Moroccan slum called Sidi Moumim."

"Is al-Zahra known to you?" LeGrand asked.

"We picked up an intercept after Casa that mentioned the *Falcon*," French said. "There is an historical figure known as the Falcon of Andalus, a great Muslim caliph in Spain in the eighth century. Real name: Abdur-Rahman al-Zahra. That's all we know."

"Someone has taken a *nom de terror*," said LeGrand.

"Yes, that's how we see it," French replied.

"Have you spoken to al-Siddiq?" LeGrand asked.

"Yes. He said he was talking to Raimondi about a conference they planned on attending together in the spring. They had formed a friendship, apparently."

"And the fax?"

"He said it was a conference schedule."

"Did you check?"

"Yes. The conference is on the issue of enhancing co-operation between law enforcement and embassies in handling visa applications. We called the organizers. There is no five-page schedule."

"What about the Saudi agents?"

"Al-Siddiq says the credentials must have been forged."

"Is Megan Nolan a terrorist?"

"We don't know," Orlofsky answered. "She is an expatriate, a writer. Her agent in New York hasn't heard from her in two years. She wrote for women's magazines for ten years or so, but lately has been writing about the Arab problem in Europe. She was in Morocco from January until May, then in Spain, then of course in Paris to fake her suicide. That's all we know. We are looking for friends and other relatives, but for now that's it."

"What about the woman who actually did kill herself?" Geneviève asked.

"Nothing," Orlofsky answered. "Her prints were not on record. She had Megan Nolan's ID. No one's reported anyone matching her description missing. Nothing."

"What is your next step?"

"We have put a Europol bulletin out for Laurence's car. We are going through airline manifests for entries from Morocco and Saudi Arabia in the last ten days. We may get lucky."

"Is there a target? Any intelligence about a terrorist operation?"

"Nothing," said Orlofsky. "We are looking and listening. We have people in Muslim communities all over France and we are monitoring telephone and e-mail traffic to the top of our capacity."

"Can I help?" Geneviève asked.

"Yes," said Orlofsky. "You can call Catherine Laurence on her cell phone. We have brought a phone for you to use. If she answers, it will triangulate nearly instantly. We will know where she is."

"Anyone could answer."

"Yes, of course. But if someone has her cell phone, we will very much want to talk to that person."

"Now?"

"Yes, now."

"What shall I say?"

"Anything. Just keep her talking for fifteen seconds or so."

"And then what?"

"And then you will return to Paris, Inspector LeGrand, and speak to your chief and to the interior minister, who will tell you if you still have a job, and if you do what it might be."

Geneviève LeGrand looked at the men confronting her. There were no smiles on their faces, no satisfaction in their eyes, only grim determination. And something else, something she recognized as fear, fear of the consequences of their failure. They were trying to stop, with little in the way of leads, a terrorist attack inside France. An attack that it appeared she had unwittingly, stupidly, helped facilitate. Reaching for the phone, which Dionne had already dialed, she prayed that Catherine Laurence would answer, and that whether or not she lost her job or her reputation, she would not go down as a footnote in the history of mass murder.

~ 25 ~

Morocco, May 15-16, 2003

Casablanca's French colonial quarter was within walking distance of the city"s modern center. As a result, the explosions Megan heard while she was eating dinner in her room at the Porte Rouge seemed to have occurred right outside her door. One nearly did, in the cemetery around the block, where earlier the neighborhood boys had been playing. Looking out her fourth-floor window, she could see over the rooftops to the chaos that was once the pleasant and orderly burial ground: the tops of trees burning like giant torches, the doors blown off charred mausoleums that glowed like furnaces on the inside, and smoke everywhere, rising into the night. There were no televisions in the rooms, so she joined the handful of Porte Rouge's other guests in the lobby to watch CNN's local French language station. The others, two middle-aged couples and a female lawyer, all French, were swift to blame America's adventure in Iraq for the bombings. They spoke openly in their native tongue, not seeming to care whether Megan, an obvious American, could understand them or not. They soon left to go out for dinner, but Megan stayed for several hours, watching and listening and smoking. Five suicide bombings had been staged simultaneously around the city, two at Jewish restaurants, one at the Jewish cemetery in the old quarter (she could hear the fire trucks outside all night), one at the Farah Hotel, and one at a Spanish social club. Speculation as to the Farah centered around a conference held there some months ago that included a delegation from Israel. Commentators could not understand the targeting of the *Casa de España*, the popular Spanish gathering place, but Megan knew of the burning hatred in the hearts of some jihadists for Christian Spain. She was not surprised to hear Salafist Jihad mentioned along with al-Qaeda as possible responsible parties.

Two of the fourteen suicide bombers had survived. One was badly injured and said to be hospitalized under police guard. The detonator of the second survivor's bomb pack had failed and he had crashed his car into a pillar at the Farah, apparently hoping the impact would arm the bomb. At least two bombers had attacked each site, either on foot or by car, and it was the second bomber who did the damage, very extensive, at the Farah. The lobby, where he set off his bomb, was completely gutted and fully aflame, and the first five floors above it were bombed out, their furniture, accoutrements, and occupants now either strewn about the street or among the burning debris of what used to be the lobby. Megan's room had been on the third floor, above the lobby.

Around midnight, the second surviving bomber's picture was flashed on the screen. He was Moroccan, in his early twenties, with a scraggly beard and a shaved head, his eyes dull and unfocused. Megan recognized him immediately as Sirhan al-Majid, the young man with the toothache who had come barging into Abdullah's shop and who she later saw talking with Mohammed in the rear courtyard. That conversation, she now recalled, she had both photographed and taped. She stubbed out what she promised herself would be her last cigarette—she forgot for long stretches that she was pregnant—and left the remainder of the pack on the lobby coffee table. In her room, she found the Mohammed/ toothache-man and the Lahani/Mohammed tapes and put them in her bag. Outside, she walked in the opposite direction from all the police and firefighting activity until she was able to hail a cab, which she took to the Carrières Thomas market. Thick clouds covered the moon, and when she exited the cab, she was plunged into near-total darkness. She made her way as swiftly as she could through the souk's maze of streets, praying she would not make a wrong turn in the dark. She knew that Abdullah slept most nights on a cot in the rear room of his shop. When she arrived at his door, she knocked hard, anxious to talk to him, anxious to be out of sight of the robbers and rapists who were said to roam the entire Sidi Moumim slum at night.

Abdullah peered at her through the bead curtain and then swiftly let her in. Except for one candle on the counter, the shop was dark. She could hear a television's peculiarly insistent noise coming from the back room.

"You have seen his picture?" Abdullah asked.

"Yes."

"You should not have come here. It is not safe."

"I need a favor."

"Of course."

"It may put you in danger."

Megan knew that she was not herself and that she looked it. She thought she had actually recognized her bombed-out room at the Farah on television earlier. This image, coupled with the highly suspect coincidence of her being asked to leave that morning and the constantly surprising thought of her pregnancy, had, together, finally unnerved her. She had decided to have the baby, but if what she was thinking was true, then what would she do? She did not know. Abdullah took both of her hands in his and drew her into the back room. "Sit," he said, pointing to a stuffed chair next to the cot. Megan sat while the pharmacist poured her mint tea from the clay pot he always kept on a warm electric burner. She could see the Coptic cross tattooed on his wrist as he extended his arm to pour the tea. He turned off the television and sat on the edge of the cot. "Drink," he said, and Megan did, finding the ubiquitous thick sweet tea delicious for once.

"What is it?" Abdullah asked when Megan finished.

"I have two tapes that I would like you to listen to and translate for me."

"Arabic?"

"Yes."

"Child's play."

Abdullah watched as Megan fumbled in her bag for the tapes and the tiny recorder/player on which they could be heard.

"I thought you had come to talk about our friend with the toothache," he said.

"No."

"He will be tortured and killed."

"Yes. That sounds about right to me," Megan said. "Here it is." She had found what she was looking for and inserted the first tape into the machine. She pushed the play button and turned the volume up, pointing the small device in Abdullah's direction. He listened intently as it spit out guttural Arab for about ten minutes.

"It is al-Majid and his two friends, and one other man," said Abdullah. "The fourth is older. Who is he?"

"His name is Mohammed," Megan replied."I don't know his last name."

"Do you know this man?"

"Yes. He works for the man I have been dating, Abdel al-Lahani."

"What does Lahani do?"

"He is a Saudi businessman."

"How did you come to tape this?" Abdullah asked, tapping the tape player with his finger.

"They were in the courtyard behind the shop. You were out. I recognized Mohammed. If you recall, I wanted to interview al-Majid. I just turned the recorder on."

"It is a marvelous recorder."

"Yes. Very expensive. What are they saying?"

"Your Mohammed has recruited the boys as suicide bombers. He is telling them that the day is soon coming when they will be in paradise. He is assigning them targets. Our boy Sirhan is to have the Farah Hotel, made foul, says Mohammed, by the stench of Jews.' The Falcon, he says, 'is aloft and has reached his hunting weight, and you are his wings, his sinews, his talons.'"

"The Falcon."

"Yes, the Falcon."

"Does he say who the Falcon is?"

"No."

"How about this one?" Megan asked, slipping the cassette from the recorder and replacing it with the one from the previous night. Again Abdullah listened intently, his eyes closed, his ten fingers forming a temple of his hands in front of him.

"It is our friend Mohammed," he said when the tape ended, "and another man."

"Lahani."

"I see," Abdullah replied, "the Saudi businessman."

"Yes. Go on."

"Mohammed says that all is in readiness, that the day's final *salat* will be one of gratitude to Allah for the success of their mission." Abdullah stopped to look at Megan.

"What?" she said, meeting his gaze.

"Mohammed is to follow you, to bring you to Lahani when he gives the order. Lahani's friends in the Interior Ministry will see to it that you do not leave the country. Your passport has been flagged. You are carrying his child, and you will be made to bear it, and then you will be discarded, killed. The child will be raised to be a great leader of the *jihad*, a half-American spilling American blood. A fitting heir to the Falcon of Andalus."

Megan reached into her bag for her cigarettes, but they weren't there. She threw the bag on the cot and sat back in her chair, bringing her hands to cover her face.

"Megan ... ," said Abdullah.

"I"m not crying," she said. "I'm thinking."

"Megan, child. There is a remedy. I can make it for you tonight."

"Kill the baby? What about your own salvation?"

"This man is evil. I will do whatever penance is necessary."

"No, Abdullah, I will have this child. But I do need you to make me something."

"Of course. What?"

"As soon as possible. Tonight."

"What is it you want?"

"A poison. I will kill Lahani and then I'll run. I'll go south into the Sahara. No one will ask me for a passport there."

"Megan, my dear Megan," said Abdullah, "I would gladly help you kill Lahani, but it is too dangerous. If something goes wrong, you will be killed. He will find another American woman to breed with. I can get you a passport and drive you to Tangier, where you can get on the ferry to Spain. Once in Europe, you can use your own passport. We can leave within the hour. You must save yourself and your baby."

"No," Megan replied. "He thinks that I love him, that I have acquiesced to his control over me. I will go to him as a lover, a supplicant. He will not be suspicious, and I will kill him."

"Megan, please. I am an old man. I cannot protect you."

"You don't have to protect me. Just make me the poison."

Abdullah was silent. Megan did not change the expression on her face or look away. "I will kill him with a kitchen knife," she said, "if you won't help me. I will find a way."

Abdullah shook his head and rose to pour them both tea. "I suppose we have crossed paths for a reason," he said, his back to Megan.

"I suppose," she answered.

"When do you plan on doing this?" The pharmacist had turned to face her, and now handed her a cup.

"Today, daybreak."

"Come back here when it is done. You would not last long in the desert. I will have your passport. But you must do as I say: wear a djellaba, and cut and dye your hair. I have henna here that you can use. Then I will drive you to Tangier. You must do it this way."

Megan nodded. "I will," she said.

"Good. Now try to sleep. It is two hours until dawn, and what I am making will take some thinking, and some time."

~ ~ ~

While Megan slept and Abdullah worked, Abdel al-Lahani and his trusted lieutenant, Mohammed Abdul-Rafi, known as the Silent One among his family and friends, sat in the near-dark of Lahani's living room on the same handsome English-made chairs that they had sat on the night before. A teapot and two finely made china teacups were on the inlaid table between them. They had prayed together just before midnight, and Mohammed had been right, it had been a prayer of thanksgiving. In another hour they would pray again, and then Mohammed would leave for Saudi Arabia. The fires around the city had died out—the fires they had set—but the glow of the successful fanatic remained in their eyes. They had spilled blood like this before, and each time the surge of omnipotence that had filled their hearts had taken days to subside. They thought it was Allah's approval, what they felt, and that as a result they could not be harmed or make a mistake. They were themselves gods while this surge lasted. For this reason, the fact that Sirhan al-Majid had been captured did not bother them. Al-Majid had only met Mohammed once, and knew neither his real name nor anything else about him. The two mujahideen who had done the real recruiting, both Moroccans trained in Afghanistan before the Taliban were ousted, had blown themselves up in the attacks. In any event, Mohammed would soon be home, where he would have the full protection of the royal family.

It was Megan Nolan that they were worried about. It appeared that she had deliberately hidden herself from them, and that, if Lalla was to be believed, she had been spying on them. Lalla had also told her husband that she had seen a small tape recorder in Megan's bag. With Lahani's consent, Lalla had kept such tabs on all of his women over the years, especially the Western women he favored so much, as there was no telling what they would say or do or carry in their bags.

"Why this child, emir?" Mohammed said. "There have been others."

Lahani looked at his longtime aide-de-camp and raised his eyebrows. Only Mohammed could get away with asking him a question like this. It was, he admitted to himself, a question worth asking. Why this child and not another? If not for the child, Megan could be found and killed immediately. She did not speak Arabic, and it was highly doubtful that she had learned anything, either deliberately or inadvertently, about his covert life, his true business. Yet why take a chance? She was intelligent, and perhaps guessed or had somehow confirmed that he was the one who had forced her to leave the Farah before it was bombed. Both Mohammed and Lalla, whose experience of Americans was one of unfailing naïvité and stupidity, had been highly suspicious of Megan from the beginning. So why hesitate? Because he had been suspicious, too. Not of her motives; she could never hurt him. But of her core, which was, he believed—despite her quite good attempts to fool him with displays of Western femininity and softness—inaccessible, cold, and unsympathetic, much like his own. There would never be another one to breed a son with quite like Megan Nolan. And of course there was the wonderful irony. The coup de grace. A *half-American son raised as a Wahabi killer of Americans*. He could not pass up such an opportunity. Megan would have to be found and, if necessary, made a prisoner until the child was born. There was no need, however, to articulate any of this to Mohammed.

"I have decided," he said.

"Yes, emir."

"Your flight is at eleven?"

"Yes."

"That will give you time to make one more stop."

"Yes."

"Go to the pharmacist she has been visiting so much. She knows no one else in all of Morocco. Perhaps she is with him. If she is, call me and I will send someone to collect her. If not, talk to the pharmacist. He may know where she is. Call me if you learn anything from him. Then get on your plane. I will see you at home next week, *inshallah*."

"Yes, emir, *inshallah*."

~ 26 ~

Morocco, May 16, 2003

An hour and a half after sunrise, Megan's cab pulled into the two-hundred-year-old cobblestone dead-end street at the end of which was located Abdel al-Lahani's apartment building. She told the driver to turn his cab around and to wait for her, giving him fifty euros and telling him that she would give him fifty more plus double his fare when she returned in thirty minutes, maybe less. She fingered the plastic vial in the slit pocket of her linen slacks as she rode up on the elevator. She had stopped at the Porte Rouge to shower, apply light makeup, change, and check out. She noted now, with grim satisfaction, the reflection, in the lift's polished brass sidewall, of her classic features framed by her lustrous, reddish-blond hair. She wore the same pale green silk blouse and thin-strapped gold sandals she had worn when she first met Lahani at the train siding on the way to Marrakech in January, just over four months ago. Before getting on the elevator she had stopped to listen at the door of Lalla's first-floor apartment, hoping that the nosy and ever-present servant would not show up at the wrong time, as she always seemed to do. She heard nothing, but of course the mute but sharp-eyed Lalla could be anywhere, including somewhere in Lahani's large and spacious penthouse. So be it. She knocked confidently on Lahani's door, ready to be, one last time, the most beautiful woman the Saudi terrorist had ever met and would ever hope to meet.

"Abdel," she said when he swung the door open.

"Megan."

They stared at each other across the threshold for a moment, Lahani looking taller and stronger and more handsome than ever in his cream-colored silk shirt and dark slacks. *So confident,* Megan thought, *so supremely confident.*

"Will you invite me in?" she said.

She watched carefully, half smiling, as Lahani hesitated before nodding and saying, "Yes, of course." She knew that in that small pause he had begun assessing: her motive, her credibility, and, involuntarily, her beauty. She entered and stood for a moment in the foyer, facing him. He was about to speak, but she stopped him, placing two fingers on his lips and saying, "No, let me explain," and then taking his hand and leading him into the living room, where she sat, her legs under her, on a plush lemon-yellow sofa that rested on the long edge of an oversized Persian rug of such intricacy and beauty that standing alone it was a piece of art. Lahani sat across from her on an aged leather easy chair. He stared at her, his face impassive, drumming his fingers on the arm of his chair.

"I came to celebrate with you," Megan said.

"Celebrate?"

"Yes."

"Celebrate what?"

No, Megan thought, *not your successful terrorist mission. What mission would that be?* And then out loud she said, "Our child, of course."

"We had that celebration two nights ago. Where have you been, Megan. I have been calling you at the Hyatt. They tell me your bags are there but you never checked in. I'm confused."

"I stayed at a small place in the old quarter last night. I wanted to be alone, to think. I should have called you, but you said you would be busy all day yesterday and last night."

"Air Maroc has you booked on their one PM flight today to New York."

"Yes. I'm sorry," Megan said. Then she paused, as any woman would before saying what she said next. "I was thinking of aborting the child. I changed my mind. I'd like to stay here with you."

"Aborting the child?"

Megan hesitated again, and again it was part of her act, her act of contrition: for having fled, for having considered aborting—killing—the innocent child of the great slaughterer of innocents, Abdel al-Lahani, the Falcon of Andalus, returned from the dead to bring his people back to glory.

"I'm sorry, Abdel. I was frightened. You never mentioned marriage. Your culture and mine are not the same. I truly never thought I would be a mother. I have always been so independent. These thoughts overwhelmed me."

"What made you change your mind?"

"You," Megan replied, without hesitation this time. "I would be proud to have your child."

Lahani's face was still grimly set, but Megan could see the light of victory, easy victory, in his eyes.

"You would have to convert to Islam in order to marry me."

"I will do it."

"You would not make a good Muslim wife, Megan. It is very restricting." Lahani allowed himself to smile as he said this, a sign, Megan thought, that he felt like he had totally regained control. *He probably already has a wife or two.*

"Then I will remain your mistress," she said.

Lahani rose and walked around the sofa to stand behind Megan. He placed his hands—large and brown and perfectly manicured—on her shoulders and gently kneaded them. Then he lifted her cascading hair and rubbed the nape of her neck with his thumbs, while slowly encircling her throat with his fingers, his touch light.

"You would not deceive me, Megan?" he said, squeezing her throat slightly harder.

"I have deceived other men, Abdel, but not you," Megan replied, willing herself to remain cool and calm.

"It is an honor in my culture to acknowledge a bastard child. Do you feel honored?" He increased his hold—not by much, but enough to begin the restriction of air to the lungs.

"Yes," Megan answered, suppressing by nerve she did not know she had the feral instinct of any human in these circumstances to twist and flinch. "I do."

Lahani removed his hands from Megan's neck, but stayed behind her. "I leave for Saudi Arabia on Monday," he said.

"Oh," Megan said, turning to face him. "Shall I come with you?"

"No, you must stay here."

"Where? Here in the apartment?"

"No, in my house in Marrakech, with Lalla. She has two brothers who work for me. They will stay in the house as well. They will be with you at all times. A Western woman, pregnant, unwed, will draw attention. If you are seen as under my protection, you will be treated properly. Is this understood?"

"Yes. It is. When will you be back?" *I will miss you so, of course. What woman would not pine for the great Falcon?*

"In two weeks, perhaps three."

"And the child?"

"Lalla will deliver the child. She is an excellent midwife."

"Will you be there?"

"I am a very busy man, as you know. I make no promises. But as I have made clear, the child will want for nothing. And he will know I am his father."

That's one thing he'll never know, Megan thought. Out loud, she said, "I am grateful. And now can we celebrate? In the bedroom?"

"Yes," Lahani replied. "I am glad you are back."

"Do you have champagne?"

"In the wine cooler, yes."

"Go ahead," Megan said with a smile. "I'll meet you in bed."

In the kitchen, Megan found and popped the champagne quickly, and just as quickly emptied the vial of white powder Abdullah had given her into Lahani's glass, stirring it with her finger. In the bedroom, she set the fizzing glasses down on the window sill and then swiftly took off her clothes, her back to the bed. Lahani, in bed, naked, was smiling broadly when she turned to face him, holding up the two fluted champagne glasses. His smile got bigger when she dipped her finger in her glass and wiped it on his large erect penis, and even bigger when she bent and slowly licked it off. Rising to a kneeling position on the bed, she handed Lahani his glass, and, raising hers, said, "To us, and to our child."

"To us," Lahani said. Megan drank, watching over the edge of her glass as her lover of four months, the father of her child, a master terrorist about to die, lifted his glass to his lips.

He took one or two sips and then his cell phone, on the night table on his side of the bed, rang sharply. He put his glass down and picked up the phone. Megan put her glass down, too, and watched as Lahani, listening intently, stood up and walked out of the bedroom, the phone to his ear, saying, "Yes, yes," in Arabic. A second or two later she heard a thud. Still naked, she ran out of the room and saw the Saudi's body sprawled in the doorway to his study. The phone was on the floor nearby. She picked it up and held it to her ear, instantly recognizing Mohammed's voice as he said, "Emir? Emir?" She clicked off the phone, threw it on the floor, and bent to check Lahani"s pulse, which was very shallow. Then she ran back into the bedroom, got dressed, and came back out carrying Abdel's three-quarter full glass, the contents of which she tried to pour down his throat, forcing his mouth open with her free hand. It didn't work. She could get the champagne into his mouth but couldn't make him swallow. In fact, he gagged most of it up and out.

She checked his pulse again. Still shallow. As she was doing this, she heard the front door swing open. Turning, she saw Lalla walking swiftly toward her saying something loud and angry in Arabic. Before Megan could react, Lalla shoved her aside and knelt down over Lahani, putting her ear to his chest and then his mouth. Lalla's shove had been surprisingly strong, knocking Megan against the hallway wall. When she recovered and saw Lalla bent over Abdel, she ran into the kitchen, grabbed the three-quarter-full bottle of Dom Perignon, ran back, and smashed it over Lalla's head. Lalla went down amidst a shower of broken glass and fizzing champagne. Megan then ran to the bedroom, grabbed her bag, and left the apartment. In the elevator, willing it to move faster, she remembered her idea of the kitchen knife, but going back now would be too scary. Lalla may have recovered and called the police, or Mohammed, sensing trouble, could be rushing to the apartment. The cab was still there, but the driver was not. Looking around, she saw him at the corner talking to two other men outside a tobacco shop. She waved to him and he saw her. She tried to stay calm as he walked toward her at a normal pace. "Money," he said when they were in the cab. "Euros. Dollars." She handed him a wad that was way too much and they were on their way.

~ ~ ~

The cab driver refused to drive into the Carrières Thomas neighborhood, leaving Megan off at the ancient stone portal that marked one of the four entrances to the market square. She walked around the outside of the market and turned into the old souk on the first available street. She decided not to ask Yasmine's son to guide her because she feared that anyone coming into her orbit now would be suspected of complicity in what she hoped was Lahani's death. On this issue she was not confident. He had sipped only a small amount of the poisonous champagne. Perhaps he was paralyzed or had had a severe stroke, as this was, according to Abdullah, the physiology of the curare-based concoction he had hastily put together for her. She feared though that he was alive and well and that there would be hell, or worse, to pay.

The door to Abdullah's shop was open, only the colorful bead curtain separating the street from the interior. Megan was comforted, as the door was always open in the heat of the day. Inside, the shop was quiet. She called Abdullah's name, thinking he was in the back room, but there was no response. Something made her step around the counter. Perhaps Abdullah was sleeping, or had gone out and left her a note. As she made the turn, her foot struck something and, looking down, she saw Abdullah lying on his back on the floor behind the counter. His throat was slit and a large nail had been driven through his right wrist—through his Coptic cross tattoo—into the floor. His eyes were wide open, and for a second she thought he was alive. She knelt beside him and touched his chest, which was still warm, but he was not breathing and his face was a death mask. She closed his eyes, gently kissing each lid to keep it closed. Then she placed her face against his chest and whispered, "I did this to you, Abdullah. I'm sorry. Please forgive me. Please forgive me." Her tears stained his cotton djellaba and the blood from his neck wound coated her hair.

Before getting up, she took hold of the nail in Abdullah's wrist and tried to pull it out, not thinking why, just that she had to do it. But it was impossible. The nail was more like a large spike, and had been driven deeply into the hardwood floor. Numb, she remained kneeling, trying to collect herself and think what to do. As she was thinking, she heard a rustling sound in the back room, whose entrance, covered by a thick cotton curtain, was only a step away. She rose and pulled the curtain aside slowly and there, sitting on Abdullah's bed, his knees drawn into his chest, his large brown eyes wide with fear, was Hakim, Yasmine's boy. She sat down next to him and put her arms around him, and he leaned into her but did not cry or speak.

There was nothing for Megan to say, either. As she held the boy, she looked around the room and saw on the table next to the electric burner a brown manila envelope, an ornately painted tin canister, and a set of keys. Rising, she took the envelope and opened it. Inside was a Moroccan passport with a fourteen-day Spanish visitor's visa clipped to it. The picture inside was of a woman of Megan's age and complexion, with short brown hair. The tin contained a brown powder. Henna, she thought. Outside, in the shop, Megan shut and locked the front door and then found Abdullah's scissors in a drawer behind the counter. She hacked away at her hair until it was a ragged two inches long in front and an even more ragged three inches in back. Then, at the small sink in the back room, she mixed the henna with water in a bowl and applied it to what was left of her hair, rinsed, and applied it again, and then again until it was a uniform dark brown and the dye did not wash away.

While she was doing this she glanced over at Hakim several times and saw that he was watching her intently. She found a worn towel to dry her hair, hands, and face. Her two small bags were still under Abdullah's bed. She fished them out and pulled from one a striped cotton djellaba—one of the four she had bought from Hakim's mother's shop on the day they met. She slipped it on over the clothes she was wearing and then stuffed the rest of her things into one bag. Picking up the keys, she turned to Hakim.

"They are going kill me, too, Hakim," she said. "Tell me where the car is and I will leave."

Hakim rose and took Megan by the hand, pulling her gently in the direction of the front door. "Come," he said. "Follow."

~ 27 ~

Waldsassen, January 7, 2004

"Did you have a honeymoon?" Catherine asked.

"Yes," Pat replied, "why do you ask?"

"Because this feels like one."

"This place, you mean?"

"Yes, this little inn, the snow, the featherbed. I have finally gotten one, a real honeymoon."

Pat remained silent, idly caressing Catherine's hip and breathing in the scent of her hair, his mind going back thirty years, a trip he rarely let it take.

"We went to the Grand Canyon," he said finally. "I wanted to see the Hoover Dam before we left for Paraguay."

"Why?"

"Inspiration."

They were lying naked under clean sheets and a down quilt on a large bed in the Hotel Peterhof in Waldsassen. Outside, snow was falling at a rapid rate, the town and the woods surrounding it already under several inches. They were in a garret room on the third floor—small but very charming with its pitched ceiling and gabled windows. From the window next to the bed, which was at waist level, they could look out across Waldsassen's little central square to St. Peter's church, a squat medieval affair with an incongruously beautiful spire whose tolling bells had woken them from a deep sleep. The night was windless, and in the cones of the square's ancient lamps they could see the snow falling straight down. All was still except for a solitary figure crossing the square carrying a sack over his shoulder, bent under it and trudging along, determined to be home and out of the cold.

"How old were you?"

"Twenty-one."

"And your wife?"

"Twenty."

"So young."

"Yes."

They held each other in silence for a long moment.

"And you?" Pat asked. "Did you have one?"

"Yes. We went to Mykonos. I was very unhappy."

"Why?"

"I had made a big mistake and I thought myself a fool and a failure."

"But you tried to make the marriage work."

"Yes. For a brief time, I tried."

"After Lorrie died, I never allowed myself to make any mistakes. I never tried to make anything work."

"Are you saying you were more of a fool and a failure than me? I won't have it."

Pat smiled and said, "I don't know how to answer that."

"Yes, you're trapped."

"I love this trap." His hand was on her buttock now, kneading it gently, caressing the roundness of it, and he was beginning to think that soon they would make love again.

"Did you love her, your young wife?"

"Yes, I did."

"Very much?"

"Yes."

"And did she love you very much?"

"Yes."

"It's better that way."

Another silence, their slow breathing the only sound.

"Do we love each other, Patrick?"

"Yes, Catherine, I believe we do. I believe we love each other very much."

"I am not so young... not a real bride."

"Catherine, the past is over. It's taken this awful thing that has happened for me to see it. This terror. All this death. I thought I had lost so much, but did not realize I had gained a child, a daughter. Now she may be lost to me. But it has brought me you. And you I will not lose. I will die before I lose you."

~ ~ ~

They had reached Waldsassen in late afternoon and were at the carousel in the center of the deserted amusement park by five thirty. While they were waiting, the snow began to fall. At six thirty, cold and wet, they returned to town, where they were lucky to get a room. A crowd had arrived for the wedding tomorrow of the children of two local officials. Before locating the Peterhof they had driven past the Altes Rathaus, a beautiful old building where festivities were already underway. Their innkeeper was a stout, kindly woman, built along the same lines as the church in the square except for the spire. They paid her in advance and asked for a wake-up call at eleven. She put them in the garret and brought up a full dinner, with local white wine and strudel, which they devoured before making love and then falling into a heavy sleep. Now all was quiet, in their room, in the hotel, and outside in the town. They did not make love a second time, but rather held each other while the quiet drifted over them, falling asleep again, this time fitfully, the distant past now contending with the near future for preeminence among their worries. The ringing of Catherine's cell phone woke them a few minutes later with a start.

"I'll get it," Pat said, rousing himself and swinging out of bed. He had been dreaming of the flower girl, Megan's flower girl. She had been standing at the edge of a sunlit meadow ringing a bell with one hand and gesturing for him to follow her with the other.

"It's the flower girl."

"The flower girl?" said Catherine, who had sat up and was peering into the room, waiting for her eyesight to adjust to the darkness. "The flower girl? What time is it?"

"I mean Doro," said Pat, remembering that they had turned Catherine's phone on in anticipation of a call from him." It must be him. It's just ten thirty. Where's the phone?"

"In my bag on the chair," Catherine answered, pointing to a stuffed chair across the small room, in an alcove under a gabled window, where she had thrown her bag on entering. "I'll help you."

"No, stay there. I'll get it." Pat was standing next to the bed. He did not know how long the phone had been ringing, but it seemed like a long time. Still naked, he crossed the room quickly and, rather than groping for the phone, he dumped the contents of the bag on the chair.

"Hello," he said, picking the slim, glowing cell phone out of the darkness and swiftly bringing it to his ear.

"Oh, Monsieur Nolan," a strangely familiar female voice said. "I was hoping to speak to Officer Laurence."

"Officer Laurence?"

"Yes, Catherine Laurence. I assigned her to your daughter's case. This is Inspector LeGrand. It is Catherine's phone you are on, is it not?"

"Inspector LeGrand?"

"Yes. We met in my office last week."

"I'm afraid you're mistaken, Inspector. I ..."

Before Pat could finish his sentence, Catherine had leaped from the bed, crossed the room in two long strides, snatched the phone from his hand, and clicked it off. She stared at it for a second and then threw it on the floor.

"We have ten minutes," she said, "no more."

"Ten minutes?"

"Yes. They have our location. I'll explain later. Get dressed, we must leave. Quickly, Patrick, quickly, *vite*, the local police station is just around the corner."

~ 28 ~

Waldsassen, January 7, 2004

Max French turned the collar of his trench coat up and stood with his back to the wind. He had slept on the plane from New York, about thirty-six hours ago, and then not at all since. Luckily, the coat was lined and he had brought along gloves and a scarf, but no boots. His size-thirteen feet, a little too large for his six-foot body, were wet and cold. Tomorrow he would beg, steal, or borrow a pair of boots. Or find a store that carried extra-large sizes. The Waldsassen police chief's SUV, a sleekly black BMW, was parked nearby. It was running and its headlights were trained on the river Ohře. Their beams penetrated the dark night only thirty feet or so, but that was enough to see the tracks of Catherine Laurence's Peugeot leading to the edge of the three-foot-high bank and then, about ten feet out, its rear bumper sticking up at a forty-five-degree angle as the river rushed around it. A man in hip boots and foul-weather gear, tethered to a line from shore, was in the tricky process of hooking a tow chain to the Peugeot. This man, who looked to be about seven feet tall, had strode into the swollen river fearlessly, like it was a wading pool. Before attempting the hookup, he had managed to pry open the car's rear passenger door, signaling with a wave of both hands across his face that the car was empty.

The helicopter French had come in with agents Orlofsky and Dionne was parked in a field about a half mile away. The snow had stopped about halfway through their twenty-minute flight, to be replaced almost immediately by strong winds crisscrossing their path. The pilot was a pro, his hands rock steady on the controls, his face stony in concentration as he negotiated first the snow and then the winds like he was riding a powerful horse through a storm. It had been Max who, when he was told that Waldsassen was only eighty miles away, had insisted on the helicopter, a heroic gesture that he came to regret in mid-flight. It turned out not to be worth the effort, as either Nolan and Laurence had drowned or a boat had shown up by some miracle and carried them away.

"You'll dredge the river?" Max said to André Orlofsky, who had walked over to stand beside him.

"Yes, but it can't be done tonight. The current is too swift."

"What's downriver?"

"Forest and then the town of Cheb, in the Czech Republic. The border is only a few kilometers from here."

"Is there a crossing station on the river?"

"Yes. We have spoken to the guard, a boy of nineteen. He says he saw nothing. He was probably sleeping."

"One guard?"

"Yes."

"Why bother?"

"Yes, I agree. They will be officially in the EU in June and then no border stations."

"Our boy will be out of a job."

"Yes."

"I don't believe they're drowned."

"I don't either."

"Of course your German friends have fucked up the scene."

Max did not look at Orlofsky as he said this. He looked at the river-bank, a crime scene whose features had once been stenciled in pristine snow, but that was now trashed, the footprints of the tow truck man and of the Waldsassen deputy all over the place. Behind him, near the carousel, it was the same: a welter of footprints belonging to the deputy, the chief, and several others, but how many others and what their movements might have been had been obliterated by the Germans' heedless trudging around as if they were in the amusement park for amusement. Dionne was at the carousel, where it looked like the Peugeot had stopped before proceeding to the river. He was taking pictures with a digital camera, which they would study in the car, but French was not hopeful that they would be any help. In fact, he was certain they wouldn't.

"Yes, they have," said Orlofsky."But we *do* know there were others here. Here's our deputy now."

The Waldsassen deputy, a woman of about thirty in a fur-lined parka and bulky boots, had been the first to the scene. When her chief arrived he sent her downriver to talk to the people in the farmhouses on the German side to see if by chance they had seen a boat pass in the storm and to tell them to be on the lookout for strangers traipsing through their fields. She had parked her four-wheel-drive Audi cruiser behind the carousel and was walking toward them. The chief was in his car trying to raise the Czech police.

"Do you mind if I speak to her?" Max asked. "My German is pretty good."

"Proceed."

"Proceed?"

"Yes, proceed."

When Orlofsky picked Max up at the airport in Paris, he had made a point of saying that there had been no terror attacks inside France since 9/11. He did not have to mention how ironic it would be if the first one came at the hands of an American. He had been prickly, in other words, but not too prickly. Just the normal French prickliness that was probably in the water, or the wine. Max had spent two years as an AP reporter in Paris before going to law school in California and then joining the FBI in 1993. This was to him as good a theory as any as to why the French were the way they were. Plus, of course, their deep resentment at the United States for having done, twice, what they, the French, were incapable of doing: liberating themselves from the Germans in two world wars.

"Good evening," Max said to the deputy in German, "I'm Max French."

"Max French?"

"Yes, that's my name."

"Oh, pardon. I thought you were telling me you were the top Frenchman. American slang I"ve picked up. You're not French?"

"No, I'm American. FBI. How is the rest of your English? My German is rusty."

"Good," the deputy answered, "shall we switch?"

"Yes. You were the first to arrive?"

"Yes."

"What led you here?"

"I was home. The chief called from the party. I went to the Peterhof. I live only a few minutes away. Laurence and Nolan had left about ten minutes prior. There is only the one main road out of town. I took it. I saw tire tracks going into the park. Very unusual, as it is closed for the winter. I followed. There was a light on on the carousel. I drove to it and checked it out. Nothing."

"Were there footprints?"

The deputy did not answer. Max could see in her eyes that she was embarrassed.

"Speak!" Orlofsky said in perfect German.

"I did not notice."

"Go on," said Max.

"I saw the car tracks heading toward the river. I followed with my flashlight and saw the car in the water. I called the tow truck and the chief. They arrived at the same time. Then the chief sent me to talk to the neighbors."

"Did they see anything?"

"No."

While they were talking, the Peugeot had been dragged from the river. It was now dangling, rear end up, from the back of the tow truck. The operator, the river still dripping from his foul-weather suit, was standing next to it, his hand on the rear fender, proud of his catch.

"Lower it," Orlofsky said, again in perfect German. The operator complied, pulling a lever on the side of his truck and easing the back of the car to the ground.

"Get the trunk open," Orlofsky said, and again the wet giant complied, wielding the same crowbar he had used earlier to open the car's rear door. "At least we have one competent German," Orlofsky muttered in French. Inside the trunk, besides a great deal of water from the river Ohře, were three AK-47s and a dozen or so loaded clips. The chief, also in a parka and boots, had come over, and all four eyed the rifles.

"Where is the nearest ballistics lab?" Orlofsky asked.

"In Nuremburg," the chief replied. He was a big man. Not perhaps as big as the tow truck driver, but well over six feet and bulky, with a big gut, in his late forties. *Born after the war,* Max thought, apropos of nothing, except that when he was living in France, this was how he had routinely categorized people. Were they alive when all that bad shit was happening? Or had they been born since, into the dream life of postwar Europe, content to drift with the pack from state school to state job to state-paid retirement? He had been feeling particularly anti-France since the French had sandbagged the US in the run-up to the war in Iraq, and had been praying, sort of, that Megan Nolan was not a terrorist. Though that was pretty unprofessional, he had to admit.

"We'll send them back in the helicopter," Orlofsky said. Max knew that the rounds taken from one of the dead Arabs at the Cap de la Hague farm had been from a Kalashnikov, but he saw this attention to detail, this meticulous *police-work* as a waste of time. They should be organizing a man-hunt right now: bloodhounds, helicopters, military units, the whole ball of wax. Nolan and Laurence could not be far.

His thoughts were interrupted by the loud ringing of the chief's cell phone, which he swiftly extracted from his coat pocket and brought to his ear. *"Ja,"* he said, and then after a moment, *"ja"* again. Then, in French, looking over at Orlofsky, "We'll be right there."

"What?" said Orlofsky.

"The Czech police have fished a man from the river. A young gypsy. In his wallet they found a telephone number which they have traced to a cell phone owned by a Daniel Peletier in Brittany."

"Is the gypsy alive?" Max asked.

"Yes."

"Where is he?" This from Orlofsky.

"In a hospital in Cheb."

"Let's go," Orlofsky said to the chief. "You can drive us in your car. I want to talk to this gypsy. Can we trust your deputy?"

"Yes."

The deputy was standing no more than five feet away. Turning to her, Orlofsky said, "You're in charge. Secure this area. Get a search going up and down the river on both sides. Get something from the hotel room and use hounds. Get the pilot to fly low along both banks, get more helicopters if you can. We are looking for terrorists. Do you understand? *Terroristes.*"

"What is this all about, exactly?" the chief asked. "I would like to know."

"We"ll tell you in the car," Max answered. "Just so you know, it'll ruin your night."

"Its already been ruined," said the chief, heading toward his still-running SUV.

~ 29 ~

Morocco, May 16, 2003

Sitting at a small table outside the ticket office, Megan, her head and much of her face covered with the hood of her djellaba, watched as customs agents in gray-and-blue uniforms processed a long line of Moroccan nationals boarding the Tangier-to-Tafira ferry. Each one was questioned closely in Arabic or Berber, yesterday's bombings very much on everyone's minds. There was no proffering of baksheesh—the small bribes paid to bureaucrats across the Middle East to get them to do their jobs. Not today and probably not for the foreseeable future. Beyond the pier, with its hustle of activity, lay the long crescent-shaped spit of land that formed Tangier Bay. The day was windless and cloudless, and the sun beat down with all its strength and heat on the bay, turning it into a sheet of fiery turquoise rolling monotonously flat to the horizon. The ferry made the seventeen-mile-trip across the Strait of Gibraltar a dozen times a day. Europe lay there for the taking, so close you could see it from the hills above the bay. Megan watched three arrivals and departures, holding the neck of her hood across her distinctly Western mouth and nose. She spoke no Arabic or Berber, and the cash she had on her, about ten thousand euros, would do her no good. She thought briefly of returning to Abdullah's family, of asking them to hide her or help her out of the country, but she quickly rejected this idea. Her last image of Hakim flashed into her mind. She had given him two thousand euros to bury Abdullah, which he had placed carefully into a brown paper bag that for some reason he had carried out of his uncle's shop. As she drove off, before turning her attention to the side streets and alleys she would have to negotiate to get out of Sidi Moumim, she glanced in her rearview mirror, where she saw the boy looking intently into the bag. Then she remembered that while she was dying her hair he had swept up the thick clumps of it scattered around the floor and placed them with the same care into the bag, as if it were the most important thing he would ever do. No, she had visited enough upon Abdullah and his family.

She hoped that Abdel al-Lahani was dead, but even assuming he was, she had no illusions that she was safe. Mohammed, who had probably killed Abdullah while trying to find her, would come after her. And if his master was alive, there would be no limit to his desire to find and kill her. She had nearly taken the life of the great Falcon. Had wounded his alpha male pride terribly. Had run off with his child in her belly. And worse, she knew his true identity. She could go to the authorities and help bring the Falcon to earth.

This last option she had considered and rejected. She had the feeling that Lahani's reach was very long. A Saudi national, he had easily gotten the Moroccan government to do his bidding in several instances that Megan knew of. Her special diplomatic visa was one example, the flagging of her passport another. Maybe she would go to the police one day, but first she would have her baby and make sure it was safe. In the meantime she would run and she would hide, using her wits and finally putting to good use the money she had made by selling her body, and more—the mystique of Megan Nolan—to men for the past twelve years.

She was about to leave, to try to figure out another way of getting out of the country, when an elderly man in an expensive suit that hung loosely on his small, thin frame, sat down across from her at the table. She had been scanning her surroundings at regular intervals, but this man had not come on her radar screen. Until now.

"I would like to make you an offer," he said in French, without any preliminaries.

Megan did not reply. She did not think the man was a threat to her. He was at least eighty, maybe more, and very frail-looking, his skin stretched across his facial bones like parchment, tendrils of his wispy white hair plastered to his forehead by sweat. Only his eyes, dark brown and alert like a bird's, contained any sense of energy or strength.

"You can board the ferry with me," the old man said. "If you don't have papers, I can get them for you."

"I have papers," Megan said.

"What kind of visa?"

"Visitor's."

"And a passport?"

"Of course."

The old man looked around. The next ferry had arrived at the dock and the line of native boarders was beginning to form, though the customs agents had not yet set up their portable office, a podium and collapsible table. They would come out at the last minute, when the line of mostly Moroccan men in Western clothes had baked to a frazzle in the hot midday sun. The foreign national line, perhaps twenty people, had already passed through their checkpoint and were waiting in the shade of a frayed awning near the boarding ramp.

"I have been watching you for the past two hours," the man said, returning his steady gaze to Megan. "You are very beautiful, though you are quite obviously trying to hide it. You are also brave, but afraid."

Megan smiled for the first time in two days. "What am I afraid of?" she asked. If he answered this question correctly the old man was a genius.

"Your destiny has arrived."

"My destiny?" Megan smiled again. "Are you a fortune-teller?"

"I am *roma*," the old man said. "Gypsy. Yes, I have the second sight. The eyes of heaven are on you. You must be in great trouble to require such help."

Megan shook her head and looked over at the native customs line that had now begun to move in fits and starts as the two uniformed officers carefully checked the papers of each supplicant coming before them. Abdullah's car was parked on a side street a few blocks away. She could drive south over the mountains and into the Sahara, or she could drive east and try to cross the border into Libya. There were no other options. To the west was the Atlantic ocean.

"And in return?" she asked.

"I am dying of cancer," the old man said. "I would like to look at a beautiful young face as much as possible in the few months I have left."

"That's all?"

"The pain is starting," the gypsy answered. "I will need morphine, medical-quality morphine secured and administered. I do not believe in *gadgo* doctors and hospitals."

"How will you get me through? I don't speak Arabic. The picture on my passport is not a good match."

"You are American, yes?"

"Yes."

"I usually smuggle Moroccans into Spain, not Americans. But it will not be difficult. Who is looking for you?"

"You don't want to know."

"It is not a matter of want. I must assess the level of danger."

"It is very high."

"So it is not a lover, or a husband."

"It *is* a lover: the man who planned the bombings in Casa yesterday."

The old man's thin white eyebrows raised slightly and the lids of his eyes lowered like curtains drawn halfway down a window. He stared at Megan for a long moment through the lower half.

Your destiny has arrived as well, thought Megan.

"Have you lost interest?" she asked.

The old man shook his head. "Who has helped you to this point?" he asked.

"A friend. He's been killed." Megan closed her eyes as images of Abdullah crossed her mind. He had kissed her on both cheeks and both hands when he handed her the vial of poison just after daybreak this morning. An ancient Coptic blessing on work to be done. His killer had nailed him to the floor through his Coptic cross.

"You will become a gypsy," the old man said. "With me you will never be found."

"Where would we live?"

"In Paris."

"I will be hunted."

"I am wealthy and respected in my tribe. If I order it, you will be guarded day and night by people you will never see. A hundred eyes will watch over you. The curse of the dead, the *mulo,* would be visited on any gypsy who disobeyed me. Do you understand?"

"Yes."

"What is your name?"

"Megan Nolan. And you are ... ?"

"My name is François Duval."

Megan stared again at the line approaching the customs agents.

"There is no baksheesh today," she said.

"No, but I know these agents well. I have made them rich in the past ten years. And of course I have certain evidence that I can use against them if I wished to. It is the secret to success in my trade. You must have a man's testicles in your pocket before you can trust him."

Megan smiled again despite herself. "Do you want money?" she asked.

"No. I just want to look at you as I lay dying. What is the name on your passport?"

"I don't know."

"Show it to me and we will get in line."

~ ~ ~

Abdel al-Lahani lay on the plush custom-made sofa in his Casablanca penthouse. The corner of his left eye was ticking about once every five seconds, down substantially from the ten-times-per-second flutter of an hour ago, as if a hummingbird had landed on his eyelid. Sitting across from him were Mohammed and Ismael Saboori, an Iranian neurologist on the staff at the King Hassan University Medical School. Saboori held his small black leather physician's bag on his lap, his untouched tea on a table beside him. Lalla, who had induced vomiting and then cleaned and dressed Lahani before calling Mohammed, could be heard in the kitchen. It was Mohammed who had called Saboori. The blood sample that the doctor had taken from Lahani's arm lay in its ampule on the coffee table between them, next to an envelope that contained one thousand American dollars in new hundred-dollar bills.

"And there is no antidote?" Lahani asked. The back of his left hand lay across his forehead, inside of which his brain seemed to be expanding and contracting in slow, exquisitely painful waves.

"No," Saboori replied, "just flushing, which has been done. The ticking and the headache should subside in a few hours. You apparently swallowed very little."

"And if they don't?"

"I will prescribe something, but they should."

"And the numbness?"

"It should subside as well. The Amazon Indians use curare to kill their enemies. One milligram on the end of a dart is lethal. Orally it takes more. You will be fine."

Lahani nodded in dismissal. Saboori rose and picked up the envelope. "The blood should be tested soon," he said.

"We'll do it," Mohammed said. With a nod, Saboori turned and left.

"I will leave for home tomorrow," Lahani said to Mohammed when the doctor was gone. "You will stay here to see if she turns up."

"She may have left the country. She has money and could get papers. If that is the case, we will not easily find her."

"I will call Uncle al-Siddiq. He will put her on a watch list. She will appear. When she does we will go and kill her."

"It could be America."

"Wherever she turns up, we will go and kill her. I don't care if it's the White House or the vacant pit where the trade centers used to be. We will go and kill her. Do you understand?"

"Yes, emir," said Mohammed. "I understand."

~ 30 ~

Paris, December 16, 2003

On the day of François Duval's funeral in mid-December, Megan was awoken from a deep sleep by the sound of a mournful violin. By raising herself on one elbow, she could see down into the street. Her pregnant belly spread out on the bed. She could feel its weight and the baby kicking to start his day. For the past week, dozens of gypsy men of all shapes, sizes, and ages had gathered around a barrel fire in the cul-de-sac below, drinking whiskey, talking in whispers, and going off occasionally to pee in the weeds or berate their women. Standing alone by the barrel now was one of these men in a long dirty duster and wool cap playing the violin. He was leaning into the fire as he played. The low flames seemed to be dancing in response to his long piercing notes. The day was breaking warm and sunny, one of the beautiful late fall days that sometimes extend deep into a Paris winter. The music was both shrill and sweet, a metaphor for the gypsies themselves, Megan thought, reflecting on the last seven months of her life. An outcast among outcasts, she had been protected by the unchallenged and seemingly unchallengeable authority of the wily and feared Francois Duval. François had kept his word, and so had Megan. When the old man had died last night at midnight, she had been by his side.

The old gypsy, bantering in perfect Arabic, had slipped the head customs agent in Tangier the key to a storage locker at the pier's passenger depot and they were let on the ferry with zero fuss. Megan changed into her Western clothes on the boat and, at Duval's polite urging, used her own passport to enter Spain, applying for and being routinely issued a three-month visitor's visa. She returned with him to Montmartre, to the fourth-floor flat of a small apartment building he owned on a weed-covered cul-de-sac. Gypsies lived in all four apartments. The men hung out in the street-level coffee shop all day while the women went out to hustle, looking for *gadgo* widows or old men to con out of their life savings, or simply steal from if they could gain access to their homes. The kids, about ten or twelve of them, played all day in the street or the littered lot behind the building.

As the end drew near, most of François's relatives and friends had shown up, some from Paris, others from Hungary and the Czech Republic. One family of ten claimed to be from Russia. Their banged up, cannibalized cars and trucks, which doubled as sleeping quarters for many of them, lined the dead-end street. One day, François asked to be carried down to the coffee shop. The move exhausted him. He weighed about ninety pounds and had trouble breathing after any kind of exertion, even lifting his head to sip some water. He slept for an hour, and when he woke he refused the morphine that Megan had been giving him at increasingly shorter intervals. Megan watched as perhaps a hundred gypsies entered the coffee shop over the next three days to speak to the dying man. A fierce-looking crone named Ya Ya, once apparently Duval's lover but now his head house-keeper, told her that this was not simply to say good-bye. A gypsy must not be allowed to go to his grave bearing resentment or envy or ill feelings toward any other gypsy. If he did, his *mulo*—his ghost, basically—would return to haunt the person who had caused this state of affairs. Any doubt as to any lingering ill will, going back as far as childhood, had to be resolved face-to-face before the old man died.It was the fear of *marime,* contamination by the dead, Ya Ya said, that had brought these people to the old man's deathbed.

By ten AM, the entire group, perhaps a hundred and fifty men, women, and children had gathered in the street to watch as François's coffin was lifted onto the back of a rusted-out pickup truck. One of the pallbearers was François Duval Jr., paunchy and balding but with his father's sly eyes and careful, calculated movements. Another was a large muscular man, perhaps fifty, with a head of wild black hair, an eye patch, and a prominent gold tooth. Doro, the handsome, too-solemn teenaged grandson of Annabella Jeritza was the third. The last was a young man of perhaps twenty-five, with silky black hair, dark burning eyes, and fine, feminine features, including a cruel but beautiful slash of a mouth. Corozzo's son. No gypsy would touch a dead body, and so Megan had washed and done her best to groom old François after he died, and then she and Ya Ya had sat with the body until a local undertaker, familiar with the odd ways of the *roma,* had arrived to prepare it properly for interment. While they were waiting, the man with the eye patch had entered the candlelit coffee shop. He had first glanced at Ya Ya, who immediately left, and then had taken her vacated chair across from Megan.

Megan, dressing slowly in her room, getting ready to join the crowd gathering below, recalled their conversation:

"I am Corozzo. François was my uncle, my father's brother. As a young man I ran off and married one of his daughters without his permission. In the gypsy world, daughters are worth only the money they can bring when they are married off. François did not kill me because my father intervened. But I owe him a large debt. With you I will repay it."

"How?"

"I will take you into my clan. You will be under my protection."

"How do I know you can protect me?"

This question had stopped Corozzo cold. Gypsy men were not used to being questioned by women. But Megan didn't care. She had to assert some control, some independence, lest she be totally enslaved by the large beast of a man before her. She had met Corozzo's harsh stare with one of her own.

"Because if I don't," Corozzo said, "François's mulo will enter my home, my clan. I will become an outcast myself."

"Where will we go?"

"The Czech Republic at first. We will leave tomorrow, after the old man is buried."

"No."

"No?"

"My baby is due in a few days. François promised me it would be born here, in France. I have a midwife who I have been seeing. You have to wait."

"The French police want to talk to me," Corozzo said. "About a murder." The light from a nearby candle bathed his face, softening his harsh features, but not the sharp, feral look in his good eye.

"One more thing," Megan went on, ignoring this statement and his scowl, "no sex. But if you need money, I will give it to you."

Now the one-eyed man smiled, his gold tooth gleaming in the candlelight. "François did not mention money," he said, "but you will be expensive, and there is the question of your keep. As to sex, we will see. You might change your mind. I am charming and very brave."

"I doubt it. But I will pay my way, and my baby's. I don't know how long I'll be with you. It may be a while. As much as a year. Did François tell you why I am in hiding?"

"A mad lover."

"Yes, quite mad. And dangerous."

Corozzo rose. He towered over Megan. His smell—liquor and leather and sweat—filled the small windowless room. François Duval's body, his wispy white hair neatly combed, his face clean-shaven, lay in his ornate brass bed a few feet away. A candle on a nightstand illuminated his face. Megan had looked over at him while waiting for Corozzo's answer.

"I will wait," Corozzo said. "I will want a thousand euros for every month you are with me. If I am arrested you will lose your protection."

"And you will lose a thousand euros a month."

Corozzo shrugged his large shoulders, then abruptly turned and left.

At the cemetery, the grave was already dug. A mound of red earth was heaped next to it with two coiled canvas straps resting on top. Gypsies lower the caskets of their dead themselves and fill in the grave. Megan, who had made the arrangements on François's and Ya Ya's instructions, was relieved to see that they had been followed. As the mourners neared the gravesite, the women began to wail, at first one or two and then it seemed like all of them. The violinist had arrived early and was playing as they approached. Several old women were propping up Ya Ya, whose wailing grew louder, as if she were in competition with the others. Everyone had the same clothes on as they had on at seven in the morning. Jogging suits, patched skirts, kerchiefs of every color on the women's heads, trousers fifty years old on the men, the teenagers in jeans and worn-out running shoes. An Eastern Orthodox priest said some words that Megan could not hear over the din of the wailing and the violin. The younger kids were scampering around the knees of the adults and a few had ran to jump over nearby headstones.

These were chased down and cuffed by their mothers. The same pallbearers lowered the heavy bronze casket into the grave, pulling the straps up after it. Everyone shoveled or kicked in the red dirt. Those who had been carrying flowers—most of them plastic—threw them in. When the grave was covered, two battered trumpets were produced and the clan filed out to their trucks and cars to a tune that seemed to put a wild melody to the women's wailing. Megan, feeling what she thought might be the first twinge of a contraction, didn't know whether to laugh or cry.

Annabella Jeritza, her orange hair covered by a black kerchief, took Megan's arm and they walked out of the cemetery together.

"Is your baby coming?" the old woman asked.

"I think it is."

"Yes, I do, too. But don't fret. The first one takes his time. Come, I will introduce you to Miss Pia."

Megan had lied to Corozzo. She had not been seeing a midwife, but rather she had relied on Annabella, who told her that when the time came she would produce one. It seemed the time had come.

"She is just there," said the fortune-teller as they walked through the cemetery's arched wrought iron gateway, "there with Doro and her daughter at his car."

While they waited for traffic to ease so they could cross the busy Avenue de Clichy, Megan stared at the trio Annabella had pointed out. Doro she had met and trusted. The two women were strangers. When they reached them, Annabella introduced Megan, and then began a conversation in rom with the midwife, a severe-looking woman of about fifty with a cocked eye and a mole on her upper lip. While they were talking, presumably about the delivery of Megan's baby, Megan eyed the daughter—who was perhaps thirty and about Megan's height—and was at once struck by two things: how fair she was for a gypsy, her complexion and her hair color quite close to Megan's, and how frail she looked, her bones showing through her thin cotton dress and long wool sweater. Then Miss Pia and her daughter left and Megan and Annabella got into Doro's car. They were joined by Doro's friend Ephrem, who had been in a nearby shop buying cigarettes. As they neared home, Megan pulled Annabella's hand over onto her stomach for her to feel what she believed was her next contraction. She and the fortune-teller were in the backseat.

"Yes," said Annabella, "Miss Pia will be stopping by in about an hour. I think the child is coming, but she will know for sure."

"Will she want money?"

"Yes. She lives for gold."

Megan had learned that this question was not crass in the gypsy culture. They loved money more than any material thing it could buy, and they spent a large part of their day discussing it. Only a gadgo fool did not look for the opportunity to turn any situation—tragic, comic, or in between—into a source of money.

"And the daughter?" Megan asked. "Is she sick?"

"Yes, she has a cancer somewhere. She will be dead soon."

"How soon?"

"A week or two, maybe a bit more."

Megan turned to stare out the car window, trying to rein in her racing thoughts. When Doro slowed to make a turn, she recognized the street. It was Annabella's.

"Are we stopping at your place?" she asked.

"Yes. You will not be welcome at François's any longer. Corozzo has asked me to take care of you until you are ready

to travel. You and the baby. I know a family who has an extra room. You can stay with them. They will want money,
too."

"Where does Miss Pia live?"

"In the same building you will be staying in."

"Her daughter lives with her?"

"Yes."

"Has she been to a hospital? A doctor?"

"No."

"What is her name?"

"Little Pia."

"Why is she so fair?"

"No one knows. We think her father was *gadgo*. Miss
Pia ran off when she was young and was not heard from for
years. She returned with the red-haired child. People keep
away from her. They think her cocked eye is a mark of the
devil."

"Is it?"

"She is a good midwife, but as I said, she is very greedy,
greedier than most, and she has no friends."

~ 31 ~

The River Ohre, January 7, 2004

Ephrem was knocked from the bow of the boat by a branch that nobody saw coming until it was too late. They watched helplessly as he was swept away by the current, and rushed to the waterfall about fifty yards ahead. They knew the waterfall was there because they heard it and because their skipper, a bearded, thick-set Hungarian gypsy, had anticipated that the dam on the outskirts of Cheb would be raised to prevent flooding in the small but densely populated city. Better to flood the forest for a half mile or so on either side of the river than to destroy homes and businesses and lives. The problem was that as he slowed and veered toward the left bank in the pitch dark, he did not know just how much of the forest had been submerged. The branch that swept Ephrem away was normally ten feet above dry ground. The small beach used by locals to launch their pleasure boats must have been flooded as well. They looked for it, but once they heard the falls the skipper steered sharply to starboard and, in the blink of an eye, Ephrem was gone.

The Hungarian, who had earned the five hundred euros Pat had paid him, went back upstream after off-loading his passengers. He would tie up to a tree and wait out the flood tide. With his passengers gone, he would be safe from official inquiry. Not so Pat, Catherine, Doro, and Steve Luna, Doro's young colleague, the third gypsy boy they had met in Rambouillet but never been introduced to until tonight. There was a car waiting for them at a boatyard in Cheb, no more than three or four miles away. Getting there was the problem.

"We should search along the bank for Ephrem," said Pat. "He might have made it to shore."

"No," Doro replied, "there is no shore. The river is still rising. We have to move inland."

They were standing in a small muddy clearing, all of them soaked hip-high, all exhausted from their hundred-yard trudge through icy cold, waist-high water to dry ground.

"There will be police around," said Catherine. "We cannot use the roads."

"Whose car is it?" Pat asked. "We could call them and ask them to pick us up."

"Steve bought the car today from a gypsy family. He parked it, and then he had to hire the boat. That's why we weren't at the carousel at six olock."

"Thank God you were there when we got there," said Catherine. "We were very lucky."

"The captain insisted on leaving early. He knew the river was rising and didn't know how long it might take."

This was the first chance they had had to talk. Pat and Catherine had driven from the Waldsassen municipal parking lot, near their hotel, to the amusement park in under ten minutes. They were happily surprised to see Doro waiting for them at the carousel, but in too much of a hurry to do anything but blurt out their predicament and rush to the boat, which was another surprise, and a relief, until they actually got under way. The river was dark and swift and the boat, under very little power, raced headlong downstream. It had been Doro's idea to stop and push the Peugeot into the river. As their boat was taking them away from the park's dock, they could see that their ploy hadn't worked. The car was hung up on some rocks. They could also see headlights approaching the carousel.

Once under way, Pat immediately paid the captain, who cursed and asked for another hundred euros when he was told by Catherine that he could not use his running lights. He sent Ephrem to the bow to look out for floating logs and other boat-sinking debris. The others huddled as best they could on the stern deck of the twenty-five-foot boat, watching the Hungarian skipper's back as he handled the wheel in the forward cabin. They all stood up when they felt themselves going to the left and the next thing they heard was the thud of the branch knocking Ephrem into the river. A sound they wouldn't forget for a long time, if ever.

"We'll walk through the forest," said Doro, "keeping close to the water. When we reach the city, I will go for the car."

"There will be hounds," said Catherine, "but the water and the mud will make it difficult for them. And no boat could reach us here."

In the boat, Pat's adrenaline had risen along with the tide. Now it was starting to ebb. But the cold and the possibility of hypothermia were not their biggest problems. In the distance, upriver, he heard the whir of a helicopter, or thought he did. And then it was gone and they set out.

~ 32 ~

Czech Republic, January 8, 2004

At dawn, Pat and Catherine were kneeling at a low stone wall overlooking a small but steep valley through the center of which ran an unnamed tributary of the Labe River. Fifty yards or so away, at perhaps a fifty-foot-drop from their level, was a clearing cut out from the forest on the far side of the stream. At one end, the clearing was bordered by three pyramid-shaped piles of dark gray tailings. Here and there a glint or two of ore sparkled as the strange dense masses, three times as tall as a grown man, caught the first light of the sun rising over a series of low hills in the east. At the other end, a decaying two-story brick building squatted against a denuded hillside. The building's two rows of windows were shattered and covered with odds and ends of plywood and other scraps of weathered lumber. Next to it gaped the timber-framed opening, perhaps ten feet high, to a long abandoned mine. On the hardpan near the building were parked six vehicles: a pickup truck, a box truck, and four passenger cars. The road in, at one time paved but now crumbling and overgrown with weeds, ended at the foot of the hill next to the mine building. The snow of the night before had barely reached this part of the Czech Republic, some twenty miles due east of Prague. A light dusting of it covered the clearing and surrounding countryside, just enough to make the abandoned mine compound look picturesque in the early light and the clearing look like a small but perfect stage that nature had prepared for its next important, secret event.

"Glasses would help," said Catherine.

Confused, Pat did not immediately reply. They were sipping from cardboard mugs of hot coffee, and at first he thought she meant they needed coffee cups. Then, realizing his mistake, he said, "You mean binoculars."

"Yes."

"We've got a good view here. We won't miss them."

They were waiting for Doro and Steve Luna to appear in the compound below. After trekking through water and mud for three hours and then driving through the night, they had found the fire road that led them to their current lookout about a half hour ago. Tired and wet, their shoes and jeans coated with mud, they were in need of hot food, dry clothes, and sleep. But the growl of helicopters and the howl of bloodhounds still echoed in their heads. They backtracked to a truck stop they had passed to pick up coffee and decided to make contact with the infamous Corozzo then and there. If Megan was in the camp below, she needed to be told that the world was closing in on her. And on her new friends as well.

"Look," Catherine said, "someone's awake."

Below they could see smoke curling from a chimney in the middle of the roof of the mine building. The pale gray smoke cut through the cold morning air and then drifted gently west, chased away by the sun's first heat.

"Our Arab friends may have been here already," said Catherine, keeping her voice low and her eyes straight ahead.

Pat nodded, his eyes on the entry road near the piles of tailings, where he would have his first sight of the twenty-year-old Czech-made Skoda Favorit Doro had purchased in Cheb and that had miraculously transported them all here. They both knew that whoever had beheaded François Duval must have first tried very hard to extract Megan's whereabouts from him. Which made it almost a certainty, the way things were going, that more Arab killers would pop up.

Megan, Pat thought, Megan. What did you do to draw such a nasty crowd?

"We are in a bind with Doro," Catherine said.

"How?"

"You promised he could use Megan as bait to lure the Arabs."

"I told him I would do my best to convince her."

"Megan could be killed."

"Not to mention you and me."

"She may not agree."

"I'll talk her into it."

Pat had not talked Megan into anything since she was in high school, maybe even grammar school. But this was not as hollow a statement as it would have been a few weeks ago. He was convinced that his one-of-a-kind daughter had laid down a trail for him, a trail through a minefield, trip wires everywhere. Having followed that trail to what he now hoped was its end, having passed her test, he *might* have the moral standing for once in his life to ask her to go on the line. For him, for herself, for her dead child, for Annabella Jeritza, for François Duval, for Daniel Peletier. For Catherine. These were big thoughts, but somehow not too big, not pretentious. This was where his life had led him, and Megan's hers. He would see it through and was confident without really knowing why that Megan would, too.

"We'll avenge Uncle Daniel," he said.

"I see."

They scanned the scene before them for a moment in silence—the smoke curling and drifting away, the hushed, snow-covered clearing, the stream rushing along and sparkling in the early sun as it went—then Catherine said, "He was alive, Patrick, wasn't he?"

Pat nodded, keeping his head forward. He was about to speak when the front door of the mine building suddenly flew open. A second or two later a young man in jeans and a black, hooded UCLA sweatshirt was catapulted out head-first. His forward motion was stopped abruptly when his shoulder slammed against the fender of the pickup. As he was rising, shaking his head, an older, taller, bulkier man, wearing a black eye patch, stepped through the doorway.

"Corozzo," said Catherine.

The young man stood his ground, but did not resist, or was unable to, when Corozzo grabbed him by the front of his shirt and dragged him around the pickup truck into the clearing. Still holding him by his sweatshirt, the older and much larger man struck the younger man a long sweeping blow to his face, a blow which sent the young man flying onto his back. Again the young man rose, and again he stood his ground, his body swaying from side to side like a puppet whose strings were being pulled in slow motion. Again Corozzo advanced, the balled fist at the end of his right arm swinging down by his knee. But before he could strike again, Doro pulled up in the boxy, Soviet-era Skoda. Both men stared at the car as Doro slowly looped around them in the snow, a *what the fuck?* look on their faces. Then Doro parked, facing the direction he had come from, exited the car, and approached the two men, his hands at his sides. Steve Luna got out as well, but he stayed close to the Skoda—which Doro had left running—his hands in his jacket pockets. In the cold morning air, steam was coming from the mouths of all four men as well as the car's rusty exhaust.

"That must be Corozzo's son," said Catherine, nodding toward the young man who was the object of Corozzo's blows, his face cut and bleeding above the right eye, "or possibly his son-in-law."

Pat eyed the tall, barrel-shaped Corozzo as he greeted Doro. He was smiling, his domestic dispute, Pat supposed, put aside for conclusion at a later time. His gold tooth gleamed as the sun's low slanting rays glanced off his face. He was wearing dark woolen slacks, a pair of sturdy boots, and an aging leather vest over a bulky red sweater. His long, unruly black hair spilled down his neck and over his ears. Though in his fifties, he looked much younger, more wholesome and more vibrant than Pat had pictured him. The gypsy leader's smile vanished as Doro began to speak. He listened and nodded, listened and nodded, and then turned to the young man he had been pummeling, said something, and gestured toward the mine building. The young man walked to the building and went in. Corozzo and Doro continued talking for a moment or two and then both turned as someone—a person in an open overcoat, its hood up, came out of the mine building and walked toward them.

The walk was at once familiar to Pat: erect, poised, regal. *Megan.* When she reached the men, she drew her hood back and shook her hair out as Corozzo spoke, apparently making introductions. Smiling, she shook hands with Doro, who was staring at her as if he struck gold. The young man whom Corozzo was beating on did not reappear. Corozzo smiled as well, and the three fell to talking. As they did, Pat assessed his daughter: clean, healthy, her hair coppery bright but much shorter; in tight jeans and black fur boots, she looked as proud and defiant and in control as ever. Pat's sigh of relief was audible.

"She looks well," Catherine murmured.

Pat nodded, but did not speak or take his eyes from the scene below. He watched intently as Megan once again shook hands with Doro before turning and walking back to the mine building next to Corozzo, and Doro and Steve Luna got into the Skoda and drove away.

"She always looks good," Pat said when the Skoda was out of sight and the clearing once again empty. "She refuses to ever look bad." Pat smiled tightly as he said this, thinking of Megan in command of her situation, in charge, he would not hesitate to say, of that small group of men in the clearing. He could not remember the last time he had been proud of her.

Whatever went before and whatever happened now—and a bad death was a good possibility—he had found his daughter. He had done what he had to do.

~ ~ ~

Inside the mine building, the young man who had been on the receiving end of Corozzo's blows was sitting on a slat-backed wooden chair while a young, black-haired gypsy woman dabbed a wet cloth on the wound on his swollen face. Nearby, a fire blazed in a wood-burning stove. Smoke, seeping from cracks in the stove's ramshackle sheet-metal chimney, drifted around the large room. When he saw Corozzo and Megan enter, the young man pushed the black-haired woman away, knocking her to the floor with a sweeping shove of his arm. Rising slowly, the woman glared at Megan and seemed about to say or do something—*spit at me,* Megan thought, *or lift her dirty wool skirt to curse me with her menstruating pussy*—but did not, held in check at the sight of Corozzo casting his one eye blackly in her direction.

Along the far wall, blankets hung on rope marked off the living quarters of the six or seven families who were wintering with Corozzo. Several of them stopped what they were doing to watch the scene near the stove. The men, mustachioed, unshaven, already started in on their day's drinking, smiled. The women muttered and glanced at one another.

On the opposite wall were two glass-walled cubicles that had once been offices. Blankets hung behind the glass of the room on the right. On the naked glass of the room on the left the letters "URO," in large grandiose Cyrillic script, were all that was left of the name of the mining company that the Soviets had abandoned long before the breakup of their bleak empire. Behind the "U," Megan could see Sasha, the old crone who was her roommate, sitting in a rocking chair, her head down, quietly, steadily rocking, ignoring the scene in the outer room. Megan tried to catch her eye, but did not linger when Sasha did not look up. Sasha, a girlhood friend of Annabella Jeritza, had done her best to protect Megan, trading spit and Roma curses with the young women of the clan who resented Megan with the deadly passion that only gypsies can muster.

Megan slowly took off her coat and, placing it under her arm, surveyed the scene: the young man's bruised, sullen face; his woman backing away from Corozzo as if under a spell; the plebes along the wall staring at her, the *outré*, arrogant American. She could smell the fear and hatred amid the unwashed bodies in the smoky room.

One more day, she thought, turning toward her room. One more day of these fucking wackos.

~ ~ ~

"You saw?" said Doro.

"Yes," Pat answered.

"She is well."

"Yes."

"She will meet you tomorrow at noon. I am to pick her up and bring her."

"Where?"

"I won't know until tomorrow."

"Why not right now?"

"It is Corozzo's decision."

They were standing on the dirt fire road near its intersection with the local highway, where Pat and Catherine had walked down to meet the Skoda. A mass of low clouds was now blotting out the sun and the air suddenly smelled of snow. They were hidden by the forest, but they could hear the occasional rushing sound of a truck or a car as it sped by on the paved road only fifty yards or so away.

"What was that fight all about?" Catherine asked.

"That was Corozzo's son."

Doro did not elaborate, as if this were enough.

"Gypsy fathers and sons always fight," said Steve Luna, who was standing nearby listening.

"About what?" Catherine asked.

"Money, women."

"Power," said Catherine.

"Yes."

Catherine knew what it was like to stir up lust in a man by doing nothing but existing. She wondered what the dynamic was like inside the old mine building, with the striking and self-assured Megan Nolan doing nothing much but going about her business. And possibly—likely—sleeping with one of the men. While the others watched.

"Corozzo says a fat Arab stopped by yesterday looking for Megan," said Doro, "He showed him a picture."

Catherine had expected this. After killing Duval, the Saudis, or whoever they were, would have had a thirty-six-hour head start in finding Corozzo's camp.

"How did he handle it?"

"He laughed and said he *wished* he could have such a beautiful piece of gadgo ass."

"We should go back and warn him," Pat said. "They could attack the camp, or blow it up. They're capable of anything."

"Corozzo had the man followed," said Doro. "He is being watched."

"Where is he?"

"Corozzo would not say."

"What did this Arab look like?" Catherine asked.

"Short, bulky, balding. Corozzo's age."

"We should go," said Steve Luna, "before we get soaked again." The first stray drops of wet snow had begun to fall.

"One more thing," said Doro. "She gave me this." He handed Pat a small mustard-colored envelope, the kind a druggist might put two pills in for a customer. Pat took it, tore open the seal, and extracted a small audio cassette and what looked like a miniature CD with black plastic borders. "What's this?" he said, holding up the CD.

"It looks like a disk for a digital camera," said Catherine. "I have one at home."

Pat put the cassette and CD back in the small envelope and put it in the inside pocket of his leather jacket.

"Let's go," Doro said. "We can eat and dry out at the truck stop. Maybe rent rooms. We have no choice but to wait until tomorrow."

Over the rise behind them, Catherine heard one of the vehicles in the mine compound start up and then backfire twice before driving off.

"Yes," said Catherine, looking at Pat and seeing the frustration and worry on his handsome face. "We have no choice. Tomorrow will come soon enough."

~ 33 ~

Czech Republic, January 8-9, 2004

The first thing that Ephrem did when he left police headquarters in Cheb was to buy a cell phone. Max French, André Orlofsky, and Marcel Dionne, sitting in a car across the street, watched as the young gypsy made a call from the sidewalk outside the EuroTel store. André immediately radioed the Czech police to get the number of the phone and begin monitoring it. Also to find out the recipient of that first call. But that would take a while. The three agents then followed Ephrem as he walked the ten blocks to the train station. Inside, Orlofsky got in line several spots behind the boy. At the window, he discretely flashed his ID and asked for two tickets to the same destination as the gypsy boy with the red backpack. He then radioed Dionne, in the car outside, to start driving to Kolin. On the train, he and Max sat in the same car as Ephrem, five or six rows behind him.

"A rock concert, perhaps?" Orlofsky whispered as the train got underway. It had been Max's idea to let Ephrem go, in the hope that he would lead them to Catherine Laurence or the men who had killed Daniel Peletier. They could have held the boy on any number of things, including the fact that he had three sets of identification in his wallet, all forged or stolen, along with Peletier's cell phone number. Orlofsky had asked the youthful-looking Dionne to interrogate the boy, hoping that he could quickly strike a sympathetic chord. But the teenager, obviously much savvier than his years, wasn't talking, and there was no time to bring in the experts with their psychological and physical methods of extracting information from recalcitrant suspects. And even if they did, who was to guarantee that that information would be any good? Orlofsky had agreed—their options were limited—but he did not forego the opportunity to take a few jabs at Max. His other suggestions as to where the gypsy boy might be leading them had included the circus and a day at a shopping mall.

"Perhaps he's going to see the EU bureaucrat assigned to run his life," Max replied, more curtness than sly humor in his voice. He had been thinking about Megan Nolan, her writing in particular, and wanted to return to her. He whispered also, although there was no need to, as Ephrem had not been able to see them through the one-way window as they watched him being questioned. Both men kept their eyes on the boy, who appeared to be sleeping. He had coughed up half of the River Ohře and was lucky to be alive. The guard at the border bridge had been peeing over the parapet and seen him climbing onto the cement footing of a pier below.

"Ah, *touché,*" the Frenchman replied.

With a quick sideways glance, Max caught the end of the acerbic Frenchman's tight half smile. He remained silent. Max, who spoke four languages and had been a Rhodes Scholar, was neither surprised nor bothered by Orlofsky's attitude toward him. He had left France because he had grown weary of the subtle condescension, the elusive deniable snobbery of the so-called French intellectual.

"Speaking of bureaucrats, did you talk to your people this morning?" Orlofsky asked.

"Yes, I did."

"What did they say? Anything new?"

"They finally had a long talk with General al-Siddiq in Riyadh. There was never a Saudi operation in Morocco prior to the bombings. Which, as you know, the Moroccans confirm. As to one inside France, he laughed. Your Raimondi character had his own agenda. That's al-Siddiq's story."

"Do your people believe him?"

"No. They think al-Siddiq got Raimondi to do his bidding. They think its possible that bin-Shalib works for the Saudis, that he was compromised somehow, possibly via Megan Nolan, that Raimondi was their ace in the hole, a mole they cultivated for years and finally put to use."

"I don't believe it. Raimondi was an idiot and a coward, and he came from money."

"He's the one who went to LeGrand. He knew about the faked suicide. He brought up al-Zahra, the terrorist plot."

"So Nolan's on the run from the Saudis, who want to kill her because she can somehow expose their connection to bin-Shalib?"

"That's the theory in Washington."

"Who is this woman?"

"She's a total fucking mystery, but if she leads us to bin-Shalib ... If we find her, they want us to use her as bait."

"Enlist her in the war on terror."

"Yes."

"Will she have a choice?"

"Do any of us?"

"Not according to Sartre, who you probably despise."

"I do despise him, and the answer is yes, she will."

Ephrem stirred and then awoke as the passenger beside him got up to go to the men's room. Stretching first, he stood also and reached for his knapsack on the rack above. As he did, he turned and scanned the car. Max and Orlofsky stared vacantly ahead, and Max was able to return for a moment to Megan Nolan and the little he knew about her. There had not been even a hint of irony in the dozen or so articles she had written for *Vogue* and *Cosmopolitan*, although Max did like the titles, especially the last one. Otherwise they were straightforward inanities. Then, after 9/11, came the pieces, obviously deeply researched, on the Trojan Horse that was Muslim immigration to Europe. Had she suddenly become patriotic and a scholar at the same time? Her past was just as puzzling. Two weeks at Bennington in 1992 followed by twelve years of capital hopping in Europe. A lifestyle supported, it seemed, by a continually replenished balance of about fifty thousand euros in a Paris bank. The bank code for the source of these deposits, all wire transfers, indicated that they came from private Swiss houses. Orlofsky's people were working on obtaining the records of these accounts, but Max was sure they would simply show a series of cash deposits over the past ten years or so. Could this money have come from al-Qaeda-type sources? Was her whole adult life an elaborate cover as she prepared for a career in terrorism? Stranger things had happened. People went bonkers with hate and anger. He hoped Megan Nolan wasn't one of them. He was starting to like her in the strange way that was familiar to him under a certain set of circumstances. He did not want to have to kill her.

"Max French," said Orlofsky, stirring Max from his thoughts, "Where did you get that name?"

"From my parents, where else?"

"Are you actually French?"

"French-Canadian, German, American Indian."

"American Indian?"

"My great grandfather was a miner. He married a Shoshone squaw and brought her to San Francisco."

"You seem distracted. Have you been thinking of our Miss Nolan? I notice you keep her picture in your jacket pocket."

"Where else would I keep it?"

"And that you study it often."

Max smiled wryly and remained silent. Once, when he was a reporter in Paris, he had covered the story of a woman who had been suspected by the French police of murdering her husband by mixing small amounts of rat poison in his food over a period of two years. A beautiful brunette with sad, haunting eyes, he had carried her picture around as well, not disposing of it until two years later when he returned to the States to start law school.

"Perhaps it is a good thing," said Orlofsky.

"What?"

"To fall in love with your prey. It sharpens the senses."

Max had slept for three or four hours last night, laying across four chairs at the police station in Cheb, his buckskin shoes drying on a radiator nearby. The radiator's intermittent muttering and the quiet hissing of his soft leather shoes had lulled him to sleep.

"Dry shoes help, too," Max answered.

They changed trains in Prague and a half hour later they were disembarking in Kolin. On the platform Ephrem was met by another gypsy boy, this one perhaps two or three years older, darkly handsome, his black hair pulled into a ponytail, wearing a black motorcycle jacket à la Marlon Brando in *The Wild Ones*. Max and Orlofsky watched as the two boys hugged as if they had not seen each other for years, or as if the older boy had thought the younger one dead, perhaps having fallen from a boat into a swollen river. Leaning against a nearby post, pretending to read a Czech newspaper, was Marcel Dionne. Outside, the boys got into a beat-up gray Skoda. The three policemen followed as they drove out of town and picked up the main east-west highway. After only a few miles, they pulled into a truck stop complex that contained a restaurant, a truck wash, a large parking area half filled with behemoth tractor-trailers, and a drab one-story motel of about twenty rooms. The boys parked the Skoda in front of room nineteen and went in. Orlofsky was driving. He parked behind a Dumpster, but with a direct view of the boys' room, the next to the last on the right, and then sent Dionne to check out the back. The baby-faced detective returned in a few minutes to report that there was a small bathroom window at the rear of each room. No door.

"Go and get us some food," Orlofsky said to Dionne, nodding toward the busy restaurant. "And coffee."

"And blankets," said Max, looking at his watch and then the cold gray day outside. "We could be here a while."

It was one PM. Max and Orlofsky watched Dionne as he walked around the motel to the left and through the maze of parked trucks, taking a circuitous route to the restaurant so as not to be seen by the occupants of room nineteen. While Dionne was gone, a car pulled up—another Skoda, this one a grimy white—and parked next to the gray one. A third gypsy boy, with dark curly hair, perhaps eighteen, got out and entered room nineteen using his own key.

"Two cars," said Max.

"Yes," Orlofsky replied. "I'll call for help. We should be watching the back window, anyway." They had already checked in with the Kolin police, and now the French agent called his contact there, a Sergeant Ruzika, and asked him to send out an unmarked car, with food and blankets for a possible all-night stakeout. Ruzika himself arrived twenty minutes later in a Ford pickup and parked alongside one of the tractor-trailers, at an angle that gave him a good view of the rear of the motel. Once he settled in, he buzzed Orlofsky on the radio.

"There are two Skodas," Orlofsky said, "one gray, one white, parked on our side of the motel. You take the white one when it leaves. I'll buzz you. Plate number: CF553. Do you have backup?"

"Yes. A car near the entrance."

"Have you heard from Prague?"

"Yes. Your boy called a party here in Kolin. Arturo Toscanini, a Paris address. Phony."

"Our gypsies are great kidders. Any other calls?"

"No."

"What about *your* gypsies?"

"There is a family of ten or twelve in an apartment near the square. They've been there for about six months. There is also another group of about twenty in an abandoned Soviet mining camp a few miles from here. Shall I send someone?"

"No. They'd warn their friends."

"I agree."

"Did you bring supplies?"

"Yes."

"Keep an eye on that back window."

Marcel had been unable to get blankets in the restaurant and they spent a cold night. But it was worth it. At around two AM, the door to room twenty swung open and Catherine Laurence stepped outside to smoke a cigarette. Max had also studied her photograph, taken on the day five years earlier when she was promoted to detective sergeant, though not as much and not with the same interest as Megan Nolan's. When she emerged, Orlofsky and Dionne were dozing. Max did not wake them immediately. He watched Laurence, her face lit by the dim glow from a yellow lamp above the door, struck by her beauty. *You're not obsessed with her, Max,* he said to himself, *you're very cool with respect to Catherine Laurence. You could kill her and not skip a beat.*

There was a low railing, made of plastic or cheap, painted wood that separated the parking lot from the cement apron that ran along the front of the motel. Max watched as Laurence stepped closer to it to flick her half finished cigarette away. When the door behind her opened, she did not turn. A large man, perhaps six-four, with a strong face and deep-set eyes came out of room twenty and, stepping behind Laurence, rested his hands on her shoulders. Even in the dim yellow light, Max could see that these were large hands, the hands of a working man or of a great lover. Laurence, her arms folded across her chest, raised her hands to take hold of Patrick Nolan's. Max's father, one of the first casualties of the Vietnam War, had had large hands. So Max had been told. Hands that caressed a weapon, and his nineteen-year-old wife, before leaving Fort Lewis for Nam. Would that man have traveled halfway around the world to track down a runaway son who was suspected of high crimes?

Max shook this thought from his head. When you were an orphan, you had many many more questions than you had answers. Then he nudged Orlofsky, and when the Frenchman raised his head, he pointed to the couple under the yellow light, and whispered, *"Voilà."*

~ 34 ~

Czech Republic, January 8-9, 2004

Mohammed, Abdel al-Lahani, and their army of two were staying in a motel on the outskirts of Kolin. Most of the fifteen or so rooms were empty. There were a few back-packing, marijuana-smoking young people. A middle-aged couple checked in and out within two hours. Tedious examples of the corruption of the West. But the old crone that owned the place did not ask for passports or car registration information. Illicit love, drugs, foreign nationals that fit the typical terrorist profile, these did not bother her as long as cash was paid in advance. Lahani paid for a week, though they did not plan on staying that long. They needed only a day or two more of isolation and anonymity.

On his way back from the gypsy camp yesterday, Mohammed had stopped in Kolin to purchase a second car for their mujahideen to use. They were now sitting in it, perched above the old mining camp, their orders to phone Lahani immediately if they saw someone who could be Megan or if the gypsies appeared to be breaking camp. Mohammed was sure that the leader, Corozzo, a wild-looking man with a gold tooth and an eye patch, had lied. Either Megan was in the camp or the chief knew where she was. Mohammed had mentioned a large sum of money to Corozzo as a reward to anyone helping them locate Megan. If nothing developed soon, Lahani's plan was to raid the camp and extract Megan if she was there, or information as to her whereabouts if she was not. By any means necessary.

At two in the morning, Lahani and Mohammed were awakened by a rapping on their door. They had been sleeping lightly, fully dressed, expecting gypsy greed to bring them either a traitor or an attempted robbery. Through the door, their visitor identified himself as Sebastian, Corozzo's son, having come with information about Megan Nolan. Nine-millimeter pistols in hand, they let the man in and invited him to sit in the room's one rickety chair. He was wearing a heavy overcoat with a woolen scarf wrapped around his neck and a hunter's cap on his head. When he took these latter two off, his blackened and swollen right eye and the ugly welt along his right jawline were revealed.

"Would you like a drink?" Sebastian asked, reaching inside his coat and pulling out a half-full pint bottle of whiskey. The two Saudis shook their heads, but the gypsy did not seem to notice, taking a long swig and returning the bottle to the folds of his voluminous winter coat.

"Where is the Nolan woman?" Lahani asked. He was sitting on the edge of one of the room's two beds, across from Sebastian, leaning forward, his hands clasped in front of him. Mohammed was standing to the right of Sebastian, his pistol held at his side.

"Who is she?" Sebastian asked. He had to cock his head to one side to look at Lahani through his good eye.

"She is a dangerous criminal," Lahani answered.

"A criminal? Yes, I believe it. And a bitch."

Mohammed looked closely at the young gypsy's face, handsome beneath its bruises and its growth of beard. There was fear in the depths of his watery drunken eyes, which was to be expected. And something else. A *bitch,* he had called Megan.

"Where is she?" Lahani asked.

"I heard you mention twenty-five thousand euros," the gypsy said to Mohammed, turning his head in exaggerated slowness, as if in full control, the way a drunk will.

"Where is Miss Nolan?" Lahani asked, an edge now in his voice. "Is she at the camp?"

"No, she has left."

"Where is she?"

"I don't know, but tomorrow she is to meet her father. I will find out where and call you."

"How will you find out?"

"There are people in the camp who hate the woman. It won't be hard."

"How was the meeting with her father arranged?"

"A gypsy from our tribe arrived this morning. He made the arrangements with Corozzo."

"Just the father? Anyone else? Are the police involved?"

"No, my father would not deal with the police."

"What happened to your face?"

"A quarrel with Corozzo. With the money I will be free."

"Yes, you will get your money when you have delivered Megan Nolan to me."

"I would like some now. Half."

With a nod from Lahani to Mohammed, this Sebastian would be dead. Corozzo would probably thank him. But Lahani believed his story. There was the truth of hatred in his eyes. He could kill him later, once he was sure he had Megan in his sights.

Lahani reached for his jacket, hanging on the back of a chair, and took his billfold from it, extracting a roll of hundred euro notes, counting off ten, and handing them to Sebastian. He then wrote his cell phone number on a slip of notepaper and handed it to the gypsy.

"You will call me, I know," Lahani said. "You would not risk your life and your entire family's for a thousand euros."

"One more thing," Sebastian said.

"Yes."

"Corozzo has someone watching you, to warn him if you head for the camp. He is a boy of fifteen, driving a red Volkswagon Beetle."

"Thank you. We will take care of him."

"Yes, I'm sure you will."

~ ~ ~

Sebastian did call late the next morning. Afterward, Lahani had Mohammed call their two men in from their stakeout. While waiting for them, the Saudi prince savored his situation. A week ago, a French policewoman had made a routine call to the Foreign Office in Rabat regarding a female suicide possessing a Moroccan diplomatic visa. The inquiry had reached the person who had issued the visa, who indeed issued all such visas in Morocco, a jihadist in league with the Falcon of Andalus. Now, after seven months of circling in frustration and muted anger, the Falcon was about to land. Where Uncle al-Siddiq, through his idiotic dupe, Charles Raimondi, had failed, he would succeed. He would kill Megan Nolan with his own hand, first looking her in the eye, and thus expiate the humiliation that had weighed so heavily upon him these past months. Afterward, he would resume his work of killing infidels, of reinstituting the caliphate in Europe, starting in Spain, the most cowardly among a continent of cowards. March 11 was only two months away.

~ 35 ~

Czech Republic, January 9, 2004

Pat had turned off the cheap electric heater when they went to bed because it made so much noise he knew he wouldn't be able to sleep. When he woke at two AM the room was very cold and Catherine wasn't there. He turned the heater on and, as he was dressing, he saw the glow of a cigarette outside through an opening in the synthetic drapes that covered the front window. Relieved, he stood for a moment and watched Catherine smoke. She was wearing Uncle Daniel's blue wool sweater and her stylish French jeans. Her hair hung down to her shoulders. Her arms were folded on her chest and her head was slightly bent. She looked younger from behind, more like a girl of twenty than a woman of thirty-five. Younger and more vulnerable. She had been subdued during their long day of waiting, and so had he. They had bought provisions, checked into the room, showered, eaten, made love on the edge of exhaustion, fallen asleep for six or seven hours, eaten again, watched CNN—understanding little—and then tried to sleep again.

As the day wore on, Pat realized that they had become disconnected somehow, a phenomenon that he gave himself credit for grasping, but the cause of which eluded him. It had been a long time since he cared whether or not he was disconnected from a woman, much less tried to figure out why. Now he cared, but was confused as to the cause.

She's probably having second thoughts. We're strangers, really, I'm older, I'm American, I'm quiet, I'm boring. Fuck. These thoughts stung him, but the sting aroused him to action.

"What's the matter, Catherine?" Pat said a few minutes later. He had gone out and brought her back in, and they were seated facing each other on the room's chrome-and-plastic chairs, the bottle of brandy they had bought earlier on the dresser next to them along with two glasses.

"Are you going to pour that?" Catherine said, nodding toward the brandy. Pat poured out the liquor and handed Catherine her glass.

"Thank you," she said. "To finding Megan well."

"To finding Megan well," Pat repeated. They drank and looked at each other, their faces in shadow. The only light in the room came from the fixture outside over the front door, spilling in through the cheap curtains. The better, Pat had thought when arranging the chairs and putting out the brandy and the glasses, not to see the cheap carpet and the rest of the cheap furniture. The room was quiet, the heater, having gone through its initial series of clanks, would not run through its annoying cycle again for another fifteen minutes or so.

"I'm afraid," Catherine said.

"Of what? Besides the obvious."

"That our lives will change after tomorrow."

"Is that why you couldn't sleep?"

Silence.

"Catherine … your husband died only seven months ago. I believe you when you say you didn't love him, but that doesn't mean you haven't been traumatized."

"You have helped me to heal."

"And now you've lost your uncle …"

"What are you saying, Patrick? That you don't want the job of caring for me? That I am too wounded a bird to take on?"

Up to this point, Pat had felt he was doing the honorable thing, easing the way for Catherine to back out. Now he was confused again. He decided to press on, though he was not feeling quite so chivalrous as he had just a moment or two ago. "No," he said, "I don't want you to wake up one day and resent me. I'm fifteen years older than you … Children are an issue."

"I thought you said you'd die before losing me?"

"Catherine … ,"

"Children are not an issue."

"You say that now, but you're young," Pat said, regaining his confidence. "I'm not sure I want more children. But it would be only natural for you to want a family."

"Natural, yes, but I am not natural."

"Of course you are."

"No, I'm not."

"I don't understand:

Pat's vision had adjusted to the semidarkness. He could see Catherine's face, half in shadow, her eyes cast downward. He wanted her to raise them, to look at him, but she did not.

"Talk to me, Catherine," he said.

"Jacques wanted children. He was very insistent. One weekend I told him I was going on a training exercise. I went to Switzerland to have my tubes tied. To sterilize myself." As she said this, Catherine lifted her eyes and looked directly at Pat. In them, Pat saw Catherine's pain, and her fear, he realized with a shock almost palpable, that she could lose him over this issue.

"I thought I was punishing him," she continued, "but of course I was punishing myself."

"Catherine."

"Yes?"

Before answering, Pat edged his chair closer to Catherine's so that he could see her face better and hold her two hands in his. "I was afraid you wanted to leave me," he said.

Smiling, Catherine replied, "I was afraid—I still am—you would not want me. It is a great sin I have committed."

"Listen to me, Catherine," Pat said. "I have lived for years in a fantasy of the past. I have neglected my daughter, a cruel and selfish thing. I have no understanding of what it is to be married. I thought I did, but how could I?"

Silence.

"I don't want to be alone anymore," Pat said. "I am not that brave."

"A moment ago you were giving me a way out."

"Yes, but I didn't mean it. I thought it was what you wanted."

"If you left me I would accept it as my penance."

Pat pushed his chair back, stood, and kneeled before Catherine, taking her in his arms and burying his face in her neck and hair. Then he pulled away and looked directly into her eyes.

"No more penance, Catherine. No more sin. Marry me."

The heater suddenly started its racket, and they turned to look at it, startled but smiling at its awful timing.

"I could fix that," Pat said.

"You could fix anything ..."

"But I don't want to."

"What do you want to do?"

"I'll tell you, but first you have to answer my question."

"Yes, I will marry you. *Mais oui.* So?"

"To make love, *mais oui.*"

"*Moi aussi,*" Catherine said, smiling. "Shall we begin?"

~ 36 ~

Czech Republic, January 9, 2004

At eleven, the two Skodas left together. Nolan, Laurence, and the oldest of the gypsy boys were in one, the other two boys in the other. The agents, Dionne driving and Sergeant Ruzika in his truck, followed. The day was quite warm for January, nearing fifty degrees Fahrenheit. The rising sun had quickly melted the light dusting of snow from the day before and there was, after a long cold night, a welcome glare on the windshield. At daybreak, Dionne had gone to the restaurant and brought back coffee, hot rolls, and egg sandwiches. Max had devoured his and then fallen into a dead sleep, thinking of the tragically beautiful Catherine Laurence and her Helen of Troy face, the long hours of static waiting having activated the melodramatic elements of his brain. He was back in the world of genuine drama now, the one that had lured him to policework in the first place, intently watching the two Skodas up ahead. They were on the A4 westbound for only a few miles when the Skodas pulled into an area off the shoulder that seemed to have been cleared of trees, a cutout from the heavy pine forest that leaned into the highway on both sides as it made its way around Kolin. The police drove their vehicles past, then made U-turns and slowly headed back, pulling over onto a grassy verge next to the forest, about a hundred yards from the parked Skodas. Ruzika trained his binoculars on the clearing for a moment, then got out of his pickup and went over to Orlofsky, who had also exited his car.

"They went on foot into the forest," the Czech policeman said, his English thickly accented but passable.

"What's back there?"

"A fire road that goes up behind the mining camp."

"That's it?"

"There's an old hunting lodge up at the head of the creek, a couple of miles in. The comrades that were more equal than us took their mistresses up there to watch American movies and fuck."

"I see. Is your backup still with us?"

"Yes."

"How many?"

"Two cars, four men."

"Then you stay with them. Watch the Skodas. If Nolan and Laurence or any of them come back, arrest them."

"Orlofsky?"

"Yes."

"There are five of them. Do you want me to call for assistance?"

"Yes, as many as you want, but they are to stay out of the forest. I don't want an army traipsing around in there, scaring them off."

"Let's go," said Max, who had also gotten out of the car and was eyeing the clearing up ahead. "Before we lose them."

In the forest, it was Max who took charge, following the stream, tracking mostly by sound, stopping for long moments to listen and then swiftly but very quietly moving on. They saw their quarry once across a large sunlit field of tall winter-brown grass, and a second time as they were reaching the top of a small rise, where Pat Nolan was reaching a hand down to Catherine Laurence to help her negotiate some rocks.

He loves her, Max thought, watching this scene, liking this thought, this idea of an American guy arriving in

Europe to confront the craziness that his daughter had cre-
ated and taking a moment to fall in love. And with such a
beauty.

A half hour later they were crouching behind a thick line
of evergreen trees and looking across a small, man-made
clearing to a low-slung rustic building with a wide veranda
running along its entire front. Catherine Laurence and the
older gypsy boy were standing on the veranda, their hands
in their coat pockets, looking out at the clearing. The other
boys were not in view. Nor was Patrick Nolan. The windows
on either side of the front door, six in all, were broken, deglazed completely. Through them could be seen only dark
shadow and the faintest outline of one or two objects that
could have been furniture.

"I think Nolan is in there meeting with his daughter,"
said Max in a low whisper.

"Or they are waiting for her to arrive," said Dionne, his
voice pitched low as well.

"We'll wait to be sure," said Orlofsky. "It's the girl we
want. You go around back," he said to Max. "Keep your radio in your hand. Do not enter the building. Do not do anything until I tell you. Understood?"

"*Oui, je comprends, mon capitain.*"

Staying well inside the tree line, Max made his way to
the back of the lodge. He had not been able to resist the
"mon capitain." Do not enter the building. *Do not do anything until I tell you*, the accent on the *anything*. Charles
de Gaulle lived. The trees here were so thick, there was no
seeing through them. Climbing, keeping quiet, he found
a rocky shelf from which he could see the lodge. The two
other gypsy boys stood on either side of the back door, their
hands in the pockets of their winter coats. The sun was directly overhead. The boys were no more than seventeen or

eighteen. On the trek in, Max' shoes had gotten wet and muddy. Again. But this would soon be over. He buzzed Orlofsky on his walkie-talkie.

"Two teenage boys at the back door," he said when the Frenchman acknowledged. "Probably carrying pistols. How long are we waiting?"

"Not long. If the boys go inside or head to the front, let me know."

"I'm in range. I can take them out and get inside whenever you say."

"Can you get a look inside?"

Max scanned the back of the building.

"I can make my way to the side. There must be a window. It"ll take a few minutes."

"Go ahead. Buzz me."

Max did as he was told, happy to be in motion, away from Orlofsky's haughty gaze. The chief of his unit, on orders from the attorney general, had told him that the French were to be in charge. Nolan had pulled her fake suicide in France, and the alleged terrorist attack was supposed to occur in France. But they were no longer in France. As far as he was concerned, he was in a no-authority zone and could do what he wanted. What he wanted was to talk to Megan Nolan. *Faked suicide. Terrorist plot. The Falcon of Andalus. Four dead Saudi Secret Police. Raimondi a traitor. Al-Siddiq lying through his teeth.* What the fuck was she up to?

The side window was not as cleanly deglazed as the ones in the front. Jagged glass surrounded a hole the size of a soccer ball. Max listened for the boys at the back before looking in. It had taken him ten minutes to circle through the trees, avoiding their line of sight, his footsteps muted by the thick layer of pine needles on the forest floor. He heard nothing. Looking in at the lower left corner, through dirty glass, he saw a wide room that once was a kitchen, its sink rusted, its cabinets ripped from the walls. The next room was a dining alcove and in it, seated on folding chairs at a metal table were Megan Nolan—her hair short but still very beautiful—and her father. Their profiles were remarkably similar: straight, strong noses; full lips; high cheekbones; full heads of thick lustrous hair. The father dark Irish, the daughter a fair colleen with a hint of the Slav in her exotic eyes. They were leaning toward each other, not talking. Suspended, Max thought, between worlds; between what had gone before, which was over forever, and what was to come, which was hard and bright like a diamond or a miracle.

~ ~ ~

"Megan," said Pat, and then again, "Megan—I feel like I'm meeting you for the first time."

"You look like you've changed, too."

"I have." Pat cast his mind back over the past week, to the attack in Volney Park, to Daniel Peletier going over the cliff, to the three dead Saudis he and Catherine had left on the ground in Cap de la Hague, to the beheaded François Duval. Any one of these events would have changed him forever.

"How did you find me?" Megan asked.

"I went to the convent. They told me about the baby. They gave me François Duval's name and address."

"Junior."

"Yes."

"How is he?"

"He's dead. Beheaded."

Megan, who had been staring steadily at her father, looked down at the table for a moment. When she looked up again, her eyes were as clear and hard as before. "So they'll be coming for me," she said.

"Yes. You have to come away with me, it's your only chance."

Megan shook her head. "I can't."

"Megan, please … They"ll find you. It"s just a matter of time."

Megan did not answer. She also was thinking, Pat could tell, about the recent past, filled with what death and destruction he could not fathom.

"What about the police?" she asked finally. "Are they aware of the faked suicide?"

"Yes. I told them it was you, but yes. We think they're helping the Saudis hunt you down. You're supposed to be planning a terrorist attack in France with your Arab boyfriend."

"I see. I'm a terrorist now. Who's *we?*"

"A French policewoman, a detective who has been helping me. Her name is Catherine Laurence. She's outside now with Doro and two other gypsy boys."

"Detective Laurence has gone off the reservation, I take it."

"Yes."

"Why?"

"Why?"

"Yes, why? You said the French police are hunting me. That means she's put her career—not to mention her life— in jeopardy. Is she in love with you?"

Pat, surprised by the swiftness and the accuracy of Megan"s insight, did not answer.

"Does she have children?" Megan asked.

"Do you want to interview her? She's right outside." Pat smiled as he said this, and shook his head. It had never occurred to him that Megan's approval—of anything in his life—would hold any value for him. Until now. Megan smiled as well and they shared a moment that most fathers and their grown daughters share often.

The moment passed, but its memory would be priceless to Pat in the years ahead.

"How did you get Doro to help you?" Megan asked.

"The Saudis killed Annabella. Doro brought me here. He wants revenge."

There was nothing to do but to say this outright. He watched Megan's eyes absorb another death. The trail she left for Pat had led directly through Annabella Jeritza and François Duval. She had led her executioners to her friends" doors.

"So I'm the bait," she said.

"He wants to talk to you when we're done."

"He's just a boy."

"He's a man now."

"I'll do whatever I can. But he'll be no match for Lahani."

"Lahani?"

"Abdel al-Lahani. My Arab boyfriend. It was probably his idea to trick the French into helping hunt me down. Brilliant, actually. Who is my fictitious boyfriend supposed to be?"

"A terrorist named Rahman al-Zahra."

"Unbelievable. That's him."

"Who?"

"Lahani."

"Talk to me Megan. What's going on?"

"I met Lahani in Morocco. We became lovers. I discovered he was a terrorist, the so-called Falcon of Andalus, Rahman al-Zahra, a Muslim who ruled Spain long ago, supposedly come to life to return Islam to world dominance.

He did the bombings in Casablanca last May. I tried to kill him, but failed. He's hunting me. I thought the fake suicide would free me, but he saw through it."

"You tried to kill him?"

"Yes."

"How?"

"Poison. It didn't work."

Corozzo had told Doro that the meeting could last no more than thirty minutes. Pat paused to absorb this amazing piece of news. *She tried to kill this asshole. She fought back.* Then he pressed on.

"Who was the girl at the morgue?" he asked.

"A gypsy named Little Pia. She was dying of ovarian cancer. I gave her ten thousand euros. It must have been a shock. I'm sorry."

"I was happy you were alive, Meg. I've never been so happy in my life."

"What made you lie to the police?"

"The note was weird. The cremation. You weren't wearing Lorrie's ring. That is, the other woman wasn't, Little Pia. My instincts told me you wanted the police—the world—to believe you were dead. You needed me to help you ..."

"We finally communicated."

"It"s a hell of a thing, the way you went about it."

"I knew you could handle it."

"When was the baby born?"

Pat had hesitated before asking this question, but only for a second, a second in which he took in the silence inside the lodge and the winter stillness outside. Despite the quiet, or because of it, he could sense the storm surrounding them. In the calm of its eye his heart drummed, its beat both driving him to pull Megan away from all this danger and riveting him to his chair, to hold on as long as possible to this moment with his daughter, to make it last a lifetime if he could.

"December 21," she answered.

"That's Lorrie"s birthday."

"I know."

Pat's mind went back to his meeting with the prioress at the convent in Lisieux, to the sadness in her eyes as she told him of the death of his grandchild. And to the question he had been wanting to ask ever since, the question he promised himself he would not ask, the one that now came to his lips as if on its own.

"It was bitter cold that night, Megan. What were you thinking?"

"The baby was already dead. It was stillborn."

It was Pat's turn to look down. *Stillborn.* Megan reached across the table and took his hand. Pat Nolan stared at his daughter's beautifully formed hand caressing his fingers. Then he remembered the round-trip train ticket to Lisieux he had found in Megan's wallet, dated December 24.

"But you went to Lisieux on December ..."

"My baby's still alive, Dad," Megan said, interrupting.

"Alive?"

"The baby I brought to Lisieux I bought from a gypsy family for another ten thousand euros. My midwife was Little Pia's mother. One of her patients delivered a stillborn boy on December 24. She persuaded them to give it up. She was part witch and gypsies are very superstitious. Or maybe she stole it. I don't know. I needed a substitute and she was greedy and got one for me."

"Your baby's alive?"

"Yes, and healthy."

Pat leaned back in his chair and stared at Megan, shaking his head.

"I know," she said, a rueful smile on her face. "I'm sorry for all these shocks."

"Where is he?" Pat asked, collecting himself.

"Back at the camp."

"You faked your own death *and* the baby's?"

"Yes."

"Why?"

"Lahani is the father. He is Saudi royalty, very rich and very powerful. He wants to kill me, but he also wants his son, to raise as a terrorist. If he went to Lisieux, he will think his son is dead. The same as you did."

"I think he did."

"Good, then you can take Patrick home with you."

"Patrick?"

"Your grandson. He's back at the mining camp."

Pat put his hands to his forehead, as if to press all of this information into his brain. He rubbed his eyes with the tips of his fingers. When he took them away, Megan was still there and his grandson was still alive and would live with him in Connecticut, far far from this place and time.

"What about you?" he said finally.

"I'll stay with Corozzo. We're leaving today. With him I'll be safe. Until I can figure out a way to change my identity."

"Change your identity? *Just come home.*"

"No. I would be unguarded, totally exposed. Lahani could reach me and kill me with ease. I tried to poison him and now he thinks I killed his son. I have to go off alone, so that Patrick will be safe. Lahani will never know he exists. Do you understand?"

Pat shook his head. He was not ready to accept that he had found and lost his daughter at the same moment. He would change her mind; he knew he could. They could *all* change their identities, move to someplace remote. Canada. Arizona. Christ, how small the world was.

"What was that fight all about yesterday when Doro showed up," he asked, changing the subject as a tactic. In a moment he would begin to convince her to come home with him. "I was watching from the fire road."

"That was Corozzo and his son, Sebastian. Sebastian has been dying to fuck me."

"Oh … I see."

"No, Dad. It's not what you think. I'm paying Corozzo for his protection. There's nothing else. The night before, Sebastian came home drunk and got into my bed, like an animal. Corozzo heard me scream. When he got to my room, Sebastian had passed out. The next morning he went after him."

Corozzo is taking better care of you than I ever did, Pat thought, and then he said, "When will I see you again?"

"Maybe never."

"Megan …"

"Dad, do you remember the night we spent at Annabella's a couple of years ago?"

"Yes."

"Do you remember her reading of you?"

"A bit."

"She saw marriage in your future, and children. Remember? You laughed at her."

"I remember."

"Go ahead and marry Detective Laurence. Raise Patrick together."

"Megan …"

"She also did a reading of Patrick. On the day he was born. She said he would be an architect and builder, that he would build great structures all over the world and become famous for his work. Who better to raise him than you, Dad. You can start teaching him young."

"Megan ..."

"Dad, I'm not coming home. I'm sorry. I'm sorry for everything. I didn't know I was testing you, but I was. Running off to Europe, living off rich men. You never quit on me. I see that now. I think I wanted you to, but you never did. And now this. I made your life miserable, but you tracked me down, did not quit. Despite all the danger and death."

Pat looked into Megan's eyes as she paused for a moment, thankful that they contained none of the cynicism that had hurt him so much in the past. What he saw in them he could not quite define. It was too new and exotic.

"I love you, Dad," Megan said finally, her eyes meeeting his. "I may never see you again, but at least I've told you. I love you."

"No, Megan," Pat replied. "I made *your* life miserable when you were a girl. I blamed you for Lorrie. I ran off whenever I could, to wallow in self-pity. I'm the one who should apologize. Megan, I love you, too. Just come home."

"I can't. I want my son to be an American, not a terrorist, not an oil pig, not a Wahabi jihadist ... an *American,* the country I abandoned. And you're the one to do it. I know you can."

~ ~ ~

For a long drawn out moment, Max could not take his eyes off of Megan and Pat, especially Megan, who was much more beautiful than her picture. The mysterious Megan Nolan come to life. To extraordinary life. Then he pulled his head down and was about to buzz Orlofsky when he heard the staccato report of an assault rifle on automatic. Two assault rifles. He heard the two boys in back scampering around to the front, and then heard return fire from the veranda. He pulled his Glock from its shoulder holster and, from a crouching position, leaped through the broken window into the wreck of the kitchen. He had his Glock out when he landed and was screaming, "FBI! Get down! Get down! I'm American, don't shoot!"

Pat and Megan were now crouching next to the table. As more shots were fired outside, Pat began to reach into his jacket pocket.

"Leave it!" French said, his voice a bit quieter but very forceful. He was on one knee now, his pistol aimed at Pat's heart. Pat complied.

"I'm going to the window," Max said. "Stay put."

"I'm going, too," Pat said. "Get back against the wall, Megan."

Max did not argue. There was no time. It was quiet outside for the moment. Running low, he went to the window to the left of the front door and Pat went to the one on the right. They peered carefully out from the windows" corners and then sat quickly down, their backs against the wall. A young man, a gypsy by his dark complection and black hair, was slumped over the veranda's wooden railing, his right arm hanging down as if reaching for something on the ground below. Catherine Laurence was sitting with her back against one of the massive posts that held up the verandah's sloped roof. She was holding her left hand against her right shoulder. Her pistol was in her right hand on her lap. She looked dazed, but when she saw Pat, she lifted her hand away from her shoulder and waved it at him slowly. It was covered with blood.

"She's saying not to come out," Max said.

"I'm going to get her," Pat said.

"Nolan, no!"

But Pat was already at the front door, crouching, swinging it open. Max rose and flattened himself against the wall next to his window. When Pat crawled out, Max emptied his clip across the front yard, giving him cover, not knowing what or who he was firing at. In a few long seconds, Pat was back at the door, dragging Catherine by her armpits into the lodge. He sat her against a wall in the alcove next to Megan.

"What happened?" he asked her.

"Shots from the woods. Automatic rifles. Several of them."

"You're shot."

"Yes, my shoulder. I'm okay."

Pat brushed a strand of Catherine's hair away from her sweating forehead, but could do no more. He hurried back to his window.

"The other two boys are down," Pat said to Max. "They're lying in the yard on the left."

"Somebody has a rifle with a scope," said Max as he snapped a new clip into his Glock.

"Are you alone?" Pat asked.

"No. There are three other agents at the tree line and some backup. They've probably called in more. It won't take long. Just stay down."

"What about the back door?"

"You're right. One of us ..."

"No," said Catherine. "I can do it. I'm okay. It's a flesh wound I have."

"I'll go with you," Megan said.

"Here," said Max, taking an old-fashioned police revolver from his ankle holster and sliding it across the floor to Megan. "You just have to pull the trigger. There are six rounds in the barrel."

Megan and Catherine crawled through the kitchen, over Max's shattered glass, to take up positions at the windows facing the backyard.

"Stay low, but keep a lookout," Max said to Pat. "If they rush us, we'll have them in a crossfire with my guys in the trees."

Pat did as Max said, showing as little of his head as possible. It occurred to him that with the veranda and its overhanging roof in the way, whoever was out there—presumably Lahani and/or his men—could not get a shot into the cabin. They would *have* to rush them. Some of the shots they heard must have come from the other cops. Their presence would make a rush very risky. Maybe the American FBI agent was right. Maybe they just had to wait. He turned to take a quick look at Megan and Catherine, who were looking out of the corners of their respective windows but appeared to be talking.

"What's your name?" he said to Max.

"Max French."

"How did you get here?"

"We've been following you. Your daughter started a mess of trouble."

"Those guys out there want her dead."

"I'm here to keep her alive."

They were looking as they were talking, but all was quiet in the yard and at the tree line. Overhead, Max heard a hum that he soon realized was a helicopter.

"The Czech cavalry," said Max, smiling. But his smile vanished as he saw a man—dark, tall, and strikingly handsome even at this distance—appear out of the woods on the far right side of the cleared yard, about fifty yards away.

"Fuck," Max said, again emptying his clip, but missing the man, who was out of range of the Glock. The man, who had been crouching, rose quickly to his feet and tossed something toward the trees that were shielding Orlofsky, Dionne, and Ruzika. "It's a grenade," Max said."Get down!" Pat hit the floor and Max heard the explosion at the same time.

When they knelt to look again, three men were racing at them across the yard. The tall dark man was tossing a second grenade at the Orlofsky group. Max, who had reloaded, waited for the three to get into range and then began firing. Pat did the same. Max's first shot hit the lead runner square in the chest and he went down like a shot horse. The second started to veer to the right, toward Pat. Both Pat and Max fired at him and hit him, but he did not go right down. He stumbled forward toward the far corner of the veranda. When he was about twenty yards away he exploded.

Max had turned his gun on the third man, who he could see now was older and much stockier than the other two. He managed to get off one shot when the explosion occurred. And then all was black.

~ ~ ~

"My father told me you were helping him," Megan said to Catherine.

"Yes."

"Why?"

They kept their eyes front as they talked, scanning as much of the truncated backyard and the rear tree line as they could. Catherine had taken off her coat and sweater and was holding the sweater against her bleeding right shoulder with her left hand. Her gun was on the floor next to her. She had managed to cut her right hand on the glass on the kitchen floor as she crawled to the window. It was bleeding as well. She would be next to useless in a gunfight, a fact which she kept to herself.

"Saudi Secret Police tried to abduct your father," she answered. "One of them was a known terrorist. Then they killed my uncle, who was trying to help us. My government appeared to be helping the Saudis."

"I don't know about your government," said Megan, "but the Saudis are working for a man named Abdel al-Lahani. He's a terrorist. He did the Casa bombings. He's after me."

"Why?"

"I tried to kill him."

"Did you say the Casablanca bombings? In May?"

"Yes."

"My husband died in them. He was staying at the Farah Hotel."

Catherine took a second to steal a sideways glance at Megan as she said this. Her face was flushed, her blood up, her green eyes sharp and intelligent. Yes, she was Pat's daughter, and yes, she was capable of many things, including trying to kill a terrorist.

"I'm sorry," Megan said.

"I wasn't, you see. And then there's your father."

"Are you lovers?"

"We are betrothed."

They were silent for a moment, and then Catherine started laughing. At the solemnity with which she made this statement, at its surreal context. Megan laughed, too, her eyes flashing with delight as they met Catherine's for one deliciously absurd second.

"Do you have children?" Megan asked when her laughter subsided.

"Do I have children? Did your father tell you ... ?"

"Tell me what?"

"No, I have no children."

"Will you take care of him? My baby?"

"We both will."

Then Pat and Max were firing their pistols and there were two explosions in the front yard, and then a third much nearer the lodge. Debris, timber, glass, smoke. Catherine was stunned senseless for a moment, but not knocked out. Through the smoke she could see a stocky Arab, dreamlike, in slow motion, aiming a handgun at Megan and firing: once, twice. Before he could fire again, Catherine found her gun, raised it, and shot the man twice in the chest. He fell on top of Megan. Catherine crawled over and pushed him off, using the last of her strength.

She put her ear to Megan's chest, but heard nothing. Then she passed out, as if Megan were her lover and she had fallen asleep in her arms.

Except that Megan's arms were at her sides, palms up in supplication.

~ ~ ~

An hour later, Pat and Sargent Ruzika pulled up to the mining camp. Pat's head was bandaged and throbbing. A veranda post had crashed through the front wall of the lodge to strike him a glancing blow that had knocked him unconscious. When he woke, a uniformed Czech medic was leaning over him, dressing the wound. Doro and Steve Luna were dead. The three Arabs who had attacked the lodge were dead. The helicopter that had dropped off the Czech rangers was on its way to a trauma unit in Prague with Catherine and Ephrem. The Czech special forces soldiers were searching the forest for the fourth Arab, the tall dark grenade thrower. Max French, his left arm broken and hastily splinted, was with them.

And Megan was dead. The stocky Arab had made it through the explosions and killed her. Pat had seen the body. It was being wheeled on a field stretcher to join Doro's and Steve Luna's as they lay waiting for a second helicopter to arrive. "Yes, that's her," he had said to no one in particular.

I'm her father. I know that's my daughter. I remember when she was born and I thought of giving her away. Considered it only very briefly, making it less of a sin. She told me she loved me just a few minutes ago ...

He had stopped the soldiers wheeling the stretcher and stared at Megan. He put his arms under her and lifted her to him. She was still warm, and light as a rag doll. The soldiers had backed away. It must have been noisy there in the front yard of the cabin, but Pat had heard nothing, not even the sound of the helicopter landing nearby, except his own sobs. He would have gone with the body to Prague, but with a start he remembered Patrick, back at the camp.

As Pat and Sergeant Ruzika approached the mine building from the rear, along the fire road, Pat saw smoke coming from its central chimney. There were no vehicles parked in front, however, and car and truck tracks and roughshod footprints were everywhere in the mud of the yard. Ruzika went in first, his police pistol drawn. But there was no need. The place was not just empty but looked like it had never been lived in. No furniture, no clothes, no toys, no utensils, nothing. On the floor of the large front room was a pile of American comic books. *Superman. Spiderman. Green Lantern.* That was it; all that Corozzo and his small clan had left behind. Pat stared at the comic books for a moment, then spotted an open staircase on the far right wall. He climbed the stairs two at a time, only to find the second floor just as empty as the first.

The medic had wanted to give him morphine, but he had pushed him away when he saw the soldiers pushing the stretcher, saw the shock of strawberry-blond hair in the space between their arms. He had wasted too much time pleading with Orlofsky and Ruzika, who appeared to be jointly in charge, to allow him to go back to the mining camp. There was a high-caliber terrorist on the loose and they did not want him messing things up. Finally, he put his small Beretta to Orlofky's head and convinced him to let him go. Orlofsky sent Ruzika with him, threatening as they headed out to have him prosecuted. He had told Orlofsky, an officious prick, that if the baby was harmed he would come back and kill him. Crazy. A crazy thing to say. He could hear the Czech policeman's boots thudding on the empty floorboards below.

"Nolan," Ruzika called. "Down here."

Downstairs, Pat joined the Czech on the other side of the waist-high partition that surrounded the wood-burning stove. Ruzika was staring at something. Following his eyes, Pat looked down. On the floor near the stove was a plastic laundry basket. In it, in a thick white receiving blanket, was a child, perhaps two weeks old. Its hair and skin were fair and it was awake, staring at him with dark unseeing eyes. Pat knelt down and ran the back of his index finger along the child's cheek, which was soft and tender and pulsing with life.

Epilogue

Lisieux, January 18, 2004

The waiting room at the Carmelite Convent in Lisieux was hushed like a church, and Pat was worried that Patrick would cry and disturb the silence that pervaded not only the room but the entire building. But the baby was still, as he usually was when he was in Catherine's arms or lap or in the sling carrier she had bought in Paris. Her flesh wound had healed, but she had worked around it from the beginning when it came to the baby. Yesterday they had buried Megan in the United States Military Cemetery in Colleville-sur-Mer, overlooking Omaha Beach, permission having been granted by President Bush and French President Chirac.

Abdel al-Lahani had been captured in the woods near the hunting lodge, not far from the dead body of Corozzo's son, Sebastian. Lahani, a member of the Saudi royal family and a nephew of General Mustafa al-Siddiq, the head of the Saudi Secret Police, was being held in a Czech jail. Nothing of his capture or of the bloody incident in the forest outside Kolin had been reported in the press. There was cautious hope that his debriefing would reveal the identities of others in the Saud family who were actively on the side of terrorism. His name splashed in the papers and on CNN would have been a warning to his colleagues.

Tomorrow, Pat, Catherine, and Patrick II would leave for New York. They were in Lisieux to make a donation to the convent orphanage in the names of Megan Nolan and Daniel Peletier.

"I'm going to walk around," Pat said to Catherine. "I won't go far." The prioress had not been expecting them and had sent word that she could see them shortly. That had only been ten minutes ago, but Pat was restless. He would simply have left the check with the prioress's secretary, but she had insisted on seeing them. He wanted to be home.

They would spend the summer at the farm in Cap de la Hague, not far from Megan's grave. Catherine was French. Patrick II was a citizen of both France and the United States. France was now as much a part of his life as it was Megan's. But he wanted to put the key in his front door in Connecticut and start raising Pat-Two, as he had started to call him, as an American, to fulfill Megan's last request. The only request she had made of him in the last twelve years.

"*Bon*," said Catherine. "I will find you."

Pat chose a corridor to the right. At its far end, soft winter sunshine was streaming through a vaulted window. As he walked, he could hear singing and the voices of children playing. When he reached the window and looked out, there was no one there. Just a lawn sloping down to the stone and wrought iron fence that bordered the convent. He turned back and, after a few steps, saw a door ajar on his right, a heavy oaken door, black with age and with a small window at eye level. He pushed on it and it slowly swung open. This might be where the kids were singing. But the room was empty and he quickly saw that it was a small chapel containing three rows of worn wooden pews and a slightly raised marble altar. On the altar was an open casket on a low pedestal flanked by baskets of pink, red, and yellow roses. The chapel had two high windows, but its primary light came from a group of candles arrayed in tall, slender candleholders in a half circle around the altar.

Pat stepped in and shut the door. He stared at the casket—at the body in the casket—for a long time, and then stepped closer and knelt on the twelve inches of marble in front of the pedestal.

Your daughter is in danger, Monsieur. And the child, too. Have faith, Monsieur. You will be led to her.

He had forgotten the flower girl from the Street of Flowers. Now she was dead, her black hair falling in thick waves to her shoulders, her face, bathed in candlelight, composed and serene. As saintly as it had been in life. He said a prayer and then got Catherine, who also knelt and prayed at the casket for the girl's soul.

A few minutes later, they were in Mother Marie de Ganzague's austere office, sitting in the same chairs they had sat in two weeks ago when she told them about the dead baby found on the convent's doorstep on Christmas Eve. Pat told her that Megan had been killed in a car accident in the Czech Republic and that he had come to thank her for her help. The old prioress was very grateful for the check and, over Pat's objections, promised to pray for him and for his daughter's soul. She did not ask any questions, but steadily eyed the baby in Catherine's arms.

"May I?" she said, extending her arms. Catherine handed her Pat-Two, and the old abbess, standing, gently cradled him for a moment or two. "Your child is very beautiful," she said to Catherine. "So fair and full of life. May the Holy Spirit be with him always." Catherine 's smile on hearing this was like the first sunlight to fall upon a shaded valley in the morning, bringing everything in it to life.

Toward the end of their brief meeting, Pat brought up the flower girl. "Mother," he said, "I saw the dead girl in the chapel. The door was open. I have met her before. Who is she?"

"You have met her?"

"Yes, once in Paris and once here in Lisieux."

"When was this, Monsieur?"

"About two weeks ago."

"In Paris, you say?"

"Yes. My daughter met her there as well. Catherine was with me when I met her in Lisieux."

"You say you met her," the prioress said. "Did you speak to her? What were the circumstances?"

"She was selling flowers on the street. She told me that Megan was alive when I believed she was dead. She told me ... she gave me a St. Thérèse prayer card ... I remember it now .. ."

"I see," said Mother Marie, placing her right hand on her chest and fingering the rosary beads that hung there from her neck. "Her name is Marie Catherine Sancerre. It is a name we gave her when we found her on our doorstep at the age of two months. She came down with scarlet fever when she was four and has been sickly ever since. She did not like to leave the convent. Not even to go on outings that we thought she could easily withstand. She said she would rather stay behind and pray for us. She was not adoptable because of her illness, but when the other children were adopted out, she prayed fervently for their happiness. She died two nights ago in her sleep."

"I'm sure I met her, Mother," said Pat.

"It is not possible, Monsieur Nolan. Marie Catherine has been bedridden for the past six months, heavily medicated, dying in fact. How could she have gotten herself out of bed, let alone to Paris?"

Pat shook his head. A month ago, he would have said that only a miracle could have made him a real father to Megan again, and she a daughter to him. But it had happened. A month ago, he would have laughed at the suggestion that, after all these years, he would remarry and have children.

But here were Catherine and Pat-Two sitting next to him. He was about to answer when he felt Catherine's hand on his knee, her fingers squeezing lightly.

"On angel's wings, Mother," said Catherine. "After all, it is the business you are in to believe such things."